UNSPOKEN SERIES

BOOK III

FROM THE HEART

Written by

A. K. Moss

Unspoken Trilogy by A. K. Moss

Unspoken Book 1 - 2014
Finding Home Book 2 - 2016
From the Heart Book 3 - 2018

FROM THE HEART

BOOK III in

UNSPOKEN SERIES

A.K. MOSS

Book Design: Red Raven Book Design
Cover design: Red Raven Book Design

Disclaimer of liability

This story is of a fictitious plot. Horses are animals that have an instinct of survival, they are a fight-or-flight animal. Within the tenderness of understanding the horse, there is always a potential instinct that could cause one harm. Under no circumstance is the author stating all horses react the same to the same stimuli or that horses won't hurt people or themselves. Always use helmets and appropriate riding gear when on or around horses. Seek professional advice from a reputable handler, trainer or riding center and work with someone who will assist in helping you fulfill your goals. Do your own home work, explore communication with horses and have fun, but most of all be safe.

This book is written for entertainment only. The author, publisher, printer or distributor shall have neither liability or responsibility of any sort, loss, damage or accident of any kind to person or entity, alleged to be caused directly or indirectly by the content of this book.

Message from the author

I was advised to share a little bit about why this book was written.

In the editing of my second novel, *Finding Home*, my editor, Tajaré Taylor, had suggested that in my third novel of this trilogy, I would write of the effects horses have with autistic and special needs people. I was game at the prospect. Little did I know what kind of adventure that would lead me down with new understanding. The people that I would come in contact with, who have dedicated their lives to the horses and people in need of such service who are priceless. In this fictitious story of Lilly finding her voice, I wanted to share the idea that goes deeper into the connection of animals to human and human to animal.

I did not go into specifics of autism because of the spectrum being so vast and that alone will be for another person to write. But I wanted to grasp and share the possible change, emotion and growth that has been witnessed and recorded by so many people. I wanted to capture it in an unforgettable story of hope, love, growth and inner strength.

Horses, actually animals of all kinds, have helped heal people from all walks of life, they do not care of money, circumstance, of mental or physical limitations. In the animal world an understanding beyond words has been witnessed over and over again. In this new era, a deeper knowledge has now taken root. Especially now that science is beginning to understand the healing power that animals have on the human spirit, heart, mind and soul, also the commitment and energy of human to animal.

I dedicate this book to the horses who have helped bridge the gap of communication. I dedicate it to the volunteers of rescues and the therapeutic riding centers across the US who open their hearts and life to those who need a little extra time and energy for the greater good of mankind and the world we live in.

Special thanks goes out to PATH, Professional Association of Therapeutic Horsemanship, Spirit Therapeutic Riding Center, Ellensburg Washington and Gallop, Queens New York. Tajaré Taylor for her passion of taking my words and making them come together for the betterment of this story. To my husband Tracy Moss and good friend Billie Flick for the uncounted hours of listening and patience as the story was created. And finally I want to thank you the reader, for without you, a lover of words and horses, these words sit silent on the shelf.

"Look at how a single candle can both defy and define the darkness."

- Anne Frank

PROLOGUE

Craig rolled over and could feel Paige next to him. "I'm glad you're here. I missed you," he whispered. He wanted to open his eyes, but something told him not to.

He waited for a reply. He prayed for one, just one word from her lips. But he was met with only silence. He reached over to wrap his arms around her and pull her to him, but all he felt was a pillow. He pulled it to his chest instead and held it. He heard the cars outside in all the busyness. New York, home, a world away from the world he loved.

He thought to the night before he left Oregon. Paige Cason walked toward the door to leave, and he felt an ache inside, afraid it would be the last time. He willed her to look back. *Please don't go*, he thought.

As if she had heard those words, she looked back at him. He extended his arms toward her for one more embrace. Paige turned and fell back into his arms, tears streaking her face.

He gently cradled her head against his chest, holding this last embrace and allowing it to etch itself into his heart. No promises said, no wordy goodbyes, just an emptiness—an acknowledgment that only time would separate them.

He remembered watching her brush the tears away through his own blurred vision. He hugged the pillow tighter for a moment and inhaled deeply, shaking off the memory.

The end of a dream, the end of vacation. It was time to get back to reality and finish an old life before he could start anew—or begin again. How does one begin a new life when it seems a continuation of the old?

***

Craig got up like an outdated robot. *If only WD-40 worked on joints and muscles*, he thought. His muscles were stiff and sore. He slipped on his sweats and did a couple of stretches, he heard himself groaning a little as he reached for his toes. *Maybe he wouldn't run today... no, he had to.* He started a pot of coffee, smelling the freshness of the grounds as he opened the can, poured the water in the cavern of the automatic drip coffee pot, and flipped the switch. He took a couple of deep breaths, swung his arms back and forth in front of his chest, lifted his knees a couple of times then headed out of his apartment building to begin his run. The sun was just starting to come over the tops of a few buildings, and it felt good to breathe, stretch his legs and be in motion. His soreness began to melt away.

The dew thick on the concrete, the smell of tar, exhaust and oil, it all gave an acrid taste to nature's morning. Everything was a vast difference from the evergreens, juniper and sagebrush in Eastern Oregon, yet as his feet hit the paved sidewalk, he started to feel a rhythm and fell into the jog. *Mmmm…fresh coffee when I get back*, he mused.

He had felt a change in his life, a shift, since he had returned. Something had been stirring in him for some time. He had started to walk into the sergeant's office a couple of times to resign, quit, or something, but... but that something had seemed to stop him. Why? He tried to let go, or hold on, or maybe it was facing change or not facing change that challenged his emotions. Every day he went to work, he focused on his job and his purpose. Craig didn't know what that purpose was anymore, it was like he was on autopilot, only living to exist. Because he didn't know what else he could do.

John, his partner of the NYPD for the last four years, was excited to have him back and hear of all that Craig had done in Oregon. So to pass some time, Craig talked enthusiastically, bringing alive the memories of his vacation and leaving behind the hollow feel in his heart. He spoke of a big, bay-colored horse his dad called Booger, bucking one brisk morning when he and his dad were going to move cows across the sage brush country.

He told John how later that day they followed the cows down a sheer rock bluff where Booger had ducked under a bulging rock to help Craig stay on. He talked of Cougar, a golden palomino colt in a muddy bog where a mountain lion had chased it and how a foster child named Abby had single handedly chased the lion.

He talked of helping Charlie, a widowed man who owned a pregnant mare find a place to stay out in a friend's barn, and how he was now a hired hand at Craig's dad's ranch. But the one aspect of his trip he did not talk about was Paige Cason.

Craig kept quiet about the blue-eyed girl who had captured his heart since the first time he had seen her in grade school, years ago in Baker, Oregon. She had been his first crush, before life in the Big Apple, where she had faded into a distant memory of childhood dreams and happily ever afters. Then when he went to Oregon and he saw her again after years of separation, he felt like he had never left. He hadn't realized how much he missed her confidence, her imagination, her laughter, and her spunk. He also loved her kindness for all living things. To Craig she had not changed at all over the years. But, as for now, that was not for anyone to know, it was just for him to relive in his memory when he was alone.

Hardly out of breath, Craig finished his five-mile run and jogged back into the front of his apartment building. The aroma of freshly brewed coffee filled his nose as he walked through the door. He loved fresh coffee in the morning. He poured himself a cup, knowing in an hour he would be at work.

***

John's voice shook Craig. "Man, sounds like the Wild West out there, Craig. You sound like you had a great time."

Craig grinned at his partner, whose Jersey accent seemed more prominent as he got back into the conversation for a few minutes. He dove back into the story in depth, discussing all the reasons he loved country living so much.

"I can't even begin to tell you, John. It was an amazing two weeks—a life-changing experience."

"I can't imagine even getting on a horse, let alone trying to ride a bucking one."

"He was a tough one, for sure, but he wasn't mean about it. He just wanted to make sure I was seated well and sitting on my pockets." Craig smiled at his own joke.

John didn't get it, but that was alright. Craig would forgive him for not getting his ranch jokes as long as John forgave him for not getting city jokes.

What John thought was a redneck, hillbilly or cowboy way of living brought curiosity and questions in his philosophy to Craig's history and lifestyle that dampened the stereotype illusion John had grown up with.

Each time as Craig reminisced, something stirred in him—a loneliness, a calling or yearning to go back to the country, back to Eastern Oregon. Each day he would feel it, and each day he would shove it to the side and work on the tasks at hand. At the end of his shift, he would return to his empty apartment and stare at the walls of memories, of his wife that he no longer had and an unborn child that would never take its first breath. What was he living for? If he thought about it too much, the car crash would enter into his memory and hold him responsible for the outcome. How could he walk away with hardly a scratch and leave such death and carnage behind? How could he go on living, finding happiness, wanting to live again? How could he plan a future when his wife and their unborn child were both dead?

1

Paige Cason's left hand reached for the withers as her right hand grabbed the saddle horn, the leather warm to the touch from the afternoon sun. She stepped into the stirrup, gave a mild hop, then swung her right leg over the back of Cricket, her dad's five-year-old bay gelding at her parents' house in Oregon. "Come on, Abby. Jump on and let's go!"

"I am coming!" Abby snapped back. "Give me a second." Abby was trying to get on Piper, a deep mahogany bay gelding with four white socks and a blazed face. For the first time ever, she was getting on a horse without her crutches.

Paige grinned as Piper stood there with his head down waiting for the second coming of Christ and not giving a dang about the outcome.

Abby got her leg up and started to lift herself into the saddle, but her hip pockets seemed to have lead in them. She kicked her leg up and grabbed the saddle strings, like a little kid not wanting to give up.

"Pull! Pull! You got it! Climb!" Paige called out as the young girl tried not to touch the ground with her lowered leg. "You got it!"

Abby made a grab for the saddle horn and pulled

herself all the way up. She stood in the stirrup and then swung her leg over the back of the saddle. Out of breath, she grinned at Paige. "I did it!" she said with satisfaction.

"Congratulations!" Paige opened her inside leg, turned her shoulders and Cricket moved under her in the direction she wanted to go.

Piper and Abby trotted up next to her as they headed down the driveway for a ride together.

"I am glad Abe is letting you ride with me."

"Me too. Cricket here seems pretty happy to see something besides the inside of an arena, too. Look at him."

Cricket had his head down and was headed at a fast clip to wherever his rider wanted to go. Paige felt the rhythm of his walk and fell into her father's old lesson. "Left, left, left."

Abby looked at her and noticed that Paige was echoing the motion of the horse's left hind leg by the rhythm of its walk. She did the same. Feeling Piper, she mimicked, "Left, left, left."

At first the girls were not in sync with each other. One was always a pace or two off from the other. Then, as if the horses could feel what the girls wanted, they found their rhythm together and walked in unison. Both girls giggled at one another.

"Why did your dad make you learn that? It seems silly. Fun... but kind of silly."

Paige looked at her for a moment and said, "Well,

if you know where his left hind foot is, you also know where his right hind foot is."

Abby thought about it for a moment. "Why do I have to worry about his feet?"

"You don't have to worry about them, Abby. But they are connected to the body you are riding. You just want to be connected to the feet and know when his feet hit the ground." Paige thought for a moment. "Are you really interested in this stuff?"

"Well, kind of. I wondered why it is important to Abe. How can I get good if I don't understand?"

"Well, I guess it is like writing or walking or any daily activity you do, like eating. You don't think about it. You just do it now, but there was a day when you had to learn it. That is what you are doing when you count your motion with the horse. There will be a day when you won't even need to think about it because you will just know. You asked why you want to know the rhythm of his motion, and his feet, are you ready to find out?"

"Okay..." Abby answered Paige with a question in her voice.

"Alright, bring Piper over here for a minute and let me have his head." Paige took his headstall in her hand. Alright Abbs, drop your reins and feel his body."

"I know this part," Abby stated. As she dropped the reins, she felt for a moment then started saying what she anticipated Paige would ask for, "Left, left, left."

"No... Give me his right hind foot."

Abby faltered for a moment. She opened her eyes

and looked at Paige. "His what?"

"Close your eyes and give me his right hind foot."

"Alright…" Abby had to think beyond the left and find the right. She finally found the rhythm. "Left, right, left, right… right… right."

"Okay now give me his left front leg."

Abby thought a moment and tried to give Paige what she asked for.

"I don't know how," Abby answered.

"Feel it with your body, Abbs. At a walk, a horse is like riding an accordion. Feel it in your hips. Feel it in your legs and feet. Feel how every muscle in your body moves because every muscle in his body moves, too. He becomes your legs as you become his."

Abby sighed and tried again.

"Abby, don't try. Just feel. Take a breath and feel his legs like they are your own. Feel the accordion."

Paige started her out. "One, two, three, four. One, two, three, four. There are four beats to the walk, Abby. So if you were to listen to all four beats it would sound like, left hind, front, right hind, front. Left hind, front, right hind, front. Hear the rhythm?"

Abby took another breath and all of a sudden felt it, left hind, front, right hind, front. She could actually feel each foot. Opening her eyes and smiling at Paige acknowledging the rhythm, she lost it in an instant.

She closed her eyes, took a breath and found the rhythm again. "Okay, it would be…" relaxing as the accordion effect made her body sway. She let her body sway directly with the walk, feeling each foot fall with motion. She felt the hip go up, the ribs sway and the shoulder drop, the opposite hip drop, ribs sway and opposite shoulder lift. "It would be…" Abby repeated, "Left hind, front—right hind, front."

Abby counted the best she could. Then she opened her eyes and watched Paige, her body moving with the rhythm of the horse's walk. It was starting to make sense. She watched, felt, and shifted with Paige as the model. In the study of motion, Abby began to notice things she had not before and then started to giggle.

Paige looked at her. "What?"

"Did you notice that a horse's hind legs look like an ostrich's legs? They look funny."

"Paige looked over at Piper as he walked and could see the resemblance. "Oh, that is too funny," Paige laughed. "I have never noticed that before."

Paige captured her attention again. "Alright, are you ready for me to pick it up to a jog?"

Abby braced herself, took a breath and said, "Oh boy… Okay."

Paige nudged Cricket over to Piper one more time and grabbed the headstall. "Here we go." She gave a kiss cue and asked Cricket and Piper to speed up to a trot.

Abby opened her eyes as Piper left his four-beat gait of a rolling ocean and fell into a choppy two-beat clip.

"Don't think. Feel."

A couple more strides and Abby closed her eyes again. "Don't think. Feel," she repeated. Abby disengaged her back and hips to follow the motion.

"Now feel the two-beat, feel and listen to the beat… left hind and right front, land together. Right hind and left front, land together. So, all you have to do is focus on the hind and you will know where the front is."

Abby felt the strides but couldn't label them, "I can't count them…"

Again, Abby felt the horse lift itself and settle back to the ground in time to lift itself again. She let her back relax and her hips roll forward with the motion. Abby repeated with Paige, "Left, right, left, right," And then she became quiet and resumed feeling it, not saying or thinking. The world had fallen away into a sea of fluid motion.

They had come to a turnoff on the road, and Paige announced, "Okay, this is where we begin another adventure. You can play with that later."

Abby opened her eyes and took a breath. "That is so cool!" she said as she readjusted herself. "It is like a whole other world doing that."

"Well, Piper is a good one to do it on, and only do it when you feel safe or have someone guiding you, Abby. Now let's play a little."

They turned down the trail, through some timber and started across the rocky terrain. Paige let Cricket have his head and just traveled with the open mind of what he was doing—enjoying the different terrain and textures of life away from the arena.

Abby found herself still counting and finding his feet as she walked, without really thinking about it.

Paige rode up to a log, and Cricket didn't know for sure what she wanted him to do with it. As he started to side step around it. Paige held him steady.

"What are you going to do?" Abby asked.

In that moment Cricket lifted himself up and jumped the log. "We are going to jump it." Paige said as they landed.

Abby squealed, "Oh!" as Piper did the same, lifting Abby across the log and out of the saddle. She grabbed the horn, her eyes wild with excitement and fear rolled into one. As she righted herself, Piper stopped safely on the other side of the log. "Holy crap!" Abby looked over at Paige "Can we do that again?"

The log was medium in size and an easy hop for the horses.

"Sure," Paige laughed.

Abby turned Piper around and expected the same response, but Piper just stepped over it. She turned and looked at Paige, "How come he didn't jump it?"

Paige grinned. "Because you didn't want him to. You've got to want it and let him feel you wanting him to lift him across it."

Abby argued, "Yes, I did."

"No, I don't think you did because Piper would have jumped if you really wanted to." Paige stroked Cricket's neck. "More than likely you thought you wanted to jump, yet your mind was telling him you might fall off. So you didn't follow through with the jump."

With that Abby sucked in some air to defend herself, but she knew Paige was right and let it out. "How does he know what I'm thinking?"

"Horses live off an unspoken language, Abbs. It's their life of awareness and feel. If he can feel a fly on his butt, he surely can feel you tense up when you're nervous. He really likes you, Abbs, and he doesn't want to do anything that might scare you."

Abby didn't fully understand, but she took a breath and let it out. She closed her eyes for a moment and imagined Piper lifting her across the log. Then she moved her legs for Piper to respond, and Piper jumped the log, landing casually on the other side.

"That is crazy!" Abby beamed.

"Nope, it's communication at its purest form," Paige replied.

"Can I do it again?"

"Sure."

For the next hour, Abby and Paige went on an adventure of nature and wildlife, letting the horses play and be as they talked and challenged each other in different things. They walked through the creek, circled sagebrush and weaved around the pines and golden larch only using body language and legs. No reins allowed.

"Paige," Abby began when things were quiet, "do you know anything about autism?"

"No," Paige answered, "why do you ask?"

"Oh, there were a couple of kids that where teasing a kid at school, calling him a retard... Sarah, hollered at them and said that he was not a retard. He just had autism. I wanted to know what the difference was."

"Who is Sarah?"

"Oh, a girl in school, she is pretty shy and quiet, but I think I like her."

"Boy, Abby, I don't know for sure."

"Well, she was kind of quiet about it, but it seemed to upset her a lot."

"If it is really important to you, maybe we will have to look it up in the library when we are in town. Or maybe you could just ask your new friend about it and see what she has to say."

They rode out onto the trail next to the dirt road, "I guess that is all I can do is ask," Abby stated as she looked back over at Paige for a moment. "Can we lope?"

"Sounds like a great idea." Paige adjusted her seat and pressed her knee, wrapping her calf around Cricket's left rib cage. Cricket gladly responded to the request.

When they got back to the house, Abby was exhausted, vibrantly exhausted. She stepped off Piper and walked over to Paige, wrapping her arms around her, "Thank you."

"Well, you're welcome," Paige answered as she patted Abby's back.

"I can't believe I'm doing all of these things, and I jumped a tree!" Abby rambled excitedly.

"You might want to call that a log," Paige laughed. "You would have to jump really high to jump a tree."

Abby laughed at the thought. "I really jumped a log."

"Hey, you know there are plenty more where that came from," Paige said. "You wait until Dad puts you on a cow!"

Abby's mind instantly thought of herself riding a cow and laughed. "I'm not riding a cow!"

"No, you silly. You won't ride a cow, but work a cow, or cut a cow, like you saw in that book."

"Do you think I could do that?" Abby sounded doubtful.

"Yep, pretty sure you can. All you have to do is learn to talk to your horse and stay in the middle, kind of like when you jumped the log. You think that log was fun, you wait until you work a cow."

Abby stood silently. Her imagination went wild with the thought she might be able to attempt chasing a cow on horseback.

They brushed the horses and put them away, walking to the house to tell Abe and Patricia what they had done like two sisters.

2

It had been three days since Abby had ridden with Paige, and she couldn't wait to get on Piper again. Paige had said a lot of stuff that had her thinking. All this talk of trying, wanting and accepting—things she had never heard about or had listened to before. Piper was going to make her work for the rides, not just let her sit up there and look like a rodeo star. *Well maybe rodeo stars had to work at riding too*, she thought to herself. Horses weren't as easy as she thought they were.

The last bell rang at school, and class was out. Abby was gathering her things and noticed Sarah, who had gotten mad at the kids, a few days prior, for making fun of another student. Sarah was in a couple of her classes and had noticed that she like to draw horses in her notebook. A sense of pride filled her. "Sarah," Abby paused.

Sarah was surprised that Abby would talk to her. She didn't have many friends, and for the most part felt invisible at school. "Yeah?"

"Do you think maybe someday you could come out and ride horses with me?" Abby asked. "I mean, I noticed you like horses and all. I have one that you might could ride."

"I would love to!" Sarah said as she grabbed her books. "I mean, yeah, that would be nice." She was trying to hide her excitement.

Sarah grabbed her books from her desk and started to walk out of the classroom. School was over for the day, and she was anxious to get out. Her eyes were bright with excitement at the thought of riding a horse. Before she could make it out the room, she looked back at Abby. "You know, if I wanted anyone to ride a horse, I think it would be my little sister, Lilly," she said.

"I didn't know you had a sister," Abby remarked.

"I don't talk about her much. She stays at home with my mom." Sarah was quiet for a moment. Her heart was heavy about going home. She just wished her life was different. Everyone else seemed to have better lives than she did. She didn't even know why she was telling Abby, but she continued, "She is what my mom calls special."

"Oh," Abby replied. "How special is she? Aren't you special too?"

"Not like that," Sarah hesitated and then stumbled on her words. "Look… it's nothing… just forget I said anything." She continued toward the classroom door. She started to chastise herself for blurting out about her little sister "Um, my mom is coming to pick me up. I gotta go." She started to jog down the hallway to the exit.

Abby watched her leave and then ran out to the hall. "Wait, Sarah!"

Sarah stopped. She didn't know why. She just wanted to be left alone and stay invisible. Or did she? She thought of having a friend, but if anyone knew about Lilly, what would they think? She looked back at Abby, "What?"

"Does your little sister have autism?" Abby blurted out, not knowing how else to ask.

"So what if she does? It's not contagious." Sarah was defensive.

"Well, I know that. I was just wondering… if she likes horses, you can bring her out, and we could play with them." Abby hesitated in doubt for a moment but went ahead with the invite. "Paige has a really nice horse that she could pet."

"I don't know if my mom would let us. But thanks for the offer," Sarah answered, still a little defensive. Yet the thought of riding a horse was an exciting idea. She didn't dare even dream of being around horses, her mom was scared to death of them. She had hardly said a word because her mom was so dramatic, but she secretly liked them. They were a mystical animal she had seen in the movies, *Black Beauty* and _Misty_. She liked reading books about horses. But Sarah's main focus had to be helping her mom with Lilly, that was most important. She didn't have time for this foolishness… or dare she even dream of it? Does she speak of it out loud to a stranger? Not necessarily a stranger, but someone that might judge her for her little sister's condition.

Abby broke her train of thought, "Well. I don't know

for sure what autism is, but I would like to meet her sometime."

Sarah thought for a moment, hesitating to open up to Abby. "She has some issues that most people don't like, but thanks. I've got to go. Mom is waiting." Sarah turned and started to jog toward the door.

A teacher walked out of the office.

"Ms. Wright, walk!" the teacher commanded.

Abby watched Sarah Wright duck her sandy blonde head and continue at a brisk half jog through the door and down the steps with her backpack over her shoulder. *Who is this girl?*

Sarah was relieved to get outside and breathe some fresh air. *That was stupid. Why in the world would I bring up Lilly?*

Sarah was five years older than Lilly Mae. *There's no way Lilly would be able to be around horses*, she thought. Lilly was too hyper, too vocal, too short-tempered, too slow. Autism had taken over their lives, and Sarah could do nothing about it. They could barely communicate with Lilly. With her little sister's awkward sign language and babbling how would she ever understand? *Heck after six years they didn't even know for sure what Lilly understood.* How could they ever expect her to understand what a horse was, let alone the concept of an animal that she could ride? Sarah thought for a moment that horses would be something Lilly would enjoy, only because she herself would enjoy them too.

It brought a smile to her face, yet sadness filled her heart, her mind was torn between desire, dreams and responsibility. Lilly's autism seemed to disconnect her, and that disconnect filtered into every aspect of the family's life.

It was like her mom's life revolved around Lilly and Lilly alone. As for Sarah, most of the time she felt invisible, deep down she just wanted her mom to be proud of her, but she knew her mom didn't have time for foolishness like that. Lilly took both of them, and Sarah didn't have time to be childish. There was a strength in that, yet an aloneness too. She wished she could be a kid like the rest of her class was, spending the night at friends' houses, having slumber parties, birthday parties, Halloween and Christmas parties. Smiling, she let her imagination run away with her for a moment.

Sarah saw the old mustard-colored Subaru sedan parked next to the walkway and headed for it. Lilly was in the backseat, stacking her toys in quiet concentration. Her mom was sitting behind the steering wheel, drumming her fingers to pass the time.

Sarah got into the front seat. "Hey," she said quietly.

"Hi, honey," her mom said as she started the car. It sounded like a lawn mower, and Sarah ducked her head in embarrassment. Lilly covered her ears and began to rock back and forth, making a loud humming sound as her mother ground the gears to find first and headed down the street. "How was your day?"

"Good," Sarah responded. She hesitated and then quietly added, not looking at her mom, "I can go out and ride Abby's horse with her." Thinking a statement might be better than a question.

Janis was quiet for a moment as she digested what Sarah had said. "Honey, you know what I think about horses. They are dangerous and unruly. There is no way I am going to let you ride a horse!"

"But, Mom…"

"No buts, Sarah! My best friend was killed by a horse," she paused. "I have my hands full the way it is, honey. I can't be worrying about you too." She blinked back the emotion of watching her friend Debra die. Janis forced air out under her breath in an effort not to agitate Lilly as she said, "I won't have it! I just won't!"

Sarah shut down and looked out the window. She knew better than to even think that she would be able to ride a horse, let alone pet one. Her mother seemed to be scarred for life, and Sarah was going to suffer for it.

"I have got to go into the grocery store and pick up some stuff. I want you to watch Lilly while I am in there."

Sarah looked at her younger sister, rocking back and forth with her hands over her ears, humming. Not wanting to be left alone with her, Sarah asked, "Can I go in with you?"

Janis looked at her daughter for a moment. All Janis wanted was some quiet time—just a few minutes in which she didn't have to think about Lilly, worry or try to have five hands when God only gave her two. The stimulation of a grocery store—the music, the banging carts, the coolers and freezers running—would all usually send Lilly into a frenzy of banging things and screaming. That was beyond Janis' emotional capacity, especially today.

"If you think you can watch her in the store while I get my shopping done." That seemed to take the weight off her shoulders for a moment as she let Sarah decide. She hated putting that much weight on her eldest daughter, but she was the only one Janis had and they had learned how to buckle down together over the last five years.

"Never mind. I will wait here with her." Sarah looked back at Lilly. It wasn't her fault.

Janis pulled into the parking lot at the grocery store. "I will only be about ten minutes." She got out of the car and headed into the store.

Lilly seemed to be happy where she was for a few moments as Sarah opened her backpack and took out her history assignment. *Write a report on an historic person.* Sarah read through the list: *Thomas Edison, Martin Luther King, Jr., Benjamin Franklin, Anne Frank.* In the whole list, Anne Frank was the only girl, so she chose her.

Why had a Jewish girl written a diary? What could have been written that would affect the world and put her name into history books? Upon looking at the picture of the young girl, there didn't seem to be anything special about her. How was Sarah to write a report on a page and a half out of her history book? She glanced across the street, the library was sitting right there—waiting and inviting.

If only she could go over there and check out a book or two. Thinking of her mom in the grocery store, she could go ask, but already knowing the answer... Why even try? Her mom didn't have time... but if she went now, her mom wouldn't have anything to say about it.

Sarah looked in the backseat. Lilly was sitting there stacking her toy animals by species, a cat with a lion, a zebra with a horse, and so on until all the animals had their place. Sarah thought it odd that her little sister knew how to do that, when she couldn't even speak. There had to be more to Lilly than frustration and temper tantrums.

"Hey, Lilly, do you want to go to the library and look at pictures?"

Lilly did not acknowledge.

"Lilly, do you want to see pictures in a book?" Sarah so wished she could have a conversation with her sister. She had always wanted someone she could share things with, someone who could understand. But God gave her Lilly instead.

Sarah attempted again to get some kind of response. She handed her history book to her younger sister. "Look at all the pictures."

Lilly looked at the book. In a garbled voice repeated quietly, "Pichures."

Sarah was stunned. *Was that a response from her sister? Did she hear what she thought she heard?* "Do you want to see more pictures?" Sarah asked again. "Let's go to the library and look at pictures."

Sarah went to take away her history book, but Lilly grabbed it and started to scream like a chimp, "Awa! Awa!"

Crap, here we go again! Sarah thought in frustration, "Alright! Aright!" Sarah released her history book, frustrated with herself for giving her book away. Lilly instantly calmed down.

Now I have lost homework... Sarah thought, *there has got to be a way.* "Lilly, let's go to the library and get another picture book."

"Pichures," Lilly attempted to repeat.

Without actually touching her little sister, Sarah got Lilly out of the car. She scribbled a note that said, *Went to the library*, and put it under the windshield wiper.

Then she repeated, "Come on, Lilly. Let's go look at pictures."

Lilly followed with Sarah's history book in her hand.

Sarah entered the library, and in the quietness, they headed straight to the children's section. Lilly followed, seeing all the colors from the volumes of books, Lilly kept her eyes averted to the floor.

"Look at all these books, Lilly," she said, half excited, knowing that time was very short and searching for something that would attract her sister's attention. Sarah saw a horse book and instantly grabbed it. She might not be able to ride, but her mom wouldn't stop her from looking at horses. "Look, Lilly, horses. Look at all the pretty horses." Sarah thumbed through it. "Look at the dappled grey pony, and there is a bay. Look at the palomino."

"Pa meen o," Lilly repeated.

Sarah was sure Lilly had repeated a word. "Yes, look at the pretty palomino," Sarah repeated back to her as she continued the search for another book to keep Lilly busy. She found another picture of a palomino on the cover, "Look, Lilly. Here is another palomino."

Lilly repeated, "Pa meen o."

"Oh my goodness yes! Palomino!" Sarah said excitedly then looked at the time. It was ticking by too fast to get a book or two. She looked at her sister and said, "You stay right here, Lilly, and look at the book. I will be back with another book here in a few minutes."

Sarah took off toward the library desk and asked the librarian, "I have a report I am supposed to do on Anne Frank. Can you help me find a book on her?"

"Sure, if you use the index, you will be able to find what you are looking for right over there." The librarian pointed to the index cards.

"I am supposed to be babysitting my sister and I can't leave her that long. Can you help me find it?" Sarah asked as she glanced toward where Lilly was with her books.

"Well… you kids," the librarian said with a sigh. "I want to finish filing these, but let me see what I can do for you." She looked over the top of her glasses at Sarah. "You know you kids are going to have to start using the index cards. You can't expect us to keep finding books for you."

"Yes, I know," Sarah said a little rushed. "I wouldn't ask but I don't have a lot of time."

"Nobody does nowadays." The librarian glanced at the rest of the books she had to file and index back in.

As Sarah started to turn away to get back to Lilly and figure out another strategy, the librarian looked up. "Well, it looks like it's your lucky day. Here is *The Diary of a Young Girl* by Anne Frank right here. There is more on her and The Holocaust in the history section."

"Thanks! This will do for right now." Sarah said as she took the book. "I will be right back."

"You do have a library card, don't you?" the librarian questioned. "You know if you don't, you have to have your parents sign for it."

"Yes, I do," Sarah replied as she went to get her sister. Time was ticking, and she didn't want to upset her mother.

"Hey, Lilly," Sarah peeked around the corner. There on the step where Sarah had left her, lay Sarah's history book. Lilly was gone! "Lilly," Sarah called as quietly as she could. Still no one answered. Panic began to fill her chest.

Lilly had taken both horse books with her.

Sarah looked down each aisle, quietly repeating her sister's name and hoping for an answer. Still nothing.

Her heart was in her throat. When she went past the back door that went out to the town park, Lilly was standing on the bridge going across the Powder River, both books in her arms. "Lilly!" Sarah pushed the door open and started to trot toward her sister. "Lilly!" she repeated, "Come on. We have to check out the books before you can take them. Let's bring them back inside."

Lilly didn't stop.

"Lilly, come on. Bring the books back in so we can check them out. Then we can show Mom the palomino."

Lilly stopped. "Pa meen o," she repeated.

"Yes, the pretty palomino. Let's check out the books so we can show Mom the pretty palomino." Sarah had caught up with her and was trying to help guide her back to the library. "Come on. Let's go this way to check out the books."

Lilly followed.

The librarian came through the door and across the bridge with an elderly woman leading the way. "See, I told you they were trying to steal books," the woman said. "I don't know what this world is coming to. Children have no respect nowadays."

The librarian looked over at Sarah. "You know you can't take the books without checking them out."

"I know. That's why we were coming back in. My sister doesn't understand. But I will get her there."

The woman leading the librarian like a deputy with a resistant dog said, "You shouldn't leave a retard unattended. What an embarrassment. They have special schools to keep them under control."

Sarah looked at the woman speechless.

The woman continued, "They don't belong out in public. Pure embarrassment to society, and thieves to boot."

Lilly rocked back and forth repeating the one word she thought might help them understand. "Pa meen o."

The librarian looked over at the young girls and then at the older woman beside her. "Martha."

The woman looked at her with the anticipation of an assignment. "Do you want me to call the police?"

Sarah's heart was pounding. *Would the police arrest them?* She stepped closer to Lilly. She wanted to wrap her arms around her sister to protect her, but she knew Lilly would not accept the touch.

"Pa meen o," Lilly said again, rocking back and forth, tapping her finger and thumb together out of nervousness.

"No. I don't want you to call the police," the librarian said calmly. She glanced at Martha's arms. "Unless you want to be arrested too."

Martha looked at the librarian in shock. "Well! What did I do?"

The librarian calmly pointed to the romance novel nestled between Martha's arm and torso.

"Marie! You know that I would never steal a book," Martha stuttered. "I was just trying to help."

"I don't think we need your help today. Let's all go inside so this young lady can get her book."

As they walked in, the librarian walked past the

history section. With hardly a glance, she grabbed another book off the shelf and handed it to Sarah. "Here is another book on The Holocaust that might interest you." They continued to the checkout counter. "What is your sister's name?"

"Lilly."

"Well, Lilly, you bring your book back to me in two weeks, okay."

Lilly hugged her book, "Pa meen o."

Sarah smiled. "We will."

Martha went and sat back in her spot, glancing over the top of her book periodically like a monitor waiting for someone to step out of line.

Janis came through the library door just as they finished checking out. "Sarah!"

"Come on, Lilly. We've got to go home."

The librarian smiled. "Sarah, you girls come back here anytime."

"Thank you," Sarah said as she started toward her mom.

"What in the world were you thinking?" Janis started in on Sarah.

Martha was giddy with purpose. She got up from her chair and walked over to Janis. "I can't believe you would let a child like that out in public. It is an embarrassment. A complete embarrassment," she repeated to make her point. "She even tried to steal books from here! Kids like that should be locked up. They can't be trusted!"

Janis looked the older woman straight in the eyes, astonished at her judgement. Without hesitation she replied, "Is that what they said to your mom when you were a little girl?"

Martha's eyes glazed over as she brought her hand up to her mouth and gasped at the rudeness of this young mother who let her children run around town unsupervised.

The librarian walked over and in a firm voice said, "Martha, sit or leave, now."

Martha looked over at her. She couldn't think quickly enough, so she turned on her heels and sat back down like a child in trouble.

"Your girls are welcome here anytime. They are a pleasure."

"Pa meen o," Lilly said.

Janis jumped with surprise at hearing Lilly. Then, thinking it was a fluke, she looked over at Sarah. "What did she say?"

"Palomino," Sarah replied with a sheepish grin.

Janis looked over at Lilly and then back at Sarah, half angry, half unbelieving. "Really? Horses?"

Sarah grinned and shrugged her shoulders. "I didn't pick them. Lilly did."

"Thank you," Janis said curtly to the librarian.

"Good luck with the book report." Then the librarian turned and went back to filing her index cards.

"Thank you." Sarah turned toward the door, trying to escape the glare from her mother.

Janis gathered her girls and started toward the car. "What kind of book report are you doing?" She was trying to get beyond the horse thing, hoping it would blow over.

"Going to write about a girl called Anne Frank."

"Are you sure you want to do that? It was a horrific time."

"It's about a girl who lived upstairs, Mom. It's her diary."

"Oh, it is so much more than that, Sarah." Knowing not to take the conversation any further than that, she hinted, "I would love to read your report when you are done." Janis looked at her daughter for a moment. "Did you really try to steal some books?"

"No, Lilly just went on one of her walkabouts with books in her hand. Boy, it sure got that Martha worked up… I thought for sure we were going to prison there for a few minutes."

Janis looked at her eldest daughter and smiled, "Yep, she sure seemed to have had her panties in a bunch. Complete embarrassment," Janis repeated like Martha.

Sarah grinned. Her mom was funny at times. "Can you believe how well Lilly talked today? I could really understand her."

"I am really surprised, and to speak so clearly." For the first time in a long time, Janis was having a conversation with her eldest daughter. And it felt good.

Lilly rocked back and forth with her book in her hand,

her body was almost vibrating with anticipation while listening to the words but having no way to respond, other than her normal babbling. She understood but didn't know how to communicate what she wanted.

"I talked to one of my friends about Lilly today, Mom, and she was cool with Lilly being different. She said she would really like to meet her sometime. Do you think we could go over and see them?"

"Aw, honey, I don't know. It is quite a bit of work to take Lilly someplace. You know how she gets." Janis looked over at Sarah.

Sarah was disheartened, "Yeah, I suppose."

"Maybe sometime in the future, but right now let's just see what we can do for her. How about if I call her or something. Let's see how that goes first."

Sarah knew that if her mom said, "Let's see," it meant it was not happening. She crossed her arms in disappointment.

3

Janis thought of the book report Sarah was doing on Anne Frank. Having studied it in school herself she hated the thought of the pictures she had seen. To even think that millions of people lost their lives. An unimaginable act, that should never be forgotten. Lilly came walking in the room. It was almost a relief to see her. Noticing an odor from her backside.

Janis tried potty training so many times. She had changed Lilly's diet and put her on a schedule, but it always seemed that Lilly didn't like going potty in the toilet. She seemed not to like it at all. Not five minutes off the toilet, her pants would be full. Janis had her sit there for an hour one day, but no sooner she was off the toilet and down the hall, Lilly had soiled herself. That would be a miracle all on its own. Janis sighed and went to go get a diaper and washcloth.

***

Janis, a woman of thirty-five, once again washed her hands and tossed the disposable diaper in the garbage. What was she doing? Her life was limited by a little girl, who had no intention of growing up ever.

She thought back to her ex-husband, who had fathered both of the girls. He was a good man for the most part, always putting food on the table when Sarah was a baby and watching her grow but not participating in family. He kept himself at a distance. Janis did all the work around the house and made sure that everything was taken care of—the chores done, lawn mown and so on. Mike would get up, go to work, and come home after a long day to sit in the chair until bed time. That was his life.

Janis figured if she could only do more, he would be happy and maybe want to do things with her and Sarah, but he wasn't, he just watched from a distance. He was thrilled to hear when Janis said she was going to have a second child. He knew this one would be a boy. He couldn't wait. He went out and bought baseballs and mitts, he found a pedal car that his son could drive and thought of getting a dog. Janis was so happy to see her husband so elated with anticipation, she reinforced the thought of her pregnancy as a boy. But when she found out it was a girl, her heart broke.

She couldn't tell her husband. Maybe they were wrong, she convinced herself. She hadn't seen him this happy in years. She couldn't imagine the sadness he was going to feel. Maybe she was just overthinking his reaction. Maybe he would be excited. Janis finally sat down with him one afternoon and shared the news.

She had rehearsed several times all the things she wanted to say. How they would try again for boy. But as words spewed out, her attempts to make things right, a glaze fell over her husband's face. He didn't hear a word of healing or support or of trying again. He mentioned abortion. She would have none of it. He didn't feel the baby move or kick. He didn't feel the shift of life within the thin wall of her belly.

He had paced around the house for three days—and on the fourth, he left for work without saying goodbye, he didn't come home that night. He didn't come home the following night either. He didn't show up for work. Three weeks later Janis knew he wasn't coming home. What would a single mother do with a child on the way? She tried to call him and make it alright. He offered no response. Janis finally got a job as a waitress. She held the job trying to live off the tips she earned until she could no longer stand on her swollen legs with her aching back.

When Lilly was born, she figured she would be off about a week and then she would be able to get back to work. But Lilly was a fussy baby. Her sensitive tummy made it hard for her to digest food. Nothing seemed to make her happy. Janis would walk the floor at night trying to soothe the child, the only thing that seemed to soothe her was the motion of rocking with her ear to her mother's breast. After three weeks of struggling with her job and the fussy baby, Janis gave up work.

At three months, Janis knew something was not right. Her Lilly never looked at her, she would not respond to loud noise or Janis's cooing and giggling. Things did not improve with time. Lilly started to scream for no apparent reason. She would repeatedly beat her head on the floor, falling into tantrums, almost convulsions.

Janis tried different doctors, who diagnosed Lilly with schizophrenia, mental retardation, or conducted evaluations for various levels of retardation that had taken up to six months before a diagnosis was even given. She had traveled for hours in the car to make it to therapy sessions in Boise and Portland, all for nothing more than guessing games, until her funds ran so low it felt like a dead end in a treacherous tunnel. Lilly's improvements were measured at a snail's pace.

Janis started taking Lilly to local therapy sessions when her budget would allow. At least it made her feel like she was working toward something. She didn't know what that something was, but at least it was something. At night, Janis would sit in her bedroom and cry. She was at a loss. All she could do at times, was hold her child— rocking her back and forth—in tears of frustration and helplessness. The day she heard the word autism, it was an answer that created even more questions. A whole other world opened up as she searched for some type of understanding through books and different therapies.

Now here she sat, forging forward, praying for relief and answers. With tremendous effort every morning she would get up and start again.

Janis knew there would be a day when she would have to put her child into an institution. She could hear the doctors and therapists all repeating the same thing, but in Janis' mind she would only let them be words. She could not, no… She would not believe that was where Lilly would end up.

As Sarah became old enough to help with Lilly, there seemed to be light at the end of the tunnel. Through the books Janis studied, she helped guide Sarah to make sure Lilly was as safe as she could possibly be, which gave Janis much-needed relief and sanity. Every day she relied a little more on her eldest daughter to help. Soon it seemed both lives were consumed with Lilly—the habits, distraction, and temperament of an uncommunicative child.

How was she supposed to do this on her own? Raise two girls while keeping up with Lilly, her medical bills, and therapy?

And Sarah… all this talk about horses and friends and wants. A feeling of overwhelm filled Janis. She felt her eyes start to water. *No*, she thought. *I am not going to cry… I can't!*

She thought of her ex-husband again. Maybe she could call him. Maybe she could make it work. She could try a little harder if she could keep Lilly out of his way. Maybe try to be a better cook, keep the house cleaner. What could she do to get him to want her back?

It wasn't love she was after, she felt none of that for the man, but living alone as a single parent was exhausting. At one point she picked up the phone and looked at the numbers and closed her eyes. Taking a breath, she opened them and dialed the first three digits then paused. She thought of how he talked to his mother, how he claimed that Lilly was not his child. How she was supposed to do all the right things. Resistance welled up within her, and she put down the phone. *No, not today,* she had thought.

***

And now here they were with Lilly, seeming to make it work without an institution. With what her ex-husband sent her a month, she was a stay-at-home mom locked into a world where nothing made sense beyond an infant's mind frame. Somehow Janis knew it would get better. It had to. She fixed her hair and woke Lilly up, changed her diaper and got Lilly ready for her therapy session.

As they sat in the waiting room, Lilly was oddly calm, fixated on one page in her library book. She sat there quietly rocking back and forth, staring at a large black horse with a harness. Janis took the opportunity to reach down and grab a medical magazine. As she flipped page after page, she ran into an article on autism with a picture of a little girl sitting on a horse. Janis tried to ignore the article and continued looking through the book. But as she finished the last page, feeling anxious, she began to thumb through it again. The magazine fell open to the article of horses and autism. Glancing at the words, Janis recognized the emotions she had been feeling—loneliness, frustration, isolation. Maybe she could at least read the article. She just might be able to pick up something she could do with Lilly without having a thousand-pound animal involved. As she read, she realized she was reading about her own life and the trials she went through on a daily basis. She felt another mother's helplessness, anxiety and exhaustion. Then when it came to the horses, there was a dramatic shift between the authors daughter's behavior. *It could not be so simple. Could it?*

Janis finished the article wishing it would not end, she was wanting more information. Down at the bottom of the page was information about a therapeutic riding center based in New York state, where not only people with mental disorders rode, but those who had autism did as well. She glanced at it again and hoped they would eventually get something like that in Oregon, but she knew it would be years before that happened. She also knew it would never be in a remote area such as Baker. It would still most likely be a three- to six-hour commute to the west side to get the help she needed, but at least it would be something.

The nurse called Janis and Lilly in for their therapy and counseling. Janis sat and listened to the doctor elaborate on the expectations of Lilly's progress.

Janis spoke up without thinking. "What about horses and autism?"

"Excuse me?" the doctor said.

"You know horses, the four-legged animals that run

around and have saddles on their backs. Cowboys and Indians."

"What about them?"

"Do you think that horses would help handicapped people? You know like crippled people or kids like Lilly." Janis was grasping at straws. She didn't want the doctor to think she was crazy about asking about her daughter alone.

"I don't know anything about that," the doctor answered.

"Would that be something we could try?" Janis looked over at Lilly with her book still in her hand, the big, black horse standing boldly on the page. The page that held her daughter's attention longer than anything ever had. Janis pointed to the book and began to argue a case she didn't even believe in. "I have never seen Lilly so taken with a book before—and watch this."

Janis went to turn the page, and Lilly instantly began to scream, grab, and stomp. Janis returned the page and the book to her, and Lilly sat silently, running her hand over the horse. The reaction astounded not only the doctor but also Janis, who had anticipated a reaction but nothing like that.

"Babe," Lilly said quietly, rocking back and forth.

Janis looked at her daughter. "Is that your baby?"

"Babe," Lilly repeated.

"I don't do anything with horses and mental illness. Actually, I don't know anything about horses. My practice is based on scientific facts and medication.

All I can offer you is medication to keep your daughter with you for as long as you can handle her and give her rigorous auditory and communication therapy sessions. In my experience I don't know of anything that can shift the mind of an autistic child. I wish I had better news for you, Janis, but all I can do is give you my opinion."

Janis didn't want to give up on the conversation, so she continued, "I found this magazine with an article on horses, but it is clear over in New York. I can't go that far. I was wondering if there was anything closer to home."

"Janis," the doctor sighed, "I don't want to get your hopes up too high. There are studies being done on different spectrums of autism, but nothing has been proven. I have to stick with what has worked in the past. I can't risk my practice on ideas that might work. I have seen Lilly improve over the last year. She has become more sociable than what she has been in the past, and after today, there is a definite mood swing when she has something that she wants. I believe these are all good things, Janis, and even though horses worked for that woman, it doesn't mean it will work for Lilly and you." He paused looking down at his notes. "We have to be realistic and focus on what works. In my experience, you are doing the best you can for your little girl. Let's work with what we know."

"Yeah, you are probably right," Janis began, although she didn't believe her own words. She was saying them to help support the only person she thought could help her understand her own daughter. If she lost him, who would she have to help her?

As they finished up the appointment, with Lilly's little hands grasping her book as they walked out of the office and into the waiting room. On the table, the magazine was sitting like a beacon. Janis hesitated, then picked it up and tucked it under her arm. She would bring it back later. Whoever had written that article, seemed to be screaming at her, they seemed to have written her life within those few pages.

The doctor might not want to sacrifice his practice, but for the first time, Janis didn't want to sacrifice her daughter either.

When Janis got home two hours later, there was a message on her answering machine. It was Lilly's doctor.

"Ms. Wright, I did a little research from your request today and found a program that will help fund the research on autism. You might want to check it out. Here is the phone number..."

Janis fought with the pen and scribbled the numbers down.

***

When Sarah got home from school that evening, Janis could hardly wait to talk to her about what she had read and the idea of maybe a horse helping to get some kind of handle on an autistic mind.

"Sarah," Janis hesitated, knowing that what she said

afterward would open up a whole new can of worms for her teenage daughter.

"Yeah?"

"Well, when I took Lilly to her therapy session today, I found an article in this magazine." Janis handed it to her daughter. "Do you remember the other day when one of your friends offered for you to ride a horse?"

Sarah took the magazine confused as she thumbed through the pages until she found where her mother had marked it.

"I called a woman named Susan today over in New York," Janis paused. "She sounded so positive and helpful." She looked at her daughter getting giddy, "Don't you get your hopes up. I just have been doing some thinking and have an idea."

"Really, Mom? We are going to ride horses?" She glanced at the pictures, too excited to read the article.

"That doesn't mean anything. I just want to find out if there is anyone who has experience with horses and healing like what I read in this magazine who might be able to meet with Susan."

Sarah looked at her mom with hope in her eyes. "I think I know who will." But how was she supposed to get ahold of Abby. Who was she living with? She racked her brain trying to remember what Abby had said.

All of a sudden Sarah looked at her mom, tears brimming in her eyes, "I know how to get ahold of her," remembering Paige Cason's name, she grabbed the phone book.

Janis picked up the phone and looked at it, then put it down for a moment and drummed her fingers on the table, *What am I going to say to her?* Janis got up and walked into the kitchen, then turned on her heels, *What have I got to lose?* and dialed Paige's number.

4

After the conversation with Janis about Lilly, Paige started thinking long and hard about her adventures in life. The thought of desperation and frustration that Janis had spoke about really hit her heart in a way that was unexpected. Paige made a few phone calls around town, including child services to see if there was any support for Janis or families like hers. None was found. The special education at the schools was founded upon a different basis. All of the schools were working on maintaining what programs they already had in place, which were more about sitting still and gross motor skills. They could not afford new innovative ways to teach special needs children.

Thinking back to Piper and her dad, Abe, when Paige was a kid. How the bay horse seemed so confused. Every time Piper had tried to express his frustration and confusion after he had dragged young Samantha Greenly across the arena at a horse show, professional trainers were sought after to try to break him of his fears, instead of rebuilding his courage. Piper's future had hit a dead end after each trainer repeated the same thing. *There are too many good horses in this world to waste in on a bad one.* For a last resort, John Greenly asked Abe Cason for his input on his daughter's horse, thinking the connection between Samantha and Piper was as fragile as the finest crystal. Death to that horse could shatter the emotions of his fragile daughter.

Paige had watched years ago, as her dad would wait for the horse to attempt to do simple tasks, such as walk through the open stall door after hours of standing in the corner. How Piper was too scared to try or explore the boundaries beyond his stall. Yet she watched his courage grow, at each achievement of the horse playing the "What if Game" as if the horse was asking itself...

What if I step toward the door? Nothing.

What if I peak my head out? Nothing.

What if I step outside the stall? Nothing.

Piper became braver and bolder until finally, after hours, he began to explore the world beyond the walls of his stall. He had to trust that he could trust himself again and trust the man on the outside the stall walls. Abe was there for support only. The horse did all the work. Could a child learn the same way? And with the comfort that Paige had experienced with that knowledge, the deep-down healing that she had witnessed, would it be the same for those who had challenges of communication, such as Lilly?

When she met Janis at her house for a brief conversation, in a shy manner she quietly handed Paige the magazine she had lifted from the doctor's office and said, "I don't know if this is something you can help me out with, but I am at wits end here. I am afraid we are going to lose her. I know that she is smart, I can sense it, but I don't know how to reach her. I just don't know where to go from here. I talked to that woman from New York, Susan, and she said she had people come from all over to learn what she had to offer. It doesn't cost anything for her time. So it is just the trip over, which I found some funding for." Janis paused to get her wits, "I just need to find someone who knows about horses and wants to learn even more."

Paige had taken those words and dwelled on them for a few days. She studied the article and made a few phone calls. Without a second thought, here she was.

She looked at her airline ticket one more time. She was actually going to New York to experience something new and document her observations to bring back to her community. She closed her eyes in anticipation and excitement.

A small-town girl who had lived her entire life in Eastern Oregon—what was she thinking? She hadn't really been planning it, but like most things in her life, everything seemed to just fall into place or take her by surprise. Out of habit she reached for her crucifix necklace... It wasn't there. She had lost it when she got stung by the wasps. It was one of her favorites. A small, gold cross with Christ in silver. A small, delicate refined piece that had captured the true meaning of strength and fragility of the human being and the belief of the creator of God. *Make a wish...* fluttered through her mind. Paige smiled in memory of Craig reaching for her throat line and fixing the clasp behind her neck.

Just the thought gave her strength. *I am going to do this!* she thought to herself. This one was certainly a dramatic culture shock. Now she was going to see how a therapeutic riding center for special needs children was run. But, of course it had to be clear across the US in New York. On the edge of New York City—Queens to be exact—and in her mind, she had no idea if there was difference. It felt crazy yet invigorating all at once.

Paige would live at the center for two weeks with the host Susan Clark, studying different behaviors, learning how to assist and help with the children, and what type of horses to look for. For a bonus she planned to surprise Craig before heading home.

He was going to be so surprised to see her. Maybe he would be able to take her on a tour before she left. Just to see him, to take his hand—she was giddy with anticipation. It seemed like everything in life was lining up for the first time.

She couldn't turn down this opportunity, without much of a second thought, she had signed up, bought a plane ticket and was preparing for the trip.

She closed her eyes for a moment and took a breath. What an exciting adventure. The plane surged down the runway, and her body pressed back into the seat. No turning back now. She glanced out the window and watched the world fall away into a sea of patchwork below.

***

Paige stepped off the plane and stopped for a moment to find a directional marquee. People bumped into her as if she had stopped the flow of traffic. It seemed like when everyone was on the plane it was a red light with everyone seated and mostly quiet. But as soon as the plane had stopped it was a race to get where they needed to go. Where was she supposed to go to get her luggage? She saw a short-haired blonde woman holding up a small sign with *Paige Cason* written on it. Paige approached, "Susan?"

"Are you Paige?"

"I am."

"Thank God! I am Sue Clark. Are you ready to get out of here?"

"Boy, I didn't think you were coming to pick me up. I thought I had to take a taxi or something."

"Oh, honey, you couldn't afford a taxi where we are going, and I just couldn't see you driving to our place. Come on. Let's get your luggage."

Paige followed Sue to the baggage claim through the hustle of busy people. She felt like she could get swallowed up inside of all the chaos and sure appreciated a companion to help guide the way. As she walked, she realized that it was like a herd of ants. Everyone had a destination and a place to be, and they all focused on that direction. The short, stocky woman walked with direction and purpose as she spoke.

"This your first time in the city?"

"First time anywhere really, Susan," Paige answered,

as she almost jogged to keep up with the stride of the shorter woman.

"Call me, Sue," she said. "Well, I am so happy you decided to brave the crowds to come and stay with us." They brushed past several people who were obvious tourists, looking confused and lost.

Sue stepped on an escalator, but Paige paused. She watched it for a moment as it began to carry Sue down to the lower floor. Paige then stepped on so as not to hold up the people behind her or lose her escort. She fixed her feet so she wouldn't fall off the step and tentatively took four steps down to stand next to her new acquaintance.

"Never been on one of these?"

"Nope, but I have now." Paige realized they were coming to the end of the ride and was half anticipating getting swallowed up by the moving stairs.

"Just step off and keep walking," Sue said as she took two steps and was on the solid floor. Paige watched her and did the same. She found her feet felt funny at the stability of the ground.

"Luggage won't be for about another twenty minutes. You want a coffee?"

"Would love one," Paige answered. She felt exhausted yet exhilarated and lost all at once with all the commotion around her. At home she knew her complete surroundings. Wherever she went she always knew most of the people around. But here… everything was a blur. She found herself focusing on the signs to tell her where to go. Most people seemed to be in a rush to get wherever they were going with deadlines to keep, they didn't have time to look around.

Sue stopped at a small bistro and ordered a tall, sugar-free something or other, but Paige had no idea what she had said. Sue looked at Paige. "What do you want, honey?" She glanced at Paige for a moment and then back at the register. "I am buying."

"A large coffee."

Sue laughed. "Just a coffee?"

Paige was confused. "Isn't that what we stopped for?"

"Make it two of mine," she ordered.

"That will be nine fifty," the cashier said, his eyes hard and no expression on his face.

Paige swallowed hard. Confused.

"Do you want anything to eat?"

Paige hadn't eaten since she had left but she didn't feel that she could keep anything down. "No thanks. Just coffee."

The next thing Paige knew, two paper cups appeared in front of Sue. She handed one to Paige and dropped two dollars into the tip jar.

"Let's have a seat," Sue said as she walked away without a thought.

Paige looked at the guy behind the counter. "Thank you." The cashier looked questioningly at her and nodded his head. Paige sat down at the small circular table with her new acquaintance, people continuing to bump past her.

Sue took a sip of her coffee. "So, I was intrigued by your inquiry about our center and what we do. We haven't had anyone come over from as far west as Or-EE-Gone." She said Oregon with an old Jersey accent.

Paige smiled at the sound of her home state. She put her cup on the table and leaned forward to hear what Sue had to say. Then she answered, "I have been around horses all of my life and always felt they had something that most people seem to miss. I was hoping you might be able to teach me a little about the connection you have learned with handicapped children."

"We are happy to put you up for a few weeks and let you see our process. We work with all sorts of people and have found that it is the motion of the horse that triggers something deep within that helps some of our students come out of their shell."

Sue heard the conveyor belt turn on for the luggage but knew they still had a few more minutes.

Paige took a sip of her coffee and almost spit it out. It was not what she was expecting.

"Not your kind of coffee?"

"Not really." Paige smiled as she swallowed. "I usually drink mine black."

As the first of the flight's luggage came spewing out on the oval conveyor, they walked over and stood looking for recognition of Paige's suitcase. In less than ten minutes, they were heading out the door to the vast parking lot that seemed miles long to Paige.

The drive was not what she expected either. Paige

tried to digest the volume of cars and traffic and a whole new culture. Sue seemed unfazed by the congestion, visiting and talking like they were on a country road. She looked every now and again at Paige while cars whizzed past, beside and behind. They pulled into the driveway of Sue's little spread, which was tucked in a small grove of trees.

"It is little, but mighty," Sue said as she pulled in front of her barn and parked.

As they stepped out of the pickup, Paige smelled the smell that brought her mind back home—horses. It is universal.

"Welcome to our little corner of the world," Sue said. "Would you like a tour or do you want to get settled in first?"

"Let's do a tour."

5

After a long day, Craig was looking to get to his apartment and put his thoughts together. He wanted and needed some quiet time. He felt out of place here now, something had changed for him. His shift was over. "Look, John, I am going to head home for tonight. I will catch up with you tomorrow."

John had expected to go out and have a beer with his partner. "Sure," John said, a little disappointed. "If you need anything, call. Alright?" Craig had seemed to have changed while in Oregon. John couldn't put a finger on it, but there was something different about him. John patted Craig's back as they each headed to their vehicle.

Craig pulled up into his cramped parking space at his apartment building, a place he had called home, that seemed now only a shell. Out of habit, he headed to the front door out on the one-way street. He hoped for a little air before he headed into the stuffy hallways of the building. It was just before nightfall, when he caught a glimpse of a familiar woman walking out of his apartment building. He looked again. His heart jumped into his throat. Was that his wife Lisa walking out of the apartment building? He stopped dead in his tracks. The hair, the walk, her profile, that was impossible. Lisa was dead. She has been dead over a year. He jogged after the women for a moment trying to get a better look as she walked away.

"Lisa?" *What is this madness? Am I hallucinating?* He heard himself speak again before he even thought. "Lisa?"

The woman turned around. It was Lisa's younger sister, Lori. Craig stopped short. "Lori," he whispered as he could see the resemblance of his wife. He swallowed hard. He hadn't seen her since the funeral. "Hey, what are you doing around here?"

"Craig, I was hoping to find you. I didn't know if you had the same apartment or not." Lori smiled at him, "I was in town for a couple of days and thought I would touch base with you, see what you are up to."

Her voice sounded the same as Lisa's. His heart ached in recognition. "Wow, um, I'm getting by. What about you? How is your mom doing?"

"Mom is doing alright. She takes it day by day," Lori answered. "Kind of like the rest of us. Sometimes I just don't believe Lisa is gone."

"I know that feeling. I sure wish there was a way I could change things," Craig answered.

Lori looked around a moment. "Do you want to go get a drink or something?"

"Sure, I would love to. Let me get changed first. Come on up," he said, as if she was still family.

Lori walked at his side, and it was oddly familiar having her there. "So what brings you into town?"

"A conference on management," she answered. Not knowing how much he would want to hear, she kept it short. "Going to be listening to a bunch of mumble jumble the next couple of days."

"Oh, well that would be interesting," he answered, trying to get his heart out of his throat.

"Well, I would rather talk about what you have been up to more than what has been going on with me," Lori answered. "It has been a long time."

"I know." Craig couldn't believe the similarity of Lisa's younger sister. They had the same New York accent, the same nose, the same eyes. It was almost like he was in a dream.

They walked up the stairs in silence and Craig unlocked the door. "Come on in. Make yourself at home. I will change really quick and then we can go out and do some catching up."

Lori walked in the apartment, noticing the staleness of the room.

"It ain't much since Lisa has been gone, but it will do for now," he said as he grabbed his shirt off the back of a chair and his duffel bag off the couch. "I don't have company here very often." He walked into his bedroom and tossed them on the bed.

Lori wandered around the stale living room. She saw a picture of a horse's head drawn on a piece of paper—a golden buttermilk-colored horse with a black mane and hazel eyes with an eagle feather tethered behind its ear. It was, in her perception, simple art, nothing of imagination. It had no frame and handwritten under the picture it simply said, *From the heart*. Although beautifully done, it seemed to be something Craig would hang on the refrigerator.

She saw his cowboy hat upside down on the table. "What are you doing? Getting ready for Halloween by playing cowboy?" she said as she picked it up and noticed the sweat-stained band. "Did you get this at a second-hand store?" she asked as she dropped it back on the table, looked at her hands, brushed them off quickly and then headed to the sink to rinse them.

"No. I just got back from visiting with my dad in Oregon."

"Oh yeah? When did you get back?"

"A couple of weeks ago." His heart ached at the thought.

Lisa saw a small picture frame with a picture of her sister. "She was beautiful, wasn't she?"

Through the door, it sounded just like Lisa's voice, and Craig swallowed hard. He slipped on his jeans and a t-shirt and headed back into the sitting room to slip on his cowboy boots. He looked at Lisa's picture in Lori's hand. "She was the best thing that happened to me since I moved here."

"I am glad she found you. You were all she ever talked about. She had so many things she wanted to do with you."

"Well, we didn't get to do all that she wanted, but I guess life has a way of creating itself. We are just along for the ride."

He grabbed his wallet and jacket and stood up, "Are you ready to go?"

"Yes," she said as she walked toward the door.

They stepped out into the evening air and began to stroll down toward Sarge's Deli on 3rd Ave, a small 24/7 diner that had been an old standby for years. The pictures of famous actors, basketball and football players who had come in the establishment lined the walls along with a copper tin ceiling reflecting the light from Tiffany-colored shades.

Lori laughed at a memory.

It sounded just like Lisa's laugh. He felt an ache in his heart and a moment of pure happiness for old times— an odd feeling of family.

They sat in an old, tan-colored booth. Lori ordered a coffee as she placed her perfectly manicured hands on the table. Craig looked at her for the first time in the light. Her makeup was perfect, and her hair was in place. He remembered her always being that way.

When the coffee was brought, Lori looked at the waitress. "I want cream with my coffee," she requested with a bit of force in her voice.

The waitress looked at Craig. "Just black for me. Thanks."

The waitress returned with a small carafe of milk.

"That is cream. Right?" Lori stated.

"Uh, no. It is milk."

"Don't you have cream?"

"I will check in the back," the waitress stammered as she retreated to the kitchen.

"Sometimes…" Lori sighed. Then she looked back at Craig and smiled. "So how was Oregon?"

"Oregon was good. I had a great time with my dad and saw people I haven't seen in years."

The waitress came back. "Um sorry, I only have whole milk."

"I can't believe you don't have real cream." Lori looked at the waitress exasperated for a moment. "Never mind I will take what you have. It just takes out the bitterness," Lori said dismissively, putting up her hand to stop any further conversation. Then turned away, disappointed in the waitress' capabilities, and focused on Craig. "So here we are, Craig. Tell me more of what you have been up to." She put both elbows on the table and cupped her chin in her hands.

****

They drank coffee for a few hours, laughing about old times and Christmases long past. They talked of prom and when Craig first became a cop.

For the first time in a long time, Craig looked back on his past and realized how much fun they had had as a family. But after the accident, something had changed. He felt responsible for the death of his wife. He felt like he didn't belong any longer. But here tonight, it was like nothing had changed, and he would see Lisa walking in the door at any moment.

It was getting late. Minutes rolled into hours. They got up and headed back to Craig's apartment. Lori looked over at Craig for a moment and reached out her hand. Craig took it. "You know," Lori said. "I was always envious of Lisa. I wondered why I could never find a guy like you."

"A guy like me? Well, there isn't anything special about me," he said kind of caught off guard by the comment.

"Well, you always made her happy, and she always wanted to be around you. So I would say that is pretty special. I would like to have that someday."

Craig looked at Lori for a moment as they stopped at Craig's apartment building. Lori's car was parked right out front. "Lori, I hope someday you find that special someone that makes you feel like you are on top of the world. Someone who will challenge you, inspire you and will love you for who you are." Craig paused for a moment as he thought of Lisa and the life he had with her. "I wish I could turn back the clock at times and maybe do some things differently. I really, really do. But I just can't. Lisa is gone, gone for a lifetime."

"Craig, if you ever need to talk or anything, I am only a phone call away."

"Thanks, that means a lot to me. I am so sorry about your sister. I so appreciated this evening, and thanks for taking me back down memory lane." He smiled. "And just so you know, that phone rings both ways."

Lori pulled her keys out of her purse and unlocked her car. She reached out and gave Craig a hug.

Craig felt the familiar embrace as his sister-in-law held him tightly, not wanting to let go. He was saying goodbye one more time to a life intertwined by a woman who was now gone.

"I will call you when I get back into town, alright?" She said as tears ran down her cheeks.

"That would be good," Craig said as he looked into those familiar eyes one more time. "Have a good conference and pay attention to all the jibber jabber. You might learn something."

Lori laughed as she pulled a tissue out and dabbed at the makeup on her eyes, "That is mumble jumble."

Craig smiled. "See you later."

He reached for the apartment building door.

"Goodbye," Lori replied as she got in her car and started the engine.

6

Paige looked around and was intrigued at the small piece of property. She acknowledged that every inch of it was utilized. Inside the barn was a small corral they used as an arena. All of the equipment had its place. Little pens were set up for a few farm animals and a fenced garden. This place was so small compared to Paige's place, but everything was well kept, and it worked. They had class sessions for some kids in groups, teaching teamwork, responsibility, and communication. And then they had individual sessions with those who needed more isolated 3-on-1 interaction. Sue explained the work she had been doing to create a day ranch where kids and young adults had a safe place to go to work with horses and dogs and help with the garden, giving them courage and self-worth.

"This was a dream of mine, Paige, but it takes more than me. I had the intention, but it is the volunteers and the supporters that keep this place going. I know what I want to see, but the volunteers are the ones who work toward that vision and support it wholeheartedly. We have school programs and local people who come help support, along with people, such as retired school teachers, who love being around horses who also come and help support the programs here. It is amazing how it grew into a mighty little community."

Paige saw some young people helping a little girl groom an old pony, "That is Buttercup, she has been here for the last seven years, and Tia is working with her today." Sue said as she watched Paige's gaze.

Paige watched how they helped support Tia but let her do the work. She heard another woman giving directions in the little arena out on the side of the barn. Two side walkers were holding cones and the girl had to listen to the woman in the middle of the arena as to which cone to put the ring on, the left or the right.

A young man came walking toward the two women. "Ms. Sue," the young man said as they strode toward the barn.

"Hi, Danny," Sue replied. "What have you done today?"

"I got to ride Rocket today!" Danny exclaimed. "We got to trot and everything!"

"Did you go all the way around the barrels?"

"I did. All by myself!"

"Danny, that is so cool. I am really proud of you!"

"Ms. Kim said that I was so good I get to do it again tomorrow!"

"Hey, Danny, this is Ms. Paige Cason. She is going to stay with us for a while."

Danny's eyes lit up. "Ms. Paige, will you watch me ride Rocket tomorrow?"

"Danny, I think I would be honored to watch you ride Rocket."

Danny grinned from ear to ear, excited to have an audience. "I am getting really good."

"You go finish your chores, Danny, and maybe we will see you in a little while."

"Okay!" Danny started to run back to the corrals. Then he turned as if he had forgotten something and trotted back to the two women. "Nice to meet you, Ms. Paige."

"Nice to meet you too, Mr. Danny." Paige said with a smile.

Danny beamed, blushed then turned back toward the corral.

Sue grinned at the young man jogging back to his assignments for the day. "That is Danny. He has been here for the last four years. When he first got here he didn't say anything and was mad at the world, so misunderstood. His parents had horror stories of aggression, self-mutilation and depression. They had driven past here almost daily, taking Danny to doctors, psychologists, neurologists and anyone else who they thought could help them with him. When his mother told her husband to turn in to the ranch, her husband laughed and told her that was the stupidest thing she could think of. According to him," Sue laughed, as she brought her hands up to quote the word, "they needed a *professional*. They knew nothing of horses or farms. When Danny got out of the car, he never looked back. Every day he comes and spends hours here. When we started assigning him chores and horses, his confidence went through the roof. He works in the garden, feeds the horses, cleans stalls, and gathers eggs. His biggest dream was to ride Rocket. Rocket is one of the fastest horses we have here, one of the liveliest, and it took Danny this long to be good enough. I am so proud of him. He is our spokesperson. During the summer, he spends all of his extra time down here. We are so happy with his work that we were able to hire him on as one of our employees."

Paige looked after where the boy had gone and saw him pulling his little wagon over to another corral with an apple picker in it, cleaning up after the horses as Ms. Kim gave lessons. "What a young man."

"Yes, he is. I wish all the kids were like him.

"They aren't?"

"Oh no, not all of them. Each child is its own, so all we can do is offer a place for them to go. Some change very slowly and others not at all. Some kids really enjoy watching a garden grow while others are drawn to the animals. We are just here for the experience."

A little blue pot-bellied goat came trotting over to investigate the new arrival. Without a thought, Paige reached down to pet the little guy. He started chewing on her pant leg, and then he pressed his little horned head to her knee and pushed.

"Hey, Danny... Oscar is out again. Can you come and grab him?" Sue asked as she tried to get the goat away from Paige.

Danny looked over at them and came at a jog,

"Oscar!" he said as he started laughing. The little goat took off at a trot heading back toward his pen. "Oscar! You get back in your pen!" he said with authority, although a smile was on his face.

The little goat hopped on a wheelbarrow, a wooden box, and then landed on top of his goat house inside his pen. He turned around and bleated at the young man.

In feigned frustration, Danny looked over at Paige, "He does that to me all the time." He shook his head and went back to cleaning.

Paige looked back over at Oscar. The goat bleated again and hopped back onto the box and waited.

Sue started to laugh, "Danny…"

Danny looked at Oscar. "No, Oscar!"

The goat hopped into the pen again.

"Oscar is a rescue," Sue explained. "He kept getting into trouble at his old place, so they sent him to a dog shelter. The shelter called us because they were not able to keep goats. He gets into the garden and eats the veggies. I think we are going to have to tie him up because he just constantly picks on Danny."

Paige could see the connection between the boy and the goat. "Why doesn't Danny just take Oscar with him. Give the little guy a job?"

"Yeah right! That little guy… a job? He is an obnoxious nuisance." Sue shook her head and laughed. "He is good at two things… getting out and eating."

Paige laughed as she watched. "That is just because that's all anyone lets him do. From what I can tell, he seems to really like Danny and listens to him pretty well. He is really bored in the pen, so why couldn't Danny teach him to pull that little wagon and help him with chores?"

Sue looked dumbfounded. "What do you mean?"

Paige had an idea that might help out the little situation. She didn't know if it would work, but it would be fun to find out. "Can I visit with Danny for a few minutes?" She grinned. "This might get interesting."

"Sure…" Sue looked over at the boy. "Danny, come here for a few minutes, if you would."

Danny stopped his cleaning and came trotting over, excited to have so much attention.

Paige looked at the beaming face of the young man. "Danny, do you like Oscar?"

"Yes. He is kind of goofy, but he is funny how he follows me around."

"Does he do that all the time?"

"Yes."

"How would you like to give that little goat a job?"

Danny was inquisitive, at the thought of a goat having a job. "What can he do?"

"Can you get me a little halter and a couple of lead lines?"

Danny went to get them and came back as Paige and Sue walked casually to the makeshift goat pen. Sue was just as curious as Danny.

Danny called to Oscar. As they stood at the open gate, Oscar jumped on his goat house and hopped the fence to come trotting to see him.

"Okay, let's put this halter on him for a harness and see what he thinks of it," Paige stated. She grabbed his collar, slipped the nosepiece over his head and buckled the headpiece around the goat's protruding belly. Oscar nibbled on Danny as Danny watched curiously. "Okay, now we hook a lead line here and here." Paige snapped the clips on each side of the halter and then tied them to the wagon that Danny had been hauling manure in. "There. Now just don't fill the wagon too full. You don't want to hurt Oscar. You just want him to help."

Danny beamed at the concept.

"Now all we need to do is let him know he has a job to do with his best buddy. So grab his collar and take him for a walk to let him know it is okay to pull the wagon.

Danny grabbed the string on the goat's collar and called to him, "Come on, Oscar. We have work to do." The little goat pulled into the halter with purpose, like he was meant to be a draft horse, and followed Danny to the barn. The little wagon clanged behind him.

Sue was silent for a few minutes. "I'll be danged," was all she could say.

"That ought to give Oscar something to think about. He just wanted a job like Danny," Paige said as she headed back toward the barn where they first started.

Sue watched Paige walk away. *And she came here to learn.* she thought before she started to stride after her.

Danny made it back to the corral with his goat next to him. He grabbed the apple picker and put a forkful of manure in the wagon. He walked to the next pile and the goat followed, willingly pulling his little wagon. Sue shook her head.

"Look, Ms. Sue! Oscar likes it!" Danny said excitedly.

"I see that!"

"Everybody likes a job to feel like they are part of something," Paige said.

"Can't argue with that," Sue replied as they walked to the barn, along the side of the arena was a single wheelchair. Ms. Kim was giving directions to a young girl. Ms. Kim would ask to take the riders left ring and put it on the side walkers right cone. The side walker with a hand on the little girl's ankle would hold out the plastic cone so the girl could stretch her core to put the ring on.

"Amazing stuff here, Sue. You do a beautiful job." Paige had never thought of how wonderful this was. Her heart was in her throat as she watched.

"That little girl is Crystal. The doctors didn't think that she would be able to have mobility in her arms and fingers. But look at her now." Sue called out to her. "Good job, Crystal, look at you go!"

Crystal beamed.

All afternoon, Paige followed Sue around with notebook and pen, taking notes and sketching out setup plans. She met and visited with Kim, asking questions of how to keep the kids involved, temperaments of horses and so on. Kim was inviting and accommodating for the questions. She was passionate about the horses and kids. Keeping activities and lesson plans available for the kids and families seemed to be first and foremost on the priority list. The protocol was simple for most things, the tasks challenging and engaging.

Frequently checking on Danny and his sidekick, they laughed and talked through the afternoon.

***

When Paige got to her room that evening, she unpacked her things and realized she had not brought her phone charger for her little flip phone. The phone that was seldom used all of a sudden brought reality to her life in Oregon. She never thought she would want a cell phone, but she was surprised when she felt a bit of panic not having it. Two years ago, she had never heard of a mobile phone.

She flipped it open and saw that it had less than a quarter of a charge. She called her mom, filling Patricia in on the day's events with a short conversation, and explained to her mom the short battery life. She hung up the phone, thought for a moment, and then shut it off. She would ask Sue to maybe pick up a charger when she went into town. Her eyes were heavy as she finally turned down her bed and crawled into fresh sheets. She was asleep before her head hit the pillow.

The next day, Paige watched kids come and go while volunteers performed daily routines to keep the little ranch going. Danny came trotting up to Paige, little

Oscar trotting behind pulling the wagon with a dog harness on. Danny had cut long sleeves off of a shirt and put them on the breastplate of the harness to keep it from rubbing on the little goat's chest. "Look, Ms. Paige! Look what Oscar has! My Mom bought it for me last night!"

"Danny, that is a brilliant idea! Good job," Paige answered.

Danny beamed.

Paige stood in the middle of the arena with Ms. Kim and listened while she gave direction to Danny as he rode Rocket around the barrels and trotted the old horse home, just like at a rodeo. Little Oscar, not wanting to be left out, came trotting out to follow them. They laughed at his courage and stamina. Paige admired his devotion to Danny and Danny's devotion to the farm. Paige constantly wrote notes in her notebook of the ideas for creating something similar to this farm back in Oregon.

*∗∗∗

Sue filled Paige's mind with how the place was run, protocols, daily plans, challenges, paperwork, dedication and struggles. The days flew by as Paige studied written material of different types of special needs, including autism. When Paige saw the faces of the kids and young adults coming in to the place, she knew why Sue did it. It was all worth it. The world beyond this little ranch seemed to fade away into routine and accomplishments.

Before Paige knew it, it was time for her to go. She packed the last of her belongings and looked around her little room. It seemed odd how she felt at home here yet she was ready to get back. She loaded her stuff in the back of the little pickup then went out to say goodbye to Danny, Ms. Kim and the rest of the volunteers. She went and scratched the pony Butterscotch, and ole racing Rocket. Oscar came trotting over as not to be forgotten. He butted his head up to Paige's knee, "I will never forget you my little friend. Danny is taking good care of you." She reached down and scratched his neck a few moments, then she reached out and gave Danny a hug.

"Danny it was a pleasure to meet you." she opened the door to the pickup to get in. She was ready to finish the last leg of her visit.

"Wait Ms. Paige, I have something for you!" Danny reached in his pocket and pulled out a picture of Oscar and him with the wagon. "Ms. Sue took it for us."

Paige felt her eyes well up with tears. "Danny you are the best! Thank you!" Paige gave him another hug. It was almost hard to leave the place.

"Sue you have a wonderful place here, thank you so much for sharing with me."

Sue nodded her head, feeling a bit of remorse sending this woman away, she had so much she could offer this little place and a quiet respect had developed in the last few weeks. Sue started the pickup and headed back toward the airport to her hotel room. It was a quick goodbye with the promise of keeping in touch, they exchanged phone numbers and addresses.

"If you ever come out to Oregon, I want you to know that you will always have a place to stay," Paige said as she got her luggage out of the back of the truck.

Sue smiled. "If I ever have the opportunity, I would love to come and see you."

Paige reached out and gave Sue a hug like they were sisters. Sue turned, got back in her truck, and pulled out of the parking lot as Paige walked inside to settle into her reserved room.

7

Craig walked up the two flights of stairs. He didn't know for sure what to do with his emotions. Lisa was gone. She was really gone. He walked into his apartment and sat down in the darkness. He grabbed the little framed picture and stared at it for a few moments. Tears started to form and a sob came from his lips.

He thought he was through all the emotional roller coaster rides. He could have a new beginning, but something seemed to be holding him back. Every time he walked into this apartment, he looked at her clothes still hanging in the closet and that damned huge refrigerator that she had to have. He'd had to drag it up two flights of stairs and take the doors off to make it fit through the apartment door. He smiled as he wiped away the tears.

"Lisa, I am so sorry. How do I let you and the baby go?" He looked back down at the little picture and ran his finger around her face. He closed his eyes and lifted the picture to his forehead. "Forgive me." Then brought it down to his heart and held it. "Goodbye, baby," he sobbed. "I will never forget you. Goodbye." He lay back on the couch and allowed his anguish to overtake his body.

***

When Craig awoke, it was still dark. His eyes were heavy, but his mind seemed clearer. He lifted the picture from his chest, looked at it for a long moment, and gave it a kiss before he closed the frame. He walked into the kitchen and opened the glass door onto the little balcony. The moon was almost full, its light so many miles away, and he thought of Paige. Her memory was like a beacon in the night. He thought of the evening they had gone swimming and laid under the stars. He thought of her laugh. He thought of her waiting in Oregon.

He walked into the bedroom with a box, and with a clear mind, he took a dress out of the closet. He held it to his face and took a breath in, trying to find Lisa's familiar scent. It smelled of stale closet. He paused for a moment and then gently laid it in the box. He took another dress off the hanger and began to pack up the last of her belongings. He took the last of her clothes out of her dresser and gently laid them in the box. The beginning of the end had started, and there was no turning back now.

He walked out of the bedroom, closed his eyes and took a breath in, blowing it out forcefully. He had one more room to do. One he had not opened since the accident. Slowly he walked down the hall, paused, and then took hold of the knob, turning it slowly and opening the door to the nursery.

He didn't turn on the light. The faded glow from the hallway muted the bright colors of baby animals that lined the walls. He allowed the skeletal shadows of the crib, with its zoo animal carousel and changing table, to bear witness to a dream never to come true. The room had the smell of baby powder as he looked at the beginning of a new life that never started.

He opened the top drawer of the dresser and took out a rattle and baby book that lay there. He thumbed through the empty pages, and a photo fell out. As he picked it up, he saw Lisa posing with her little pooch of a belly. On the bottom of the photo it said, four months.

I took that picture. He could remember the laughter and embarrassment of the pose. He held it to his chest for a moment and then set it in the box with his wife's things.

He opened the second drawer and pulled out one of Lisa's favorite baby dresses. Craig's mind quietly reminisced the day and how excited she was to have found it at the store. She knew this was the dress she was going to bring her baby home in. He lifted it up and held it for a moment. He cradled it in his arms, with a tear running down his cheek, and laid it to rest with her mom's things. He thought they needed to be together. He quietly closed the lid.

As he had filled the last box, it was just becoming daylight. He sat down at the kitchen table with a cup of coffee in the quiet moments of reflection. He paused. It was done. He ran his hand through his hair and grabbed a pen and paper. Then he began to write a letter. He didn't know what he was going to write, but the pen crossed the paper leaving a permanent mark.

> *Dear Paige,*
> *I am writing this from the heart. Life is filled with change, and our lives are led by the choices we make after the changes. I have been trying to put the pieces together here and pack up to move on, but it seems so hard to do. For these last few weeks, I feel like I have been two people divided by past and future...*

He continued writing from his heart all the emotion locked up, and finally turning them loose. He finished the last few lines. He grabbed an envelope, printing Paige's name on the outside of it. He paused a moment, kissed the envelope then set it down on the table. He would send it later after he got back from his run. He picked up the phone and called Lori. He knew it would be a little too early for her and got her voicemail. "Hey Lori, this is Craig. There are a few things of Lisa's you might want here at the apartment. If you would like, you can come by and pick them up after your conference before you head back home. Talk soon."

Craig put on his running shoes and stretched a little, preparing for a short, five-mile run before heading into work. The morning air was fresh, even with the busyness of the people preparing to open their shops.

He felt alive and free of some decisions that had been weighing him down.

He got to the stoplight and jogged around the corner when he saw a yellow ball roll off the sidewalk and a little toddler trotting after it in between a couple of parked cars. Seeing a car coming, the driver unaware of the little boy running after his ball, Craig whispered, "Not today," as he dodged between the parked cars, scooped the child up in one swoop, and then set him back on the sidewalk. The car drove past without even slowing down. The mother came running off the steps and grabbed her son. The toddler twisted in his mother's arms as he reached out for his little yellow ball still in the road.

"I got it," Craig said as he jogged back out between the parked cars. He glanced at the red stoplight as he again ventured out into the street, grabbing the ball and grinning broadly at his prize for the boy.

A car came around the corner a little too fast. Craig, startled by the vehicle, let his instincts take over—and with pure perfection—anticipated the impact. He managed to jump and roll over the hood of the car. The impact was not hard, but enough to roll him off the other side. As he felt himself falling, he thought, *Just tuck and roll.* As he landed, the momentum kept him rolling forward, casting him into a parked car. He felt his head crack against a tire rim. All went black.

8

Jim Curry heard the phone ring. He was a big frame of a man as he walked from the barn back into the house after saddling Mouse, his grulla colt. The morning Oregon air had a sweet taste of fall coming, and it seemed to be coming early this year. Fall was his favorite time of year, when the golden needles of western larch and the tamaracks mingled with the evergreens and juniper, while the aspen leaves fluttered their windy dance, preparing for their final release later in the season to rest in a blanket on the forest floor. It was coming soon. Jim inhaled the brisk air as he jogged to answer the phone.

He and Charlie were going out to check the cows out by Keating today where his neighbor said a couple of calves had gotten out next to the highway.

Boy, I hope we don't have more out, he thought as he jogged to the phone. "Hello?" Jim said as he picked up the receiver.

"Jim? This is Alison," she paused.

Jim had not heard from his ex-wife in a couple of years, he was surprised to hear her voice now.

"There has been an accident. Craig has been hit by a car and is in Bellevue Hospital on First Street." She paused again to regain her composure. "He is in a coma. Jim, I don't know what to do."

Jim swallowed hard, trying to digest the words being said.

"I need you here."

Jim could hear the hospital noise in the background as Alison spoke. "What happened? How serious?" Jim's hands began to shake as he listened. "I will see what I can do to get over there."

"Here is my phone number and he is staying at…"

Jim grabbed a pen and scribbled down as much as he could. His mind was racing.

"He is in the trauma center," she said. "Let me know when you can get here."

"I will get there as soon as I can."

"I have got to go, Jim. The doctor is coming."

Jim heard a click, and the phone was dead.

He sat stunned for a moment trying to get things lined out in his head. Craig, his only son, was in a coma three-thousand miles away. He picked up the phone and called Abe Cason. The Cason family was one a person could rely on. Jim always enjoyed their company and he trusted and respected their opinions, from Patricia, Abe and their daughter and his neighbor, Paige.

He remembered when Paige had found one of his baby colts on her place stuck in a bog a little over a month ago. Had she not known what to do, it would have been certain death for the little guy. Now he stood out in the pasture with his momma and sibling, bucking, playing and enjoying the good life. He was a late colt but he was a good one, out of Abe's stud horse affectionately called Shorty.

Patricia, Abe's wife, answered the phone, "Hey, Patricia, this is Jim." His voice was firm, deep, and serious.

"Good morning, Jim," Patricia happily responded.

He didn't go into the pleasantries of the day. He didn't have time. He went right to the point. "There has been an accident, Patricia. Craig is in a coma. I was wondering if you and Abe could help Charlie watch the place for me while I am gone?"

"Whatever you need, Jim."

"I will call my neighbors and see if they can help out until I get back, but I just thought…" He went quiet. "Paige…"

The realization that Craig had spent a lot of time with Paige while he was here on vacation made him stop in awareness.

Patricia was as silent for a moment. "Jim, I will send Abe over. I will call Paige. You go ahead and get your things packed and make your travel arrangements."

"Alison is supposed to call me back with some more information. I will wait until Abe gets here. Thanks, Patricia." Jim hung up the phone.

***

Patricia got off the phone and headed out toward

the barn of their fifteen-acre ranch at the base of the Elkhorn Mountains. Abe Cason had just finished up feeding his boarding horses and cleaning a few corrals of the messes all horses make when fed well.

Charlie Thomas was staying out at the Cason place, sleeping in the tack room in the barn until he could save enough money to get his own place after his bankruptcy and losing his wife to cancer. Abe had offered him a room in the house, but he felt most comfortable out in the barn and didn't want to be a burden to this family. He was throwing a little hay to his Plaudit mare and her two-week-old buckskin filly. She was like a new beginning for Charlie, a breath of fresh air. Charlie had been hired by Jim to do some, 'day riding', and helping Abe around the place. He had hopes to have a place before the first snow.

Patricia jogged out to see them. "Abe, Charlie," she called half breathless. They both looked at her, surprised to see her at the barn. She didn't know how to say it, so she just blurted it out. "Craig has been in an accident. He is in a coma."

They both just stopped and stared at her, trying to register her words.

"Jim is getting ready to leave and wants to know if we could help out. I told him I would send you right over and you guys can make some sort of plan.

Without thought, both Abe and Charlie headed to Abe's truck. Flick, Charlie's border collie jumped in the back before either of them could get in. Abe looked at Patricia, his heart seemed to have stopped. "What about Paige?"

"I am going to call her."

Abe put the truck into gear and headed out of the driveway.

Patricia dialed Paige's number, her heart thumping in her chest. After four rings, it went to voicemail. Patricia paused. She felt a tear run down her cheek but then cleared her throat and left a message. When she got off the phone, she hollered at Abby and headed to the car.

***

Jim's mind was swimming with everything that needed to be done. Heading out to unsaddle his horse, Mouse, he made a mental list of things that needed to be done. As he started to jog off the porch, he felt his foot begin to slip on the wood deck, and as if in slow motion, he felt his leg give way. His arms outstretched only grabbing air, he landed hard on the ground as he heard his lower leg snap. He felt sick to his stomach.

"You have got to be kidding me!" he gritted his teeth but lay there for a moment trying to catch his breath and gather his wits. He rolled around on the ground, a searing pain in his leg. Grabbing the guard rail, he pulled himself up to standing. Maybe it is just a sprain, he thought as he cautiously put his foot down and felt his leg give to the pressure.

"Damn!" he cursed under his breath. He fell back to the steps. He had to stop and think and gather his wits. He dug the heel of his good leg into the ground, and with his hands, he scooted back up the steps and through the door into the mud room.

Grabbing the countertop, Jim climbed back up to standing to reach some vet wrap that he would normally use for horses. He scooted over to the wood stove, took two pieces of thin kindling, and posting them outside his cowboy boot. He took the vet wrap and, as tightly as he could, began to wrap his entire lower leg, gritting his teeth through pain.

That ought to hold it for a while, he thought as he scooted back over to the mud room and grabbed the broom. With a bath towel, he wrapped the bristle side as tightly as he could to make a soft spot for under his arm and bound it together with the last of the vet wrap to make a crutch. He pulled himself up to a standing position and tested his crutch. *That should work for a bit*, he thought as he hopped out the door toward the barn.

With care, Jim slowly crutched out to where Mouse stood saddled and ready to ride. Mouse, shy and fidgety, twitched and paced at the uncertain object hobbling toward him.

"Well, little man, this is your lucky day," Jim said as he eased up to the colt slowly, wiping the sweat from his brow.

Mouse watched warily then side-stepped away. The

voice was familiar, but there was a different energy from this man that he tried to trust. He flickered his ears back and forth unsure of the makeshift broom crutch. Jim untied the horse and turned his back toward the colt's head to begin loosening the cinch. Jim was feeling lightheaded, his hands began to shake, and he couldn't make his fingers work the leather. He blinked a couple times then leaned his head against the saddle seat for a few moments.

As Jim regained a little of his strength, he loosened the saddle and started to pull it off, Mouse began to get nervous, his ears snapping back and forth between the voice of the man he thought he knew and the odd object he was holding. Self-preservation took over as he felt the saddle on his back being pulled away. Mouse jumped to the side and hid behind Jim, rollers blowing out of his nose.

Jim knew at that moment his saddle was going to hit the dirt. With a cringe, there was a heavy thud as the hunk of rawhide and leather lay in a heap on the ground. *Just not my day*, he thought to himself. Mouse circled behind Jim, looking for understanding to the unnatural stimulus. He had to put something between him and the saddle, he peaked around Jim's shoulder at the lump on the ground.

"Easy, Mouse, easy. It's just a saddle," Jim said, trying to remind himself of that too. "Just a saddle," he repeated as his custom-made rig lay in the dirt. Jim felt sweat roll off his temple. He seemed hot for such a chilly morning. Maybe he would just leave the saddle there and pick it up after he took care of his horse.

Again, he crossed his hand to wipe the sweat from his brow. Jim was thankful that the colt was curious enough to stay. He hobbled to the gate of the corral with Mouse in tow and started to turn the young horse loose. Booger, a large bay, raised his head from the feed bunk and watched as the gate was opened.

As he reached up to turn the colt loose, he felt lightheaded again. *Just get him turned loose*, he thought opening the gate to lead Mouse through. He reached up to untie the halter, but Mouse lifted his head away from Jim. Jim talked to him soft and low, realizing his words weren't making any sense. He finally got it untied then let the halter drop to the ground, thinking he would just pick it up later. Mouse trotted away, happy to get away from the awkwardness of this man he thought he knew.

Jim leaned up against the corral post for a moment. The gate looked too big, maybe he would just leave it open for a while. He didn't need to close it this morning. *They are good horses…* He wiped his brow again. *Gosh it seems to be hot today*. He slid down the post, his knee buckling under his weight. Maybe he might just take a rest before he headed back to the house. Pulling his light jacket close around his neck he shivered. Maybe he would just close his eyes for a moment.

9

Paige had gotten into her motel room and roamed around it for a few moments, anticipating calling Craig and letting him know she was in town. She was excited and nervous almost to the point of being giddy. She didn't know what she was going to say. She'd asked Sue to pick up a charger on their way into town, and she happily unwrapped it to charge her dead phone.

She sat at the desk in her room and went over her notes, reading the material Sue had given her. This was a whole new perspective on understanding horses and the healing effects they had on people. Paige also thought it odd that she already knew a lot of it yet had never put words to explain it.

Before she knew it, her phone beeped. Paige flipped it open and noticed she had five messages from home. Her heart pounded as she listened to them. A stillness fell upon her. She called her mom.

All the things Paige wanted to say were gone.

"Mom," was all she could say.

She let Patricia fill her in on the events. Silent tears filled her eyes. "He is at Bellevue Hospital on First Avenue."

When Paige got off the phone, she thought for only a

minute and called a cab. She had to get to the hospital. Within minutes, she was sitting in the backseat, numb at the shock of the incident. Lost in a sea of speeding vehicles and tall buildings. She glanced at the 4th Ave street sign. Across the street was a Bank of America, and down the block she noticed a tall building with NYU Medical Center. She read the names to all these places to keep her busy, but nothing digested into her mind, it seemed all a blur.

The front of the old brick building looked nothing like the St. Elizabeth Hospital back in Oregon. She stepped out of the taxi and paid the driver. She turned around, running right into a red and white sign that said No Standing Any Time. *What an odd sign*, she thought.

She turned to the glass-front building, entering into a solarium entrance. As she crossed the walkway, she noticed the entryway arc in front of her with two men facing opposite sides as the words, Bellevue Hospital, arched over the top and Administration made up the bottom. Then in more modern lettering it said Hospital and Emergency. Paige walked across the marble floor to the assistance desk to the left of the entrance where she inquired about Craig Curry.

The receptionist began typing while she said, "Go ahead and sign in."

Paige picked up the pen and put her name, state and who she was seeing.

"Second floor, the desk will advise you from there. Elevator is to your right."

Paige turned and looked for the elevator. Her heart was thumping in her throat. She pushed the number for the second floor as she stepped inside. When the elevator doors opened again she walked to the desk and asked the nurse where Craig Curry's room was. The nurse pointed down the hall and gave her the room number.

Paige cautiously walked down the hall and peeked through the door where she saw a beautiful, young woman holding a man's hand. His head was wrapped in a bandage. She backed out expecting to have found the wrong room. She went to the desk and asked again for Craig Curry's room.

"Yes, it is just down the hall. I will show you," the nurse said as Paige followed.

The nurse walked into the same room Paige had just looked in. Paige stopped outside. *This can't be Craig's room*, Paige thought as she watched the pretty woman stand up and kiss the unconscious man on the cheek before she lovingly put his hand on his chest. As she moved out of the way, so the nurse could have room to work, Paige recognized the face, it was Craig.

"Have you noticed any change, Lori?" the nurse inquired.

"No, he has been resting easy," came the reply from the woman.

"Sometimes comas are unpredictable."

"I will wait," the woman said as she grabbed Craig's hand again. "I almost lost him once. I won't allow it again."

Paige stood there for a moment as reality suddenly hit her stomach. She backed away, feeling sick. She was floating in a strange world, a strange life. She felt like she was swimming in a sea of instant reality. What she had expected was a dream, a fantasy of daydreams and future hope. This was a sea of emotions she had never recognized before. Who was she fooling? She did not belong in this place, to this man or this life. And this man did not belong to her. He had his own life here.

The nurse checked his IV and prepared to take his blood pressure.

Paige backed up and started down the hall. She heard the nurse say, "Craig has another visitor..."

Paige pushed the elevator button, and the door opened. She stumbled inside and couldn't push the button fast enough.

She remembered the last evening she saw him, how he opened his arms and welcomed her in. She could feel his heartbeat, his breathing, his hands molding around her, holding her for security, for memory until they would see each other again. She reached for his hand, and quietly lay it just below her throat line. Her heart was pounding. When she finally released her hold, she looked down at the floor. She couldn't look at him, so she headed back to the door. Taking a breath and grabbing the door knob with all the strength she could muster, she walked out. When the barrier was closed behind her, she looked back through the window. He stood in the kitchen door frame, propped against the door jam, watching her. If there were tears she couldn't see them, but she felt her own on her cheeks.

Was this the same Craig? Was he living two lives, or was she just a fling for the weeks he was in Oregon? She felt sick.

The elevator door opened on the first floor, and she ran into the bathroom, found the first stall, and heaved over the toilet, tears streaming down her face. She couldn't catch her breath. She felt weak and she sat in the stall as sobs consumed her body. Never before had she known such anguish.

***

The following morning, Paige got up two hours early and went to the JFK airport to board her flight. The sooner she left this city the better. After getting out of the taxi and handing the driver a twenty, expecting change, the driver just drove off without a backward glance.

Checking in her luggage, Paige stopped at one of the little restaurants and bought a cup of coffee. The rich, fresh aroma wafted up to her nose. It was something she always enjoyed, yet as she took a sip, it tasted like ash. She walked around the airport through the little shops of souvenirs, clothes so expensive with fancy names on them and so on. She felt even more lost. This was not her life. It never could be. It never would be.

She thought of Craig at her sixteenth birthday when

he surprised her by coming home for a few weeks. She remembered dropping all the two-liter sodas on the ground as he had walked up behind her. He didn't want to talk about New York or any part of it. He just wanted to hear what she had been up to. She remembered his laugh. He had flown from this same airport, flown the same flight.

That is enough! she thought. She had to shift her thoughts as she dropped her coffee in the trash and sat at her flight gate. She opened up her duffel bag and began to read about the spectrum of autism. She opened her paperwork and began looking through her notes. Tears started to form in her eyes. She blinked them back. *Focus on the work.*

An hour and a half later she finally scrunched herself in her seat on the plane. Her phone rang, and it was her mom. Paige did not answer. She couldn't. She didn't know what she would say. That Craig had a second life… Or that she was a fool for her thinking he loved her. She would call her when she got back home. She turned her phone off as she delved back into the reading material she had received from Sue.

10

Patricia filled Abby in as she drove. Abby was silent, listening to the sketchy details Patricia had. She had no words. Actually, she was too scared to speak as anxiety filled her heart.

Patricia drove to Jim's place. When they pulled up, they saw Abe and Charlie out by the corrals.

Abe looked over at Patricia and hollered, "Call an ambulance!"

Without a second thought, Patricia headed to the house. Abby stood and watched, almost too petrified to move.

"Abby, grab this glass and some water and take it to the barn. Grab that blanket too." Patricia picked up the phone and called an ambulance.

Abby pulled the Pendleton wool blanket off the back of the couch, then grabbed the water and glass.

She heard Patricia as she headed to the barn, "Yes, he is at the corral right now. I don't know for sure what happened… Yes, Pocahontas Road."

Abby recognized Patricia was doing the same thing that Paige had done with Cougar a little over a month ago. She headed to Abe at a trot and instantly saw the yellow vet wrap around Jim's leg. Abe was trying to get him to speak.

"Jim, hey Jim, what are you doing out here?" Abe said, trying to sound unconcerned.

Jim looked up at Abe for a moment. "Boy, it is kind of chilly out here this morning, ain't it?"

"Yeah, it's a little chilly," Abe repeated to keep him talking. "What happened to your leg?"

"Think I broke my dadgum leg. Slipped on the stairs when I went out to unsaddle my horse."

Abe looked up at Abby and took the water from her. "Here, bud, have some water. Let us get this blanket around you until we can get you to the house."

Jim took a sip of water. His mouth was bone dry. "Mmm… that is good," he said, wanting another sip.

Charlie looked at Abby staring at Abe. He knew the helplessness she must have felt.

"Abe, I think Abby and I will go check the horses and close some gates."

Abe looked at Abby and realized the fear in her eyes. "Alright, Charlie, I will stay here until we get some help."

Charlie looked over at Abby, "Hey, Abbs, do you want to go check on the horses with me and make sure they are all here?"

Mouse and Booger had both made it out with the broodmares. Cougar was chewing on Mouse. Mouse seemed to enjoy the company of a colt with a sense of humor.

Abby took her eyes off Jim and looked over at Charlie for a moment. "Sure."

The two started walking out toward the broodmares. "How long has it been since you have seen Cougar?"

Abby smiled, "It has been a little over a month, I suppose."

"Well, why don't we see how he is doing while we wait for the ambulance," Charlie said as they walked. "I hear he was bogged down in a spring and you saved him from a cougar."

Abby remembered that day, seeing the helpless two-week-old colt mired in the mud. She couldn't believe what she had done, screeching and war whooping around like a crazy woman, trying to scare a wild mountain lion. She was glad no one had seen her as she had toppled into the muddy pit after getting him out. That day had changed her life.

As they walked out into the pasture, a bright yellow palomino colt and a bay filly were out playing with Mouse. Cougar raised his head and looked at them for a moment and then almost at a run came racing toward them. Charlie raised his hand as the baby approached. Cougar slammed on his brakes and came to a sliding stop about ten feet from them. He seemed so excited to see people.

"Hey, Cougar," Abby said as she reached out her hand. Cougar walked up to her. He looked magnificent. He looked like he had grown twice the size he'd been when she had helped him out of the bog. He touched her hand with his nose and nibbled at her fingers. "Look at you," Abby said in awe of the colt he had become..

Cougar bobbed his head a couple of times and then took off at a run toward his mom, Mouse and the others—happy to have said hello and goodbye all in one quick action. "I can't believe that is him. He has grown so much."

"You wait until spring. You won't even recognize him," Charlie said as he walked the rest of the way out to check the horses legs for any injury. "That Shorty horse of Abe's can sure throw some beautiful babies."

Abby looked at him for a few moments. She thought of Charlie, who had come into their lives, was living in the barn: he'd lost everything he had, yet he always seemed happy-go-lucky. She let her mind drift back to her mom and dad, when she was living in the city and the only stress she had to worry about was if she had enough battery for her cell phone. It seemed a lifetime ago. She then thought of Paige, Abe and Patricia, and all that had gone on. She was becoming family.

"Thank you, Charlie," she said as they headed back to the barn.

Charlie grinned at the young girl. "No worries. Come on. Let's go see how Jim wants to handle the other animals before he heads to the hospital."

"Is Jim going to die?" Abby asked, her fear and anxiety fueling her imagination.

"No, don't think so, Abbs. He just fell and broke his leg. We will get him patched up here in short order."

They picked up their stride and made it back to the corrals where Jim, feeling a little better, was planning out what needed to be done. "If you could turn the geldings out with the calves and throw them a little hay once a day, that should keep them comfortable. Abe and Patricia had moved Jim onto a horse turnout blanket to get him off the frosted ground. They had his foot propped up with a saddle pad, and he was wrapped warm with the blanket Abby had brought from the house.

Patricia gave him some more water.

"Charlie, would you grab that sorrel horse and go see if you can find those two calves on the highway out by Keating? That is where you rode the first day with me. Got a call this morning that they were out. Check the fence line and see if you can find a hole in the fence. Think the elk might be migrating a little early this year."

"Sure, Jim." Charlie paused a moment and then said, "The geldings got in with the broodmares. Do we want to leave them there? They are getting along fine with the babies." Charlie paused. "I think it would do Cougar good to have some playtime with the big boys. It'd give that filly a little relief."

"If the mares don't mind. You know, keep an eye on them and we can leave them there for a few days and see what happens."

"Mouse sure likes Cougar. I will keep an eye on them, Jim."

They heard the siren of the ambulance.

11

Paige had quietly returned to Oregon. her heart heavy with how things had worked out in New York. She had isolated herself in the darkness of the house for the last couple days. She had left Abby with Patricia, she just needed some time to think. Patricia for some reason let Paige have her time alone, she was in no hurry to get rid of Abby..

Paige was riddled with guilt and if she would admit it, a broken heart, how was she going to tell Jim that she had walked out on his son? She had finished the evaluation and reports on her trip home but had made no effort to get ahold of Janis. She didn't have the stomach for trying to share information. She wanted to crawl in bed and stay there. She could hardly focus on the chores she needed to do around the house?

The sun was just beginning to rise. Paige hardly noticed her favorite time of the day. The purple and pinks were turning into a golden glowing ribbon on the horizon just before the brightness of the sun took away the vibrant colors and turned them to a distilled natural color of late summer's pale, muted yellows and sunburnt green.

Today she was going to make an effort to get back into the swing of things, and it was going to be a busy.

First helping her dad gather Jim Curry's cattle off Flagstaff and ship them closer to home before weaning. The weaner calves would have better feed and transition without their moms around on the lower ground. Then she had agreed to have Sarah come home with Abby on the bus, then have Janis and Lilly over too, to assist Lilly being around Paige's horses. She took her last sip of coffee and started for the door. Just as she grabbed for the door knob, the phone rang. She thought about not answering it. But what if it was her dad?

"Hello?"

"Is this Paige Cason?"

"Yes," she answered to the strange voice on the other end of the line. She waited.

"Uh." There was a pause. "Well, my name is Mike, and I live down the road from you." Another pause. "Well, hell I don't know how to ask this or anything, so I am just going to spit it out. I have a Percheron mare that got caught in the cattle guard a little over a month ago."

Paige wanted to listen, but she only heard words rambling together into a nonsense of sentences. What would she do with a draft horse? Why in the world would he be calling her?

She tried to focus, as his voice again started making sense.

"She was one of my best mares, but I can't seem to get her to heal up like she should." His voice shook as he continued, "She will never be able to pull again. I was wondering if you would be interested in her." Mike almost sounded like he was begging. "I would give her to you. I have my hay down and I just got another mare. I use her with my gelding to put up hay." His sentences were short and choppy, "The two mares don't get along very well. I just can't keep her and keep fences up and all." He rambled, "there are just not enough hours in the day."

"Mike, I don't know for sure what I would do with a draft horse."

Well, I just thought I would ask. I could give you hay for her for the year if that would help. I need a place for her to go. I had heard that you helped a colt that got attacked by a cougar on the same day this mare fell in the cattle guard and I thought that you might be able to help with her or something..." Mike paused again. "I just don't like the alternative."

Paige knew what he was saying. "Does she have any broken bones?"

"No, just pulled muscles on her hip, and she is pretty scraped up. The new mare ran her through the barbed wire fence this morning, I don't have any more panels to hold her. She is locked in the barn right now."

"Mike, I am gonna be riding for some cows this morning. Maybe I can get there this afternoon."

"You know, Paige, I can drop her by. I am heading into town to get some parts, and I can drop her off in the corral. I just don't trust any of my fences and these two mares in the same place." He paused. "She is a good mare, one of the best I had, Paige. I know I am complaining about fences and all of that, but I have never had an issue with her until I got this younger mare." Mike sighed, "I just got to get through haying season, and putting these two horses together is like putting a match to gasoline."

"Does she do alright by herself?"

"Never had any issues with her."

"Well, Mike, go ahead and put her in the front paddock, and I will see what we can do with her. I can't promise I can keep her, but we will see what we can do about getting her healed up."

They made arrangements and set up what was to be expected. Paige hung up the phone and sat thinking for a moment. Then she got up from her chair and headed out to catch Libby. The Palomino mare heard the door close and met Paige at the gate.

"Come on, little lady," she whispered as Libby dropped her head in the halter and followed willingly into the barn like she had done for years. Paige grabbed her grain and poured it into Libby's bucket, then grabbed the brush and began the long strokes of brushing out the dirt, it felt good to breath in the the sweet smell of warm horse scent. Her hide was losing her summer hair and beginning to grow in a coarser winter hair that would absorb the winter sun rays through the hollowness of it. Libby bobbed her head to the strokes of her brushing, appreciating the scratchy spots along her chest and at the base of her tail.

Paige didn't take a lot of time because the phone call from earlier had put her a little behind schedule. So without a thought, she grabbed her blanket and her flat-backed Hereford saddle. With a few swift stokes, she released and straightened the cinch and tugged the Latigo snug, buckled the back cinch, and then went to hook up her Chevy pickup to her little bumper-pull trailer.

There was a brisk fall feeling in the air, and it was great to be out and away from the suffocating house. The walls seemed to have closed in on her as she struggled with what had happened. The thought that she had been played a fool for thinking there could have been something between Craig and her after all this time.

And here it just didn't matter, she told herself. *It was nothing more than a fling and a one-time deal. Time to move on.* She heard the click of the hitch touching the ball of the truck. She stepped out, began to lower the hitch on the ball, flipped the lever and attached the drag chains. She headed back to the barn to get Libby to load her in the trailer. A black pickup came down the driveway pulling a large stock trailer. Paige recognized the pickup and stopped her horse for a moment. Mike waved as he pulled up next to her.

"Paige, sorry I don't want to take up too much of your time, but here is that mare.

Paige glanced at the trailer. She saw an eye looking through the six-foot-tall slat.

"Hey Mike, I will throw my horse in the trailer and show you where to put her."

Paige reached back before loading and checked her cinch, opened the tailgate and gave a kiss cue. Libby stepped forward into the trailer as Paige threw the halter rope over the saddle horn. She let Libby get comfortable any way she wanted to ride. She seldom tied her except when traveling with other horses. Libby stood quietly as Paige shut the gate and turned to help Mike with the big mare.

Mike was opening the back of the stock trailer when Paige returned. Paige added fresh water to the trough, then grabbed the door as Mike stepped in. The trailer groaned at the weight as the big mare sidestepped for the man to untie her. Mike was short on words.

"I wish I had all the answers," he said as the big mare backed her body toward the end of the trailer, the trailer vibrating and groaning as she moved. Paige could see she was tall and thin and in desperate needed some groceries, the backbone protruding and mild hip bones.

The mare hesitated about dropping her left hind leg out of the trailer but then decided to maybe use her right hind leg to take the impact of all the weight stepping out. Then she decided the left hind leg. Mike was antsy and wanted to be done with it, so he pushed on the mare to make her get out of the trailer.

She shuffled her feet but refused to step out.

Paige now knew this mare was hurt and hurt bad. She noticed the swollen left hind pastern as the mare swayed in the trailer, not wanting to put any weight on it. Her right hind quarters were rock solid with the inflammation of supporting all the weight of this large animal on one leg. She watched and cringed at the thought of backing her out.

To cut the tension, Paige quietly asked, "Can she turn around in there?"

Mike made a move, and as if the mare had the same thought, she ducked her massive head, dropped her shoulder, wedging and twisting herself around in the trailer as it almost burst at the seams. The big mare straightened herself, looking out of the back, and dropped her nose to the edge. With massive lungs, she gave a couple of rolling snorts at the edge of the trailer bed, looked at the ground, and as gently as she could, hobbled out.

Paige instantly noticed her chest sliced open by the fight in the wire this morning. A ten-inch flap of skin hung down across the shoulder. There was no question why this man needed to get this mare off his place, if there was a monster that was going to chew her up like this.

There were bite welts on her neck and on her groin, a solid, swollen hoof mark to her shoulder blade and one on her rib cage, and numerous welts and scratches throughout her body.

Mike looked at Paige for a moment, feeling shame and thinking of the judgment she would have. "Paige, I can't even tell you…" He stopped. His eyes were filled with emotion on the verge of tears.

The mare stopped next to the man and took a half breath, her head down, eyes half closed. She was not the least bit interested in her new surroundings.

Mike straightened his shoulders and gave a sigh. His eyes turned as cold as he could make them. "I have all of her paperwork here." Reached in his pocket he gave her a transfer slip and papers. "I will deliver four tons of hay in a couple of weeks."

Paige held out her hand, an emptiness, a sense of sadness, or was it loss and helplessness. She thought Mike looked like he was losing his best friend and there was nothing he could think to do to save her. Paige was his only hope, and it was better than the only alternative, which in his mind, she knew was a bullet.

"I tried to make it work, but I think I really screwed up. I didn't think that younger mare would have gone at her like that. I had been struggling trying to get weight back on her and thought she might like the company of another horse. I put them together and before I knew it the new horse just whipped around and attacked. There wasn't anything I could do until she got through the fence." He paused for a moment and then with a half sob, "I think she is giving up. I think she wants to die."

He turned and stroked the mare's neck. "She has lost about two-hundred pounds, and I can't get it back on this girl. She won't eat, and she just stands here like this."

Paige couldn't speak for a moment. Then with a dry mouth, she said, "Go ahead and turn her in the paddock. I will get some hay for her and put in the feed bunk. I will have our vet, Tom, come out and take a look at her when I get back, but for right now I have got to go. Jim Curry is counting on me."

"Alright, I will let you go, thank you," he said as he held out his hand.

Paige took it, gave him a solid shake, "You bet Mike we will see what we can do when I get back."

"I have put fly spray on her and she should be good," Mike said, he started toward the paddock, the mare walked as if on eggs, from being so sore. He turned her lose, locked the paddock gate and then headed back to his stock trailer.

Paige went and got a forkful of hay and threw it in the feed bunk, but the mare just stood at the gate. This was not going to be an easy fix, and Paige had her doubts that the mare even wanted to live.

"I will be back in a few hours. I have got to go," she said with more urgency. Libby shifted in the trailer. Paige took one more look at the black mare standing inside her little paddock. The poles looked like little match sticks and that with one swipe from a front foot, they would crumble to splinters. But from the looks of it, that mare didn't want to go anywhere. Food, water and shade—there wasn't anything else she could do for her until she got back. She jumped into her pickup and headed down the road.

12

Charlie and Abe were sitting in their pickup and waiting at the gate. They were happy to see Paige pull up. Three riders could get the cows down off the sage brush hill while it was still halfway cool. Within a few minutes, Paige had Libby unloaded, cinch tightened, her chink leggings on, and was stepping in the saddle in a matter of minutes. Libby felt the tension of Paige sitting on her back and arched her neck with the power of surging forward yet contained her energy until Paige requested it. Whatever Paige asked, Libby was willing to give. Her long flowing mane shimmering a golden blonde color in the morning sun.

"Sorry, I am late. I had a bit of an emergency at the house this morning." Paige pressed a stressed grin.

"Everything alright, sis?" Abe asked as he looked over at his daughter. He knew something had happened during her travels and was hoping that her getting out and working with cows would help her move on. He also knew that she was a strong, independent woman and if she needed some support she would ask for it.

They turned toward the east side of the field and started at a long jog, attempting to make up for lost time and letting the horses air out a little.

"Yeah, I think so, but you have got to come over and see what is in my corral. I don't know for sure what to do with her, and she is in pretty bad shape. But that is where she's at."

Abe and Charlie both looked confused and shrugged in unison at the mystery.

Paige looked at them both for a moment as if they should have been able to read her mind. Then it dawned on her. "I have a Percheron mare in my corral, a big, black Percheron mare."

"What on earth are you going to do with that?" Abe asked.

"Oh, I don't know. Maybe take up dressage." Paige grinned.

Charlie was quiet a moment but then asked, "What do you mean in bad shape?"

Paige glanced at him for a moment, "Well, last month," Paige began, "When Abby found the Cougar in the spring bog and we called the vet, he was actually headed out to help a horse that had gotten into the cattle guard." Paige hesitated for a moment. "This is that horse, but that is not the worst of it. She got run through the fence by another horse. She has bite welts and kick marks all over her, along with several wire cuts. A couple of bad ones that need to be stitched, I'm sure. Tom is coming out this afternoon to look her over."

"Well I know a couple of remedies that might help out if you don't mind me taking a look at her."

Paige had watched Charlie handle horses over the last month and had the impression that the man knew horses. "I don't mind you coming and taking a look, Charlie."

"When I get home this evening, I will grab my bag and come and see her."

They had reached the top of a little knoll, and Abe looked over at Paige. "Sis, why don't you drop down over that ridge and start those pairs back to the corral."

Paige looked toward where her father was pointing. In an instant she saw five cow-calf pairs grazing along the base of the draw. On the right was another four pairs.

"Sure, Papa," she said as she waited to hear what else was instructed to make sure nothing was missed.

"Charlie, why don't you drop over this next ridge. There should be a fence line. Take it on down, and we will all meet up at the bottom meadow in about thirty minutes."

With all that agreed, Abe headed Shorty down and across the third draw. He didn't know the country well but he had a pretty good idea that most of them would be around the water.

Shorty moved forward with grace and ease. A person would almost forget he was a stud, especially this late in the year with breeding season past. He was always a gentleman and understood when it was time for work. Abe was pleased to be able to ride him out into the country and away from the arena for a while, and

A.K.MOSS

Shorty was eager to travel some country. At his age he knew the difference between cutting cows and pushing them. He headed over the hill, his head bobbing with his stride.

As they got the pairs down into the meadow, Abe rode up to Paige, "Hey, sis, Jim has a couple of neighbors going to help us sort and load. So when we get them in the corral, you can go ahead and tend to that mare if you want."

"Alright, that would make me feel better. I sure hated leaving her this morning. Are you coming down to see her too?"

"Sure. I don't know if there is anything I can do but I can sure come and visit." Abe grinned.

"Would love to have you come over, Papa," Paige said, not realizing how much she really wanted to just visit with her dad. She was finished sulking at home, it was time to move on. She stroked Libby's sweaty neck, nudged her into a long jog, and headed back to her truck.

13

Craig felt like he was wading in thick, soupy... something... What was this stuff? It felt like it clung to him and made him feel like he couldn't breathe. He had to wade through it. A heavy, murky glue type substance just clung to him, suffocating him. His head was pounding, and he felt like he was going to die. He felt like he was in a tunnel of some sort, something that was hollow and echoing. There was light in the distance.

He saw a letter, *Dear Paige...* it fluttered in his mind and then disappeared.

There was a baby dress, a photo, all faded and muted. He tried to reach them, but they drifted away like a dream.

There was a horse, a yellow horse with a flowing mane, loping toward him. Like the wind, it passed right by him.

There was his wife. He saw her. "Lisa," he tried to say her name, but the words would not form. She faded from sight.

There was a shooting, a young boy, a father and mother dead. It all come into focus. He tried to pick up the boy, but his hands went right through his body as he faded in the murky sludge.

Then a swarm of bees, a woman, blonde hair, stings all over her body. He had to save her! He looked at her face, the deepest blue eyes he ever saw, like deep pools of the purist water he had ever seen. He felt he could get lost in them. He couldn't look away. He saw her smile and heard her laugh. It gave him peace. Then they closed. She was dead. He struggled to wake her... then all was black.

***

There was a beep, beep, beep, beep.

Craig could hear it, but it didn't make any sense to him. He heard a woman's voice. Who was that? Did he care? Where was he? He moved his hand. Someone was holding it. He felt the skin against his. That didn't make any sense. He moved his hand again. The murky glue still had a hold of him.

He heard a woman's voice. "Craig? Craig, are you awake?"

He had to see who this strange woman was. Who was Craig?

He forced his eyes to open and blinked. Everything seemed blindingly bright. They couldn't focus! Was he blind? He closed them again. His mind was racing, his whole body didn't seem to work like it should. His arms and legs felt like they were on rubber bands and pinned down to his body.

He struggled to bring his hand up to his head to

rub his temples. His once strong hand was nothing but rubber fingers. He couldn't get them to work. When he dragged his hand away to look, he could not see it or his arm, for that matter. But he knew he was holding his head.

"Craig?" the woman said again. "Get the doctor! He is waking up!"

He tried to open his eyes again. Who is waking up? Who is Craig? He squinted his eyes and tried to get them to focus.

This time he could see the silhouette of a person, but he couldn't make out the face. He waved his hand and then started to struggle to get up. He heard a voice of groans and drawls, but they made no sense.

"What the hell? Where am I?" His voice sounded garbled and drunk. Was that his voice? How did he get in here? Was this a hospital? His brain seemed constipated with thought and words that mixed together like a wad of cotton too big for his mouth.

The beep, beep, beep got faster.

"Craig, you are alright. Okay? Someone get a nurse or doctor in here!"

The woman sounded like there was something wrong. He tried to wake up faster and get out of the murky depths of the tunnel. His body started to jerk and twitch as he fought to get out.

"Let me out!" he gurgled the words, coming out in a slur of garbled speech. He couldn't talk! He struggled to get control.

He heard a soft voice speaking and firm hands holding him to steady his confusion.

"It is alright. You are okay. Don't fight it," said a man's voice. "You are safe and fine. You have been asleep for a little while. Just wake up slowly. Take a breath. That's it. Breathe. You are safe."

Craig quit struggling. The words were soothing and informative. The man did not call out an odd name or seem stressed at all. Craig focused on his own breathing. He had been asleep. *Boy, what a hell of a nightmare*, he thought as his voice tried to form the words. His arms were heavy, sludgy, and tired.

"Just rest," the doctors voice said, as the assisting nurse gave him a shot to relax. "Just rest. You are safe."

Craig did what the man requested, he relaxed and fell back sleep.

Lori looked over at both the doctor and nurse. "Are you kidding me? What the hell was that?" Her voice was raised to a piercing level. "I can't believe you would leave me in the room like that. That scared the hell out of me!"

"Please, Lori, can we take this out in the hall?" The nurse advised, "we have some work to do here."

"What do you mean you have work to do? I thought he just woke up. Wake him up again. I want to talk to him."

"We sedated him until we can wake him up slowly. We need to have a calm room. We are going to have to ask you to leave."

"What do you mean you sedated him? Wasn't the whole goal to wake him up?" Lori couldn't breathe. "Do you even know what you're doing? I thought you guys were professionals!" she spat, adrenaline far stronger than common sense.

"We need you to leave now."

"You can't kick me out!" Lori was furious.

She was under the impression that when Craig woke up he would be calm and know what was going on. She had seen it in the movies, the pacient wakes up moves around a little and then get up and walks out of the hospital. That was just the way it was supposed to be. Not a man flailing around fighting off the one person who had sat with him the whole time he was in the hospital. Those nurses didn't even give her forewarning that something like this could happen.

Lori got up from her chair and stormed out of the room, still shaking from the excitement. That was not the same person that she had coffee with a little over a week ago. That was a mad man.

She paced up and down the hall and then walked out of the building. She reached in her purse and grabbed a cigarette, lighting it with shaking hands. Normally she was not a smoker. She just packed them in case of emergencies. And right now, this seemed to be an emergency.

***

Craig felt himself floating, drifting. *What was he doing?* He was trying to make sense of it, but nothing seemed right. He couldn't get his mind to focus on one thing. Visions in his head came and went like fast flickers. Just snapshots of life seeming to flicker through his vision and then they were gone.

Bareback riding as a teen, team roping, wrestling, a birthday party at a girl's house. A palomino horse. Laughter, stars, a stabbing, a gunshot wound, a car accident, a dead family, a swarm of bees, a blonde girl, a palomino horse again, swimming in a creek, braiding reins. None of this made any sense. They were all just a snapshot and then gone. The blonde girl again with the bluest of eyes. He reached for her and said her name. Then she was gone.

He blinked his eyes open, closed them, and then opened them again. He was in a hospital somewhere. Someone was talking to him. He listened but could not respond. His arms still felt like they were glued to the bed.

"Craig, you have been in a coma. Just take it easy and let things kind of find themselves. I am Doctor Adams. I can help you get things lined out. Alright? Just trust me."

The voice was soothing. Craig opened his eyes and saw a middle-aged man in a white coat looking down at him. He had to focus on what was being said. He had so many questions.

The doctor spoke again, "I am going to ask you some

questions, and you just shake your head for no or nod your head for yes. Do you understand?"

Of course I understand, I am not in kindergarten. He tried to say okay, but the words didn't come out like he expected. So he did as Dr. Adams requested and nodded his head.

"Do you know where you are?"

Of course I know where I am ... in a hospital, he thought, but he wasn't sure, so he shook his head.

"Do you know your name?"

Craig looked at him kind of funny. He wanted to nod his head. *Of course I know my name.* He thought for a moment. He couldn't think of it at the moment, but he'd had his name his whole life. He wanted to say yes, but his head shook no. That was so odd. He would think of it in a minute.

The doctor wrote down some notes. "Do you know your birthday?"

These were stupid questions. Of course I know my birthday. He wanted to blurt it out but he just couldn't think of it right off the bat. Maybe if he took a nap or something. He began to feel really tired.

The doctor asked again, "Do you know your birthday?"

Craig gave him a dirty look and shook his head.

"One more, okay. Do you know where you live?"

Craig looked at him and was going to give him an address, but again, he couldn't remember it. *Maybe if the doctor gave me a hint., or something.* Craig one more time shook his head.

"Alright, Craig, just rest for a little while, and then we will check in on you and get you up for a bit. You will be a little weak, but that is to be expected. We will get ahold of your mom and girlfriend and have them come in to visit and be part of the consultation. Alright?"

Craig nodded his head. He was extremely tired. Maybe if he took a bit of a nap it would all make sense later. Nothing seemed to be all that important. Maybe it was all a dream… He drifted off to sleep again.

***

Craig felt like he was floating. He could hear the things going on around him, but he couldn't respond. His throat was scratchy, dry, and he wanted water. If he could just have a little water.

"War," he said. It didn't sound right, so he tried again. "Wear." That still didn't sound right. What was going on with his speech? Okay, he closed his eyes and tried to say it correctly. "Water." It was shaky but it was said. He got his eyes to focus, and a mature, beautiful woman was standing next to him with a paper cup.

"It is alright, Craig. We are going to take care of you. You are going to be just fine. Alright, honey?"

He took a sip from the offered glass and tried to get his eyes to focus. His arms were heavy as beams connected to his body. He moved his fingers and then moved his hands. He couldn't lift his arms.

"Where… am… I?" he asked in a scratchy, forced

way. His mouth wanted to move but his brain was still foggy.

"Well, honey, you are at Bellevue Hospital." Alison looked at him with a warm smile. "You had an accident and got hit by a car. You hit your head really hard."

"Who... are... you?"

"Don't be silly, honey." Alison's voice went up an octave as she tried to maintain her composure. "I am your mother." Her voice almost upset. "We have been waiting here over a week for you to wake up. Now here you are, almost ready to go home."

"I can't have slept that long. Really?" His voice was getting stronger. He reached for the water, yet his arms still felt like rocks were tied to them. He knocked it over onto the floor.

"Honey!" his mom said in a whiny voice. "Well shoot! Don't do those things. Let me help you." Alison looked around. "I guess I will have to call a nurse to clean this up." She reached over and pressed a button.

"Nurse's station..."

"Yes, my son spilled water all over the floor. We need someone to come and clean it up."

"I will send someone right down."

He wanted a drink, but his eyes were heavy. He tried to listen to the woman's ramblings, but none of it was making any sense. He closed his eyes, and instantly all went black and quiet again.

Alison sat there for a moment, shocked at how fast he went to sleep, and panic filled her. She reached for her phone, fumbling with the numbers as she called Jim.

"He has forgotten everything, and I mean everything!" she said frantically when Jim answered the phone. "He doesn't know who he is or who I am." The tears were audible in her voice. "Jim, he is almost helpless."

Jim had answered the phone. He couldn't get a word in, so he listened. His heart ached to be there, but before he could speak...

"I have got to go. The nurse is here."

Jim heard the click of the phone, the agony of sitting next to the phone waiting for any kind of news, just to be cut off and left dwelling on imagination. "Damn leg!" he said, as if that would help the situation.

***

The nurse came in the room, her eyes weary of an eleven-hour shift, and she took a couple of paper towels and wiped up the half-spilled glass of water.

Alison looked at her, "Where were you? He was just awake!"

The nurse looked at her for a moment. "I am just down the hall, so if he wakes up again, just ring me. I will document his activity and let the doctor know." She finished wiping up the little bit of water. "How long was he awake?"

"How am I supposed to know? I didn't have time to look at the clock."

The nurse wrote on the chart the time and information. "Less than five minutes?"

"Oh for pity's sake. Yes, I suppose so."

The nurse ignored the tension from Ms. Curry. She had seen and heard it all from troubled family members. She allowed her to have her say, added support where she could, and got her job done in the most professional manner she could. No sooner she was done, and her beeper went off again. She was off to another patient.

14

Charlie finished helping Abe load cattle. The day had been longer than what he had expected. He had promised Paige he would go over and look at the draft mare, but he still had to get over to Jim's, feed the leppy calves and check the water. He needed to make sure the haying crew had gotten hay in the new barn for Jim, and he still had to clean out Plaudit's stall, where Abe had so kindly let him stay for the last month.

From losing his wife to cancer and losing his ranch to medical bills, he drove away from the life he thought he would live and where he thought he'd watch his grandchildren grow up. He had lost it all. The only thing he had left was his pickup, his last broodmare, and his forever faithful dog, Flick.

It was funny how life could shift so fast. A little over a month ago, he was washing his laundry in the Snake River on the Oregon-Idaho border, eating canned chili and peanut butter and jelly sandwiches, and sleeping alongside the freeway while traveling toward a place in Washington he really didn't want to go. Everything he owned was in his pickup and a single-wide horse trailer with bald tires. His mare was so pregnant, she was due to foal within the week, and he'd contemplated whether he had enough money to buy an omelet and coffee at the truck stop, or if he needed to keep it for gas money. Not thirty minutes later, he was loading his horse into Jim's trailer. He never made it to Washington, instead he found home in Eastern Oregon on Abe and Patricia Cason's Ranch.

Charlie still didn't have his own place yet, although the tack room was cozy enough for now at Abe's place. Jim had asked Charlie to move out to his ranch so he wouldn't have to commute back and forth, but Charlie liked living at the base of the Elkhorn Mountain. The timber and sage lived in close vicinity together. The water was clear and the land rich. He loved waking to the sound of the creek behind the barn babbling and the different birds chirping their chaotic choir of native songs. It brought him peace and a feeling of stability on the Cason Ranch. Maybe it was a place for him to heal, and maybe even reinvent who he thought he was.

Before, he was a man of horses, training reining and cutting horses. He thought bloodlines and money were all that was needed to build his own empire, to be sought after by some of the best breeders to start their colts. That was his dream, his ambition. But like so many other turns in life, he found out that, dreams were only the start of a journey, and life happened between the two. He didn't need money, he didn't need a name, and he didn't need a big, fancy trailer. All he needed was to do what he loved and help support those who were doing what they loved.

He found home in this little town called Baker. The place was so diverse, it had everything from a powder-dry silt soil, salt grass with sage and juniper to the more lush, rich soil of the valley floor to grow gardens. In the vast, rocky ranges of the Cascades, seasonal aspens, larch and tamarack grew while the evergreen spruce and pines brought shade and protected the ever-elusive rocky mountain elk and large mule deer and scattered wildlife. Yes this is where Charlie had found his home.

He missed his wife. Her death would forever weigh on his heart, but she sure had to be in a better place than here. The cancer had eaten away her spunk, her zest for life. It had eaten away her love of food as well as her love of sun and spontaneity. All that was left of her was a shell of a person that once was.

As she had looked at herself in the mirror and realized her hair was falling out and her skin a putrid yellow, she'd started to cry. "What is happening to me? This is not who I am."

Charlie remembered saying the only thing that came to mind. He knew at that point there would be no more future years. There was today, tomorrow and the day after that. He took her hand in his. Her legs were shaking with weakness and her once one-hundred-and-fifteen-pound body was no more than eighty pounds. He lifted her gently and carried her to her recliner to help get her seated. Then he laid her favorite blanket on her lap.

"Babe," he swallowed as tears blurred his vision. He

spoke a truth he had not yet come to terms with. "Your soul has become bigger than your body, and your body has become tired. You are here. You are everywhere. You are in the grass and the wind. You are free to be more than what is locked within the body of blood and bone." He kissed her chilled hand.

If he had known that a week later she would be gone, would he have said something different? No, he said what needed to be said, and in one last breath it was "goodbye".

After that, it was nothing but a financial train wreck. Everyone had their hand out to take the last of his dream, the last of a life that no longer existed. Horse after horse was sold as Charlie's life deteriorated, and someone else's dream was just beginning. It was leaving him bitter and resentful.

The one thing that rang true for Charlie was that Flick was in it for the long haul. He didn't care what rig Charlie had or if they slept alongside the road. He didn't care if he had a fancy bed or if he slept on Charlie's jacket. He was going to be beside him no matter what the world threw at them. Charlie thought for a moment of when the bankruptcy took his house. He thought of his urge to die and be done with it all as he tried not to look back in the mirror and sped off as fast as his old truck would go.

Flick with his intense eyes looked at Charlie as he put his paw on his arm and whined. Charlie couldn't do it. He couldn't take his life and leave Flick or take Flick's life because of his own selfishness. He remembered pulling off to the side of the road and sobbing. Sobbing for self-pity, for what was, what is, and the vast distance between the two.

Now here he was, his forever faithful border collie dog beside him. Setting aside his memories he began to put together his todo list, wondering if he was going to get everything done that he needed to do.

Since it was midday, he figured he would get back to Jim's and put away his sorrel horse. Then he'd go take a look at the Percheron mare that Paige had apparently adopted. He had a couple of natural cures that might help with the healing process, or if nothing else ease a little bit of the pain. But all of that was in his bag at Abe's, so today maybe he could just look at the mare to give him an idea of whether he might be able to help her.

He pulled in to Jim's driveway and started to unload his horse. He had become accustomed to how things worked around here and didn't need any supervision from Jim, although he stopped in every evening to find out what else needed done. It was still early in the day to be bothering Jim, so he would drop by on his way back to Abe's. He stepped out of the truck and walked back to the trailer to get his horse.

Flick jumped out of the pickup and started to make his rounds around the barn. For a dog, he had developed a habit of checking fence lines, checking livestock and making sure there was no kitty food left in the bowl in the old milking portion of the barn.

He stopped about midway to the barn door, turned and jogged toward the house. He skipped up the steps and scratched at the door. He looked back at Charlie, who was leading the horse back to the barn. Flick barked. Charlie glanced at him for a second and then continued inside the barn. Flick barked again, and then looked back at the door for a moment. He gazed in the window beside the door. He scratched at the glass and whined again. He jumped at the door, he struck the latch, which pushed downward and clicked open.

Flick stood for a moment before digging at the door pulling it open by his paws, he tentatively walked through the washroom into the kitchen.

There, lying on the hardwood floor, was a plate along with a half sandwich, spilled milk and a shattered glass. Jim lay half delirious and moaning. Flick let out a concerned whine, approaching the fallen man slowly.

Jim heard the dog, although he couldn't see him clearly. His memory flickered back to just after he gotten married to Alison almost thirty years ago. He had one of the best dogs he ever owned, a red Aussie-border collie cross he named Honey. She was every bit a part of his bachelor life. There was a connection between the pair of them with a glance or a motion from Jim, Honey would sort a cow, push cows up into a chute or turn the lead cows into a gate.

He had known Alison for eight months, she had moved from Portland, a city girl who was infatuated by the mystical cowboy and country life. Jim was so intrigued with her, her curiosity, assertiveness and her courage to move out into the rural area, he thought for sure this was the woman he wanted to spend the rest of his life with. But after he married her and she moved onto his ranch, there was some major growing pains.

Jim had no idea that Alison didn't like dogs when he was dating her. He found out that there was a lot he didn't know about her. The romantic relationship quickly turned into a challenge to understand the phrase "give and take". From Jim's recollection, he began to realize Alison never really understood animals at all. As far as she was concerned, the house was for people, the barn was for animals. She was not a maid, so she hired one to take care of the house, then there was the complaint of being out there in the lonely ranch house all by herself, she needed friends.

Honey had just spent two days gathering cows and bucking brush with Jim, looking for calves. The miles the canine could travel had saved Jim and his horse extra hours in the saddle. After moving the last of them in they had returned to the ranch, Jim headed to the house with Honey tagging along like she always had. Being the newlywed, Jim forgot Alison's protest of animals in the house. He let Honey in to have a break from the heat of the afternoon sun. Honey took her place next to the back door. She sprawled her hind legs out so her tummy could feel the coolness of the tile. Within minutes she was fast asleep.

Jim looked at the sleeping dog with pride. That

dog was almost better than a hired hand. *If only she had thumbs so she could close gates*, Jim remembered thinking.

If only I had taken the dog into town with me to get grain on that day, maybe things would of turned out different, he reflected. He remembered just how peaceful she looked while she slept. He thought it best for her to just stay where she was and rest, the day was to hot for her to sit in the truck..

Alison had made fresh baked bread that day, cooling on the counter. Jim took a breath in to waft in the smell, he cut a warm heal off a loaf, lathered it with butter and with his mouth watering, took a bite. *I can so get used to this marriage thing,* he remembered thinking to himself. "You stay here, Honey. I will be back in a little bit." He reached down and stroked her head. Honey opened her eyes and took a sigh as Jim walked out the door, like a hundred times before.

When Jim returned an hour later loaded with grain. Alison came storming out of the house looking like she had been in a fight. Her usually beautifully styled hair was a mess. Her face was scratched, and a bruise was forming on her cheek. She was absolutely distraught.

"What the heck happened?" Jim asked in total shock as he got out of the truck and started into the house.

"That beast of a dog!" Alison was on a warpath ."That thing has eaten my bread on the counter!" Alison dove into the story with a fury. "That stupid animal had a loaf in her mouth, trying to swallow it whole. And this...

this is all I have left." She pointed to the half-eaten loaf on the counter."

Jim looked at her face. "Are you alright?"

Alison's face lit up with fury again, "Do I look alright?! I'll be damned if I am going to have that four-legged beast eat my bread. I chased her outside with a broom, tripped and fell into one of my hanging plants..." She began to cry, "Look at me...", then looking down at her fingers, "I broke a nail..."

Jim went to get a rag and try to help clean up his wife.

"Don't worry about me, you do something with that dog!"

Jim put the rag down so he could go outside to find his dog.

"Well, give me the rag, God, you had it right there in your hand."

Jim confused, walked back, got the rag again, and handed it to her. He was going to have to get used to having a woman around.

Alison was fussing in the mirror, "Oh my God, look at this..." She analyzed the scratch on her face. "That is going to leave a scar."

Jim again attempted to assist his new wife. "No, honey it won't leave a scar, it's just a scratch."

Don't you dare call me Honey! I will not be your dog."

"That is not what I meant, hone...Uh babe...uh wife..." he stumbled on what to call her.

"My name is Alison. Don't you dare give me a pet name." Alison looked again at the scratch on her face. "Damn dog."

Jim took his leave and went to get Honey and take her to the barn. "Come on girl, let's go out where things are a little quieter."

Honey followed behind him with her tail half wagging.

When Jim made it to the house a few hours later, Alison walked up behind him and wrapped her arms around his waist. "I am sorry Jim, I didn't mean to lose my temper, sometimes that dog just gets to me."

"Yeah, well," Jim started, "Maybe I should've taught her better manners or something." He was happy that Alison was at least talking to him again. He wrapped his arms around and gave her a hug.

"I guess I just get jealous that you spend so much time with that dog and I don't get any time with you at all. You are always at the barn, working those cows and horses or looking at fences, worried about water or whatever and calling that dog to go do something. I want you to do things with me."

"Oh yeah, what do you want to do?" Jim said, anxious to find something that they could do together.

"Well, I thought we could go shopping for some new furniture for the house, so it will be ours instead of all your stuff."

Jim remembered agreeing, little did he know that by the time they got done, he almost had to take out a loan to pay for everything she wanted. Not to mention that a white sofa in a ranch house didn't make sense to him. But he loved to see her smile and to hear her laugh. The way her eyes lit up when she was happy made him feel like a million bucks. And the scratch on her face had then become a distant memory, or so he hoped.

Little did he know that over the years those temper tantrums were going to be more frequent and stronger, and the woman he thought he wanted to spend the rest of his life with was not happy being a ranch wife. As for Honey, Jim kept her at the barn, and she was only allowed on the porch in the evening time. Jim had tried to see things through his wife's eyes and tried to understand the limits he was expected to follow... that was how a marriage was supposed to work, right? Give and take?

The final straw for Honey and her days with Jim was when Alison announced that she was pregnant. Within weeks, Jim found himself taking his wonderful Honey down to her new permanent home. Jim was going to be a dad and Alison was convinced that if that dog would bite cows, there was no way she was going to have a biting dog around their child.

He could not convince her that Honey would never bite or hurt anyone, and no matter how far away he kept the dog away from the house, Alison continually ribbed him about how unsafe it was. That drive was one of the longest he had ever driven, with tears in his eyes he left her, for the sake of his marriage.

Jim felt a pang in his heart at the memory over twenty years ago. He closed his eyes tightly as he heard another concerned whine come from Flick. All of a sudden, he felt a wet tongue all over his face.

Charlie had heard Flick bark again and knew something had to be up. He pulled his saddle off his sorrel horse. He put his gear in the saddle room and jogged to the house to see what Flick was so concerned about. As he walked into the room, he saw Jim trying to get up. Flick was standing beside him for support.

"What happened here?" Charlie asked as he reached in and grabbed Jim under the arm to help him up into a standing position. "Are you hurt?"

"No, I don't think so." Jim grimaced in embarrassment. "I was making myself a sandwich when I heard you drive in and looked up. I turned too fast, spilled my milk, and ended on the floor faster than I could curse." Jim grinned. "When I opened my eyes, I had a flashback about my old border collie. She was one of the best dogs I ever had, but my wife sure didn't appreciate her manners.

"Don't tell me..was she like Flick and got in trouble too?"

"Only when she got on the counters and ate fresh baked bread." Jim had to laugh. He leaned forward and wrapped his arm around his ribs.

"Let's get you into a chair, and I will fix you another sandwich." Flick was eyeing the dead half sandwich on the floor. "Go ahead. It ain't gonna get much deader."

Charlie smiled at the dog and his ways of asking for things.

With one slurp, the sandwich was gone. Flick looked over to the spilled milk. "Nope, not the milk, buddy. Leave it." Flick backed away, lay down, and waited. "Boy you keep that up, Jim, and Flick is gonna want to come here for lunch every day."

Jim gave a chuckle again, he'd be good company.

"You hurt?" Charlie asked again as he got Jim to the chair and seated.

"No, just more surprised than anything. It is amazing what happens when a feller only has one leg to walk on. I might be sore, but I am alright."

Charlie walked back into the kitchen and fixed another sandwich, poured another glass of milk, and took them into the front room to put it on a TV tray. Then he placed it in front of Jim. "There, that ought to give you something to do." He went back into the kitchen and cleaned up the broken glass and spilled milk that Flick had patiently watched in case anything was going to get it. He was sure he would be invited to help clean it up.

Charlie went back in the front room where Jim was nibbling at lunch and sat down.

"Thanks for helping me out, Charlie. I don't know for sure how I would have gotten up."

"No problem, Jim. Are you sure you are alright?"

"Yeah, I think I am gonna be fine. Just have a lot on my mind and nothing to do in here except sit and wait."

"Yeah, I know that feeling; like there isn't much we can do about it at the time. But time passes, and every day is a new day. Hey, speaking of new days, do you want to go with me and take a look at Paige's new horse? She helped us gather this morning and told us about a Percheron mare she ended up with."

Jim thought about it for a moment and then threw caution to the wind. It would be nice to get out of there for a little while. "I have got to get out and get moving around a little or these walls will surely smother me."

"Oh they only swallow you up for a little while. They usually spit you out in about six weeks. They make you feel like you were smothered, but you keep breathing."

Jim chuckled, "Say, is there any way you can bring me in some rawhide string from the barn? I have been wanting to make me a pair of reins for that spade bit that I have in the barn for a few years and have never taken the time." Jim finished his sandwich and wiped his mouth.

"Sure, you tell me where they are, and I will go get them," Charlie replied.

"Well, you know I could take you down there and show you if you don't mind walking a little slower than usual."

Just the thought of braiding made Jim feel like he could do something and not be stuck counting flies on the wall. He and his son used to braid together when Craig was growing up. They would sit on the porch in the evening and braid away the daylight after chores.

He had seen the reins Craig had braided out of hay string when he had come back home a few weeks ago, and the thought of being able to do something like that would be a good challenge while he was on extended leave.

Jim grabbed his crutches and stood up. With his one slippered foot, he crutched his way to the door while Charlie took the dishes to the sink. Flick sat and watched, feeling like he should be in two places at once and debating who needed his assistance. He moved to the door and waited with Jim while his eyes followed Charlie, making sure everything was put back and dry.

"Alright, looks like we are ready," Charlie said as he draped the rag over the sink.

Jim opened the door and hobbled down the steps.

"Got a call today from Alison, Craig's mom, in New York."

"You did?" Charlie asked. He hoped it was good news but listening to Jim's voice and how neutral it was, he didn't figure it to be. "How is it going over there?"

"Well," Jim started and then withdrew for a moment to regroup his emotion. "Craig woke up this morning."

Charlie was again expecting a more excited reaction from Jim. "And..."

"Well, he doesn't have any memory. None." He paused. "The doctor said it is common for this to happen with that kind of brain injury. But not my son." Jim was quiet for a moment. "And here I am with a broken leg and bruised ribs." He was trying hard to keep a positive outlook. "They say his memory can come back at any time, and that the loss is usually temporary. I guess we will just have to wait and see."

Charlie was quiet as he contemplated what he should say. Nothing came to mind.

"Alison and Lori are taking turns sitting with him right now. They seem to think he is going to pull out of it and be alright." Jim paused long enough for doubt to sneak in. "I don't know how they know that. How can one be so sure that all is going to be good? They say it could be a couple of hours or it could be weeks, months or even in some cases years," Jim continued. "Alison is going to move him back into her condo with her. Lori said that she has the key to his apartment, and he had called her the morning of the accident and told her he had boxes of his wife's things for her to pick up."

"Who is Lori?" Charlie asked, putting the pieces together with names but no faces.

"Well, that is Craig's former sister-in-law." Jim cleared his throat "I guess I should be happy that Alison is not having to do all of this by herself, and with my leg and all…" He paused. "Craig's wife passed away a little over a year ago. I didn't get a chance to meet the "in-laws", if you will. I didn't take the time, I guess. Well anyway Alison seems to like Lori, and right now they are going to take care of things until Craig's memory comes back."

They made it to the barn. The sorrel horse had finished his grain and was waiting quietly to be turned out. Charlie untied him and led him out the back door to the corral where Mouse and Cougar stood together in the shade.

As Charlie came back, Jim said, "Charlie if you go up that ladder you will find a burlap sack in the right-hand corner on the wall. That is what I need. It has my rawhide strings in it. I have some bee's wax here in the saddle room too. I will go and get that."

Charlie climbed up the second-story ladder, "Was this a hay loft?" he asked as he walked across the vast emptiness of floor timbers.

"Years ago, when they used teams of horses on this place, but right now it is just storage and empty space. I was hoping Craig would want this place when I am done with it." Jim sounded half empty of emotion. "But I don't know if it is what he wants. He sure seemed happy to be here this last time. He even talked of moving home before he left."

Charlie looked around the loft. Off to the right was a set of pole ends poking up from below. He walked over to investigate and saw a ten-foot-high feed bunk that the old timers would throw hay down and feed the teams from above. It could easily hold a half ton of hay if he filled it full.

He came down the ladder holding the burlap sack.

"Did you make sure there were no mice in the sack?"

Charlie dropped the sack, "Mice? No!"

Jim grinned, "Just checking."

Charlie grabbed the sack again and opened it up,

peering cautiously inside. "Nope, no mice," he said as he closed the sack really fast. "So where is your bee's wax you wanted?"

"In the saddle room on the corner shelf behind the door."

Charlie left the sack on the floor and went for the wax. When he came back, he looked at Jim. "I am so sorry to hear about your son. I hope it all works out for you and Craig. I sure like him."

"Thanks," Jim said. He looked at Charlie. "I didn't mean to unload on you today. I thought I had it all put in perspective, but for some reason it all came tumbling out."

"If nothing else in life, I have learned one thing, Jim," Charlie stated as his one bit of wisdom. "I spent my life thinking I had it all figured out, only to find out I had wasted my life on material things, thinking more money would buy my happiness. I had spent an entire year rearranging the past and predetermining the future, wishing for something I would never have again. Thinking if I suffered long enough, it would somehow magically return." Charlie was silent for a moment. "All we have in our life is today. My wife taught me that. Whatever you do with today is the life that you are living. Nothing more and nothing less. He took a breath. "Guess what I am saying is, loss is an unforgettable memory of *I wished I would of...* Jim, don't hold yourself back because of circumstance."

"For your age, Charlie, you are a wise man." Jim

sighed. "I just kind of got lost in thought after the phone call." Jim smiled, "Well, actually that is why I am out here in the barn in slippers."

Well let's go see Paige and see what she has going with that mare she got," Charlie said as they headed toward the pickup.

Jim moved his crutches and hopped along with him.

15

When Paige got home, she checked on the black mare before she unloaded Libby. The mare had moved under the weeping willow tree, resting easy. Paige left her alone while she unloaded Libby and led her to the barn. As she passed by, the black mare nickered in a half-hearted effort to acknowledge horse company at Libby. Libby cocked an ear toward her but didn't give any other sign of acknowledgment. The mare wanted to follow, took a couple of steps, and then stopped, bobbing her head and resigning herself to standing in one spot.

Paige unsaddled Libby and turned her out. She noticed that the mare had watched her, bobbing her head several times. It seemed she wanted some company. So, grabbing a couple of panels, she brought them into the paddock and divided the paddock into two. Getting another small water trough and another forkful of hay, she went out and caught Libby back up and brought her on the divided side of the paddock and turned her loose. The big mare's head came up, acknowledging the new mare across the fence. She made no effort to move.

Paige walked over with her halter in her hand, moved the untouched hay from that morning in front of the mare in the shade. The mare looked through her long, shaggy forelock that covered her eyes. Paige had never been around a horse that size, her head alone was almost the size of Paige herself. The cannon bones of her front legs were almost the size of her thigh, seeing her back bone protrude above atrophied muscles, her hip bones and ribs showing like a dehydrated hide over a skeletal structure, Paige's heart hurt for the horse

Mike always seemed to be a nice guy. He knew things weren't right with this mare and was hoping someone could give her better help than he was able to.

He had handed her papers and bill of sale, and now here she was with a mare that might not make it through the night. Paige approached slowly to get a closer look at the slices across the chest. They were ripped and jagged, not easy to stitch. Tom would be coming soon. It was getting close to three o'clock in the afternoon. The mare just stood there. Paige reached out her hand and touched the bony neck of the mare. Paige had to do something for her, but she didn't know what it would be.

Libby on the other side of the fence seemed to bring an ease to her. Paige brought her hands up behind the mare's ears and followed along the neckline feeling for knots in the muscle tissue. She got to the point of the shoulder where there was a knot holding the tension alongside the neck. Paige pressed it and held firmly but not hard. The mare dropped her head down for a moment and then yawned.

Paige walked to the other side of the mare, a ten-inch flap of skin hung open where Paige could see the meat ripped by the barbed wire. The mare raised her head as if to walk away, Paige put her hand again at the poll right behind the ear and rested it there for a moment. She felt the tension along the top line of her neck. With soft hands and gentle pressure. The mare stopped and relaxed, dropping her head and sighed.

Tom pull up in his vet truck. She went to the barn and grabbed a rope to put around the mare's neck since she didn't have a halter big enough to fit her.

Tom recognized the mare as soon as he pulled up. "Hey, Paige," he said as he got some of his gear out of the truck. "It looks like you have a new hobby."

"I don't know what I have, Tom, but I guess it is what I got."

"This is Mike's mare. Isn't it?" Tom asked as he walked up and waited for the mare to look at him.

"He dropped her off to me this morning. That new mare of his ran her through the fence and got her all cut up. I guess they really went at it."

"Boy it kind of looks that way," he said as he evaluated her before approaching. "Has she eaten today?"

Paige looked at the hay pile, "No. Didn't touch it. I don't think she drank anything either."

Tom listened to her heart, got her temp and did a quick evaluation. "Well, I am going to go ahead and start an IV and get her some fluid. We will get her a little painkiller to ease up on the stress. Looks like she has had a tough time."

Tom continued his evaluation of the mare. "If you have a blanket, I would blanket her tonight just to keep the chill off. Let's see if we can get her cleaned up. Her lungs sound good, her heart is strong, and all we can do now is put a couple stitches in her and wait."

Paige was watching what Tom was doing. With sure hands, he felt for the artery in the neck. Then with a swift, solid poke, he put the needle in and attached the little rubber tubing to begin the drip. He asked Paige if she would hold that for a bit while he got some pain medication in her. The mare didn't even flinch.

"Guess all we can do is the best we can."

"Easy, babe," Tom said as he wrapped the catheter with vet wrap around her neck. He gave her a quick shot and her head instantly began to drop. He deadened in the muscle so he could wash and clean out the wound. Then began the tedious job of stitching her up.

"I heard you took a trip to New York?" Tom said as he finished rinsing one of the gashes across the mare's chest. He took the hook needle and began to stitch up the muscle first. Luckily, the gash was not as deep as what he had first anticipated.

Paige looked over at him surprised. "Yeah, I went over to assist a ranch for horses and special needs children. I thought I might be able to help a couple of people around here. It is pretty fascinating, matching science and animals together. I always thought horses had a calming energy about them. I am just glad to see it recognized on a national level."

"I have always enjoyed the mystery of horses and their energy. You're right. It is fascinating. I heard the Curry boy got in an accident over there too. Something about a coma?"

"Yeah, that is what I heard too," Paige answered, not wanting to get in a conversation about Craig, but Tom went on.

"You went to school with him. Didn't you?"

"Yeah, I went freshman year. He moved after that." Again, Paige kept it short.

"He sure seemed like a good kid. I hope he pulls through it alright. Seems like the family is having a bad stroke of luck lately, now Jim with his broken leg."

"I do, too. We have been helping Jim keep up on a few things these last few weeks. He has a lot of good friends helping him out."

"He is a good man," Tom said as he sutured up the last of the wound on the mare's chest. It looked like hand stitching on a homemade quilt, uneven layers but each stitch done to perfection. "We will take these out in about ten days. Keep them as clean as you can, Paige.

"Let me get that other IV fluid started and then I want to take another look at her hind leg and see how that is coming along. It has been a while since I have seen her."

"What happened with the cattle guard? I mean how did she get stuck?"

"Well, from what I could tell, that cattle guard has been hit a couple of times by some big rigs and has a warp on one end, making the rails wider at some points with broken welds. Mike said he kind of panicked when he saw her cross it. She had walked across it just fine once, but when he saw her crossing it again, he said he ran up toward her and tried to get her to stop. She started to turn around and her hind leg fell between the rails. As she turned, it locked her foot into place."

"You don't think it was a cougar that made her cross it?"

"Couldn't say that for sure. It would have to be a pretty brave cat to attempt to prey on a horse like this."

"Yeah, I suppose you're right, Tom. Maybe a suicidal cat." Paige grinned.

"She is a lucky girl. She is a gentle giant, as gentle as they come." Tom stopped for a moment and looked at the mare and back at Paige. "I am sorry for Mike, but I am glad he thought of you for a place to go."

"I don't know what I am going to do with her for sure, Tom," Paige stated as she rubbed the big jaw of the mare. She brought her hand back up over the top of her poll and began to subconsciously massage her.

"That is part of it, Paige. Every day is a new adventure. When I get up in the morning, I have an idea of what I am going to be doing, but I never know for sure what I am going to do. Every phone call is different, and I have to adjust in a moment, take it for what it is, and move on. Some calls are horrific while others are loving. Some are sad, but others like today make me feel like there is peace in this world. In ten minutes that is going to change, and in thirty minutes it will change again. At times, one of my biggest challenges is to respect what I do and allow myself a little peace from the expectations of others. I am not God you know." He laughed.

Paige laughed with him. "Sometimes I feel like people think I am, and they give me their problems so I can fix them."

"Well, sometimes, we are given a gift that we think is a curse." He paused for a moment, "Or we take on a challenge that changes our life. If nothing else, you are taking on a challenge to help change this mare's life, and if anyone can do that, it would be you." He put his hand on the mare's bony hip. "As my mom always told me when she found out I wanted to be a vet." He smiled at the memory of his deceased mother. "Do what you can, as honestly as you can, and be smart enough to let the Lord take care of the rest."

He looked at Paige again with a small sigh, "In this line of business, those are the words from a saint. I live by them every day." He scratched the mare's hip, and the mare cocked back an ear in appreciation. "I have been humbled by this job, challenged, angry, upset and satisfied by it. But mainly I have found out, no matter how hard I try or my personal expectations... I have found that I am not God. I am just a man who loves animals and will do the best I can with what I have." He rested his hand again.

Paige thought of Abby and the emotions she had been through with her, redefining her strength and building on her weaknesses. She thought of what it would be like without the girl in her life and how Abby had to do the same when she had lost her parents.

"I think your mom was a saint, Tom. I think I will hold on to her words that you shared, if you don't mind." She smiled at the thought. "Do what I can, as honestly as I can, and be smart enough to let the Lord take care of the rest. It kind of takes the pressure off of having the expectation of having to know the right answers all of the time."

"I am honored, Paige. And good luck with the right answer thing." He laughed for a moment. "Hasn't worked for me at all."

Tom ran his hand over the mare's bony hip again and patted her, "Let's keep her on some pain medication for a while and see if we can increase her appetite. If you had a blanket that you could put on her at night, we will let her decide how much walking she wants to do. Keep her food and water close so she has it at any time."

Tom started packing up his equipment. "We just have to find what she is interested in and be aware. I don't want her to be completely pain free or she will do some major damage to the tendons on her hind leg. Keep her quiet." He left the IV port in her neck for future shots, so Paige didn't have to keep poking her. He stroked her neck one more time. "Alright, babe, you are gonna be fine. I am leaving you in good hands."

Paige nodded her acknowledgment as she took mental notes on what she needed to do for the mare.

"Is her name, Babe? In the rush of things this morning, I forgot to ask."

"No, I think he called her Maud. It doesn't really fit a girl like her."

"Nope, I don't think it does at all." Paige thought for a moment. "I think Babe is fitting." Paige stroked her bony neck. "Babe it is."

Babe blinked her eye under her shaggy forelock.

16

Abby was ecstatic to hear the plan that Janis had told Sarah. "Your mom is the coolest!" Abby said excitedly. I think Paige would be thrilled to be able to share Libby. I was thinking Piper, but he is out at Abe and Patricia's."

Abby still rode the bus to Paige's every night because she was still in foster care. Until the adoption went through, Paige was her legal guardian. Well that is what it looked like on paper anyway. Abby had a whole new way of seeing a lot of things.

Sarah listened for only a moment when she had heard what her mom was saying. The rest was all in her imagination. Her mom really wanted her and Lilly to meet some horses! How exciting was that?

She couldn't wait for school to be out and then go out to Abby's place and see the horses and run with the dog. It was going to be the best day ever! During math, Sarah literally lost her mind in horses. The numbers that were given randomly ran through her head, making no sense and just forming on paper. Sarah drew a number five on her paper. She looked at it and drew four legs on the bottom along with an eye for the head. Pretty soon she had a horse drawn out of the number. The minutes seemed like hours and the hours like days as she heard each second that ticked by. Instead of the subconscious tick, tick, tick… it was more like a drum to her. Boom! Boom! Boom!

How was she supposed to act? This was like a dream coming true. Was she going to ride? Boy, she hoped her mom would let her ride. Sarah had been a big sister too long, and the little girl in her was bursting at the seams to be all she ever dreamed to be. She was even going to ride the bus to Abby's house. They would get there a full hour before her mom.

The school bell rang, and it was finally the end of the day. It was time to gather her things and head out to Abby's house. The warm afternoon sun with a light breeze made the day seem perfect as they stepped off the bus and walked up the little drive to the house. For the first time ever, Sarah didn't have to worry about Lilly. She felt free and excited all at once. The only promise she had to make to her mom was that she wouldn't do anything with horses until she got there. This was just a trial run, and nothing was to be promised.

Janis had called Paige and asked if it would be alright to meet with her and see how Lilly might do meeting the horse. Janis' determination was overpowering her nervousness.. Paige was happy to oblige it was time. Lilly was one of the main reasons Paige had flown to New York. The time had come to determine if there would be any noticeable difference in Lilly once she made contact with horses.

Paige knew that Libby was going to be the best horse

to have a young girl around. That mare would stand quiet no matter what kind of events might happen. If Lilly got completely out of control, they would just remove her and possibly try another day.

As the girls came laughing up the drive, Tom was leaving. He waved at them as he drove by. "Who was that?" Sarah asked, looking at Abby.

Abby was concerned, "Um, that was Tom the vet. I hope everything is alright."

They jogged the rest of the driveway to the house. Paige was standing at the paddock looking over the fence at the mare.

"Hey, Paige," Abby said. "Did you get a new horse?"

Both girls gathered around, and Paige quietly said, "Meet Babe."

Abby was the first to put her hand through the fence. "Here, Babe. Hey, Babe," she cooed in an attempt to get the mare to respond. Babe showed no interest in the girls. Then Sarah saw the stitches across her shoulder. "Oh my goodness! What happened to her?"

"She got in a horse fight and ended up running through the fence. Tom got her fixed up, though, so she is going to be fine."

Sarah was half frightened of her. "That horse is huge!" she said as she tried to comprehend riding an animal that size. *There would be no way*, she thought.

Paige looked at the girls, surprised that Abby had someone home after school. "Oh shoot. Janis is coming over tonight with Lilly. Hey, girls, why don't you go do your homework while we wait for your mom to get here. Then we will play with the horses for a while.

"Are we riding that one?" Sarah asked, still not taking her eyes off the big, black mare.

"No, no one will be riding her.

"Come on, Sarah. Let's get our homework done so we can ride when your mom gets here," Abby said as she grabbed her backpack and headed to the house.

Sarah turned and followed, not wanting to get into any kind of trouble. "Wait!" she said as she trotted to catch up to Abby, who was already on the porch.

"Did you understand anything in math today?" Abby asked as she walked into the house.

Both girls started conversing about the math problems in class that they had for homework.

Paige grinned at the two girls, then looked around the place. She heard a pickup pull into the driveway and realized that it was not Janis. It was Charlie, and he had Jim with him.

Paige's heart skipped a beat. She hadn't seen Jim since she had taken off to New York. What was she going to say to him?

She waved at them as they pulled up. Charlie got out of the truck and went around to the passenger side to help Jim out.

"Hey, Jim, Charlie. Good to have you guys drop by," Paige said as she held the door open for Jim.

"Good to see you, Paige," Jim replied. "How are things going?" Jim started to maneuver his crutches to get out.

"They are going alright, been pretty busy these last few weeks, but I think I am doing alright."

"Charlie said you got yourself a new horse. We thought we would come over and see her."

"Yes, I am glad you did, Jim. Why don't you just stay in the truck and have Charlie pull around there. That way you don't have to stand up or walk on your leg. Are you healing alright?"

"Doing as good as can be expected. Six to eight weeks in a cast is enough time for a feller to feel like he appreciates two legs. I think sitting in the truck would be a good idea, if you don't mind. I just spent about thirty minutes in the barn at the house and I can sure feel it."

Charlie jumped back in the pickup, pulled it around parking the passenger side right next to Babe's corral. The mare still just stood there. Her ears didn't even flicker with the commotion.

Blue trotted out of the house, barked a couple of times and then trotted down the stairs to see Charlie and Jim.

Flick jumped out of the pickup and then began to play chase around the corral with Blue. Paige's quiet place seemed to have come to life, pulsing with activity.

Charlie looked over at Paige. "Do you mind if I take a look at her?"

"No, not at all," Paige said honestly. "I am curious what you'll see, Charlie."

Charlie walked through the gate and approached the mare. Her ear flickered, but she didn't move.

"Tom just got done stitching her up and gave her a light sedative about an hour and a half ago," Paige explained, giving Charlie the rundown on what was going on.

Charlie nodded his head but said nothing as he waited for the mare to acknowledge him.

Paige heard another rig pull into her driveway. The engine sounded familiar as it came around the corner. Abe and Patricia came pulling in. *Boy, this mare is drawing a lot of attention today*, Paige thought as she walked over to where her mother was getting out of the truck with an armload of groceries.

Abe got out and grabbed a bowl of potato salad sitting in the seat.

Patricia looked at her daughter for the first time since she had come back from her travels. "Hey, thought you might like to have a picnic at your house."

Paige smiled. "Um, well, I have a woman by the name of Janis coming over tonight. We are going to do a little experiment with her autistic daughter and see if she responds to horses." Paige replied, a little concerned. But she was so happy to see her mom. "I have some ground beef in the freezer that we can take out to make some patties. Maybe Janis will stay, and we could have Charlie and Jim stay as well. Shoot, we just as well make it an evening of food and fun."

"Well, I brought," Patricia started looking at the food in her hands, "corn-on-the-cob, potato salad, fresh canned green beans, baked bread and strawberry rhubarb jam."

Paige beamed at her mom with complete adoration. "I have watermelon, hamburgers and some bratwurst." Paige looked over at Charlie and Jim. "Hey, Charlie, you and Jim are staying for dinner."

Abe looked at Charlie. "I don't think that was a question."

Jim grinned. "Nope, sounded like an order."

Charlie had his hands on the point of the shoulder of the mare. Abe leaned against the fence watching. Jim had his foot propped up on the window of the pickup, absorbing the life of family in the afternoon sun.

Paige and Patricia walked into the house, arms loaded with supplies from Abe's pickup.

"Girls," Paige began. Both girls froze while Blue and Flick still danced around. Flick had a ball in his mouth anticipating them to throw it. "I want your homework done. No excuses. I will check it after we have dinner."

"Spoken as a true mother," Patricia said with a smile.

"Well, actually a big sister."

Sarah looked at Abby. "We are going to have dinner here, too?"

"Hey, maybe you can spend the night!" Abby mentioned with a brilliant smile.

"That would be so much fun!" Sarah said without thought. Her whole afternoon had been of fun and excitement. She had not even thought of Lilly or her mom since she had gotten there.

They walked back into the house, dogs trotting after. "What historical person are you going to write about?" Sarah asked.

"Thomas Edison. You?"

"Anne Frank."

"Who is she?" Abby asked as they got back to their books on the floor.

"She's a girl whose family was locked up in a house during Hitler times. She wrote a diary about it," Sarah explained. "It is kind of scary to think about all the things they had to do. They didn't have a lot to eat, so they ate rotten potatoes and had to ration out the bread and they couldn't make any noise because if they got caught they would have to go into a concentration camp."

"Wow! That sounds so much more exciting than writing about a guy creating a light bulb. We see them every day."

They opened their math books again and attempted to get through the ten problems that were on their assignment.

Paige and Patricia stood shucking corn in the kitchen, pulling the silk strands, then laying them on a paper towel. Paige had gone to the freezer, gotten out the ground beef and brats to thaw. She pulled out some pasta to make a quick Italian salad.

It was good to work next to her mother again. It had been a week since they had talked. "Mom," Paige began.

"Hmmm?"

"Sorry I didn't call you when I got back."

"I kind of figured something had happened. Do you want to talk about it now?"

"Not really."

"Okay." Patricia kept shucking the corn.

"Well, maybe I do…" Paige stammered. "I don't know." She slammed her hands on the counter. "I am kind of pissed."

Patricia raised an eyebrow.

"I mean, frustrated, confused, mad, and feeling like a fool." She paused for a moment and looked at her mom. Paige hadn't expected to spit out all those words at once. "Guess I do need to talk to someone."

"What happened?"

"Well, I went to the hospital after you called," Paige thought of her anticipation and excitement. "I found Craig's room with a young, beautiful woman sitting at his bedside, holding his hands and talking of never losing him again. I wanted to go in, but I couldn't. I just couldn't." Paige took a breath and blew it out. "I didn't belong there, Mom. I felt completely alone. I couldn't compete with that. I felt dirty, looking down at my clothes, my jeans and the dirt under my fingernails. And this woman was all dressed in a skirt, high heels, and a blazer jacket."

Paige stopped for a moment trying her best to describe her emotions. "I felt like I was a child all over again at the horse show, not having all the right stuff."

"Paige, can I ask a personal question?" Patricia was direct.

Paige paused, not knowing if she wanted to hear the question. "I suppose. I guess I was the one to bring it up."

"What did you think you were going to find when you got there?"

Paige leaned on the counter for a moment. "Oh, I don't know." She didn't know if she wanted to be honest. "At first I thought I would be able to go to the ranch and then surprise Craig. That was one of the main reasons to go to New York, the ranch was amazing. I am so excited to start something here, Mom. I learned so much. And as far as Craig, I guess I thought Craig would have been all alone and needing someone."

She looked at her hands. "I was hoping he was needing me, or maybe wanting me. Oh, Mom, I don't know," Paige said, exasperated. "I thought for sure he would need someone when I got to the hospital." She paused. "I guess when I first decided to fly over there," she smiled at the memory of it, "I thought he would take me out on the town, see the Statue of Liberty and stay up all night long looking at the city lights. I thought it would be all romantic and exciting."

Paige was embarrassed at sharing the romantic thought, but she continued. "When it came together, I realized that he has a life there, he has family and friends and apparently more than friends." Paige paused. "I just had a different thought of what our relationship was, I guess. I thought it might be like a romance in a movie, but it's not."

Paige's mind returned to the night under the stars, of Craig standing next to the corral and Libby walking over to him. "I guess I thought he was 'the one', Mom."

She bit her lower lip and then repeated, "He was the one."

"So what did you do at the horse show when you were a kid and didn't have all the right stuff?" Patricia's voice was flat and matter of fact. She stopped shucking corn and looked directly at her daughter.

Paige paused for a moment and thought of a lifetime ago when she was fifteen and had nothing but a homemade single-wide horse trailer and handmade horse blanket that her mom had made from an old canvas tent. "Well," she paused again, "I got over being mad and did what I came to do, I guess."

"How did that work out for you?"

Paige smiled. "Pretty dang good. Pretty dang good."

The microwave shut off and made four brisk beeps. Paige opened the door, took out the meat, opened some onion soup mix and began mixing the meat and soup mix together with a couple of eggs. She then started making patties as Patricia stirred the pasta in the boiling water.

As Paige finished the last of the patties, another car pulled up. It had to be Janis. The little Subaru puttered like a lawn mower up the drive. Everyone kind of glanced at it as it pulled up. The dirty, mustard-yellow vehicle came to a stop in front of the house facing toward the paddock where the men were standing.

Janis paused, looking around. There were more people here than what she thought should be, and she looked at her watch. Maybe she had the wrong day...

She glanced in the backseat at Lilly looking at her library horse book, oblivious of her surroundings. Janis glanced in the mirror and fixed her hair before she got out. Sarah and Abby came out the door.

"Hi, Ms. Wright," Abby exclaimed, excited to have her come out for the evening.

"Hi, Mom.

"Hello, Abby, Sarah."

Paige came out the door and looked at her. "Janis, glad you made it."

"Hi. Paige?"

"Yes, come on in."

Janis looked back in the car at her quiet child and then at the quiet house. This was the reason she never went anywhere. She felt panic take over her like honey poured on toast. It started to fill her emotions to the point she couldn't breathe. These people would never understand what she had to go through to get this child around the house, let alone at a strange house.

What if Lilly messed her pants again? She should just get back in the car and leave while everything was quiet. There were no messes to clean up and no tantrums to face. She had a routine down that seemed to be working. She could just do this some other day.

"Well," Janis started nervously, "maybe we should do this another time. I see you have company and I don't want to be a bother."

"Oh, you are not a bother at all," Paige replied. "I am happy you're here."

Patricia walked out the door.

"This is my mom, Patricia. Mom, this is Janis Wright. She is one of the reasons I took my trip to New York. And this is Lilly." Paige pointed to the backseat.

Lilly still did not engage.

"Do you want to bring her in, and we can sit down and visit for a while? I have iced tea and lemonade," Paige said, hopeful that she would stay.

Janis wrung her hands and then looked at her elder daughter on the porch. For the first time, she saw Sarah beaming with fun excitement, holding out the suppression of yet another night at home with Lilly and her mom. Then Janis looked in the back of the car.

Paige thought she acted like a mustang deciding to approach or jump the fence and run. "Janis, you are safe here."

Abby didn't like the tension. "Come on, Sarah. We can finish our math really quick."

Sarah stood and watched her mom. Anxiety began to fill her heart as she walked toward her mother. "I can help, Mom. I can help with Lilly." Sarah's voice had changed. The youthful excitement and energy now gone. It had left as soon as she heard the car pull up. She knew there was nothing at home for any of them. And for the first time in a long time, her mom might make some friends.

Tears started to form in Janis' eyes. "I know, baby, I know. I just wanted to..." Janis stopped. She looked at her daughter's helpless face and took a deep breath, "Alright, I guess we are not getting any younger."

She opened the back door of the sedan and began talking to Lilly.

"Hey, Lilly, do you want to get out and see some people?" Janis undid the seatbelt, but Lilly did not respond. "We can go out and play for a while, okay?"

Paige and Patricia watched, not knowing what to expect as Janis lifted the six-year-old out of her car seat. On the way out of the car, Lilly dropped her book, and the silence was gone. She began to scream and rock back and forth. "Babe! Babe! Babe!"

Janis could not get her on the ground fast enough to get her the book.

Lilly began to gulp for air. "Babe! Babe! Babe!" she screamed, as if her life depended on that book. As if she was drowning in a sea of loneliness. Janis opened the book as fast as she could, fumbling for the page that Lilly wanted, and found the picture of the big, black horse.

"There is your baby," she cooed. "There you go. You have your baby." She put the book back in the little girl's hand, and Lilly went silent, still rocking back and forth.

"Babe," she said. "Babe!"

"Yep, you have your baby," Janis reassured her.

The men at the corrals looked her way. Janis was filled with embarrassment as she tried to regain her composure. She reached in the car to get Lilly's file so they could discuss her behaviors and abilities.

In an instant, Lilly dropped her book and took off running, blindly barreling toward the paddock as fast as her little legs could take her.

Janis screamed after her, "No, Lilly!"

But in a blink of an eye, Lilly was in the corral with the big, black mare. Before anyone could comprehend the action, Lilly had wrapped herself around the horse's front leg, repeating over and over again, "Babe! Babe!"

Charlie was the closest to her. The mare had not moved the whole time the men had stood there. But when that little girl wrapped her arms around her leg, the mare responded. Not by moving a foot or by being startled. The only thing she did was bring her head around, touch the little girl's shoulder with her nose, and take in a breath.

Janis screamed, "No! It is going to eat her! Someone do something!" She started trying to get through the fence. Abe reached out to grab her. "Let go! Save my baby!" Tears of fear, anxiety, and panic were all rolled into one. She shoved Abe's hands away trying to get to her child. "It's going to kill my baby." Tears were running along with sobs and uncontrollable panic.

Abe grabbed around her waist, locking her arms to her body, and held her for a moment. "She is fine," he said soothingly. "She is fine! The mare likes your baby. Look how she is hugging her. They are fine," he said in gentle, calming words. "Charlie is right there. See, Charlie is right there."

Janis stopped her fighting and took a breath, trying to see beyond her own fear and panic. She stood shaking, vibrating with emotion and exhaustion. Her legs went limp, but Abe continued to hold her.

"My baby," she whispered as she watched.

Charlie stepped next to the mare and put his hand on her neck. Babe just stood holding her nose on the little girl's shoulder and breathing in the little girl's scent. Then, as if all had lined up, the mare reached down and started nibbling on the hay that had lain at her feet all day. Charlie squatted down by the little girl holding tightly to the leg of the mare.

He repeated what she had been saying. "Babe," he said.

"Babe," Lilly replied.

"Yes, this is Babe. Big, black Babe. Would you like to see Babe?"

"Babe," Lilly said again, but this time her hands loosened a little around the horse's leg. Charlie held out his hand to her. I can help you see Babe it you want me to.

Charlie noticed the little girl's hands moving up and down, petting and stroking the mare's leg.

Lilly was quiet for a moment and then without hesitation, she took Charlie's finger in her hand and went to him. Charlie looked over at Lilly's mom, silently asking permission to continue. With tears falling down her face, Janis nodded. Charlie lifted the little girl on his knee where he had squatted and started to rub Babe's jaw. Lilly reached out and did the same.

"Babe," he said.

"Babe," Lilly repeated. She jumped off his knee and threw her hands around Babe's neck, holding on for all she was worth. Janis gasped. Babe continued to eat, never once flinching or nervous. Charlie allowed the little girl to hold the horse. He shifted his weight to where he was between Babe's front leg and the little girl.

Charlie didn't know why, but he felt wetness on his cheek. There was an emotion of complete trust between an extremely hurt horse and a totally misunderstood girl, who for the first time in her life was accepted for who she was without judgment or fear.

Lilly took her head away from the horse for a moment and for the first time made eye contact to Charlie. "Babe," she said, her little hand still moving back and forth on the horse's neck.

"Yes, that is Babe." Charlie put his hand on the mare's leg. "Big, black, beautiful Babe."

Paige couldn't believe her eyes. The mare didn't even pick up her head. She just kept right on eating the hay.

Lilly grabbed Charlie's hand, and he let her move it to the mare's neck. She guided Charlie's hand to stroke the neck like she had done.

"Nice Babe," he said.

Paige walked up to Janis, "How did she know the mare's name was Babe?"

"I don't know." Janis looked at Paige for a moment with tear-filled eyes. "She has been staring at the library book for the last week, looking at the same picture of a black horse. I thought she was wanting to say 'baby' like it was a doll or something. I had no idea that it was the name of the horse you were going to have us see. Maybe Sarah told her that was who we were going to meet."

"Well, Janis," Paige paused trying to put the pieces together, "I didn't get this horse until this morning. I didn't name her until about two hours ago."

Janis was quiet. She glanced over at her little girl, carrying on a conversation with a strange man, allowing touch and motion. All that she had thought about horses and danger circled in her mind. As she watched again, Lilly reached herself out and hugged on the massive neck in quiet emotion.

"May I?" Janis said as she motioned to the huge horse. This was not only about her daughter. It was about reaching out and facing the challenges of what if. Standing on the outside of the fence, Janis looked at Paige, then reached out and touched the large animal. This black horse had, in a matter of seconds, changed her daughter's life.

"Momma," Lilly said quietly, "Babe."

Janis wept. "Yes, Lilly, Babe."

17

They walked to the house. Lilly was curled in her mother's arms with her head on Janis' shoulder. Before they made it to the door, she was sound asleep. Paige brought out a couple of plush blankets and laid them on her bed. Janis laid the little girl on them and wrapped her carefully.

They quietly walked out of the room, leaving the door ajar.

Abby spoke up with much anticipation, "Can we catch Libby and give Sarah a ride?"

Paige looked over at Janis who was at a loss for words. "If your mom agrees to it."

Sarah looked at her mom. "Can I, Mom? I promise I will be really careful and I will do everything just like they tell me."

Janis sighed. Had it not been for this child and her persistence, she would have never considered horses. She would have never met Paige, and she would never have heard Lilly say "Momma".

"As long as you're careful, and I want to watch you."

She took a breath as she let those words come out of her mouth. She shook her head as she fought back the tears.

Patricia came in from the kitchen. I will listen for Lilly if you want to go out and see Sarah and the horses.

Janis realized, ever since Lilly was born, she had never spent time alone with Sarah. She always had to be on guard. Her life created excuses to stay isolated away from would-be friends. Yet here she stood with a free moment, with a woman who she felt like she could trust. "If you could. I will just be here on the porch if you need me."

"I will call you if she stirs," Patricia reassured her.

Sarah looked at her mom for a moment, tears starting to run down her cheeks, she wrapped her arms around her mother, "I love you!" she said.

Abby, wrapped her arms around her too, and with a quirky smile, "I love you too!"

Janis didn't know how to act. She hugged both girls. "Go ride the horse."

Tears were welling in her eyes. She was getting tired of crying and tears. She hadn't done this for years, and now it seemed like a waterfall of emotion. Or relief? Or maybe it was a new beginning. She looked back at Lilly on the bed, sound asleep, a peaceful, deep sleep. She walked down the hall to the front porch and for the first time watched her Sarah bounce and laugh as little girls should.

Paige, Sarah and Abby walked out to the far end of the paddock to catch Libby, her golden hide reflecting the afternoon sun. Libby followed them to the gate. Paige stopped the girls' giddiness with a stern voice.

"Alright, this is where the silliness must end and where horsemanship begins." Abby and Sarah both stood at attention. "Abby, do you want to show Sarah how to put on a halter?"

"Sure!" she said remembering the first time she had tried to do it.

"Alright. Any messing around my horse, and I will pull both of you out of the corral. Then we will go into the house."

The girls agreed.

Janis watched as the two girls interacted with each other. She could hear Abby giving guiding words as Sarah tried to get the halter right.

Charlie came up beside Janis and said, "Thank you for sharing your family."

Janis was taken aback with surprise.

"Sorry, I am Charlie. Didn't mean to startle you."

"No, I was thinking the same thing about this family. I can't even begin to tell you all how much this means to me or my girls." Janis looked at Charlie for a moment, not knowing who she was talking to, but didn't really care. It was nice to have a conversation. "I am Janis, Janis Wright. And I am the one who should be thanking you. You changed my baby girl's life today."

"No, ma'am. I can't take the credit for that. You brought her here. I just happened to be the one in the corral."

"How did you know how to handle that situation?"

"What do you mean?"

"Well, you just acted like everything was fine," Janis said, taking a breath and releasing more of the anxiety that had been pent up for so long.

"Well, ma'am," Charlie sighed. "Things were fine. An over excited little girl and a horse that liked her."

"But it could have turned out differently. That big horse could have stepped on her."

"But she didn't," Charlie replied. "That mare would no more have lifted a foot to swat a fly with that little girl there."

"How did you know?"

"Oh, I probably can't explain what I can understand from a horse, but I do know that little girl is what that horse needed."

Janis looked at him puzzled.

Charlie nodded out to the corral where Babe stood. She was drinking deeply out of the shallow water trough. "According to Paige, that mare hasn't eaten a bite of hay all day or drank any water. She was drawn up and depressed because of all the injuries she has. For some reason, your little girl, Lilly, was enough energy to break the lonesomeness the mare was feeling. That is the best that I can describe it."

Janis glanced out to where Sarah and Abby were, Paige standing at the gate patiently waiting for the girls to get the halter on the horse. Libby stood there without expectation. Just happy to have someone to fuss over her.

Janis looked directly into Charlie's eyes. "Whatever you said, or did, or know, all I can say is thank you.

That is the best I have." Janis blinked back tears again. "Lilly has never engaged in conversation or in touching before. And within ten minutes of being here she called me Momma. She has never done that before." Tears ran down her cheeks. She tried to blink them back, but more fell. "This is all I have."

Charlie looked at her for a moment, "Then that is all I ask for."

She looked one more time at the girls in the corral. Paige was lifting Sarah on the back of Libby.

"Look, Mom!" Sarah said as she slid on the horse bareback.

Paige was positioned on the side, standing on the ground and holding Sarah's leg to help her find center.

Janis closed her eyes as more tears dripped down her cheek. She nodded and waved.

"I think I will go in and help Patricia with dinner." She turned away and walked back into the house. She wiped her eyes and sniffed as she went to the sink and washed her hands. She then cleared her throat, "What can I do to help?"

"I have tomatoes fresh out of the garden and a sweet onion right there if you want to slice them up," Patricia answered as she rinsed the pasta with cold water in a strainer.

"Sure, I got this," Janis stated as she picked up the paring knife and started with the onion, giving her a reason for red eyes.

Abe, Jim and Charlie sat on the porch. Jim had his foot up on a tall stool. The afternoon was perfect. Blue and Flick were romping around in the yard playing tug of war with a frayed rope. The burgers were on the grill and the sweet smell of cooking onions wafted to hungry noses.

Janis looked out the window and had the perfect view of Abby and Sarah challenging each other at who could get back on Libby again. They were aided by Paige, who guided Sarah, once Abby was on.

"Step on Abby's foot." Paige stated as she watched the attempt.

Abby was sitting on Libby's back.

Sarah looked at her puzzled. Abby's foot had to be almost three feet off the ground. How was she supposed to get her foot up that high?

"Here," Abby encouraged her as she took her right foot and tucked it under Libby's front elbow. Then she leaned over to grab Sarah's hand. "Put your foot on top of mine."

Sarah tried to lift her foot that high.

"Lean on my arm, and I will hold you up."

Sarah again lifted her foot and pulled on Abby's hand while Abby flexed her foot up.

"You got to hop and then lift yourself on behind me," Abby explained as Sarah again tried to figure out what Abby was asking.

Paige now stood outside the corral watching and wondering what life could be sweeter than this moment.

Patricia walked outside and hollered at the girls, "Dinner."

They looked at each other. "Just a minute!" they both

said in unison.

Then they looked at each other and laughed.

"Okay, here we go," Abby said again. Now when you hop, pull on my arm, and I will pull and then you can swing on behind me."

Sarah lifted her foot to the top of Abby's foot. Then she pulled on her arm and counted, "One," hop, "two," hop, "three!"

Sarah gave a big pull on Abby's arm and lifted herself up to swing on but as she was about half way up, Abby's foot slipped out from behind Libby's shoulder. Abby was pulled off to the side and Sarah was back standing on the ground. Both girls laughed as they had to try one more time. The third time was a charm.

Paige counseled from behind the fence. "Climb! Climb! Climb!"

Janis watched as her Sarah climbed and giggled and weaseled her way up the side of the yellow horse. Abby pulled and lifted and helped as much as she could. Finally, with a sigh of completion, Sarah slid on behind Abby.

The men on the porch applauded the effort and cheered.

Sarah beamed with pride. What a beautiful day.

They all gathered outside and loaded their plates with hamburgers on fresh-made bread with vine-ripe tomatoes, fresh-pulled onion, corn on the cob, pasta salad, potato salad and watermelon to top it off. For the evening, no one was a stranger.

18

The day after the BBQ, Paige got up and went to check Babe. Blue followed happily beside her. Her little front paws pranced a happy beat as they went down to the barn. Blue stopped at the gate and looked at Paige, her bright, ice blue eyes shining with mischief and excitement.

Paige walked in the corral and pulled the blanket off Babe. She had not buckled the breastplate of the blanket for fear of ripping out Babe's stitches. Babe brought her head around and looked at Paige. In the silence, the mare looked bigger than yesterday. Paige approached her with her shot of antibiotics. She was glad that Tom had left the catheter in her neck because of the volume of shot she had to give her.

This was her last injection.

Charlie said he had some stuff he called DMSO that worked for sore horse muscles, and that he would bring some by this morning. Babe looked better than the day before. She hadn't moved much, but she had pretty much cleaned up all the hay that was in front of her.

She walked over and turned on the water to fill the shallow water trough up to its twenty-gallon capacity. Paige could monitor how much water Babe was drinking by how many times she filled it up. Since last night, she had drunk about twenty-five gallons.

Paige went and got another bale of hay. At this rate, if she was going to put weight on this mare, Babe was going to need to eat enough for three horses.

Paige walked around to Babe's hind leg and looked at the injury. No open wound, just swelling and soreness. *I wonder if she would let me pick up her foot?* she thought as she reached over and ran her hand down her hip and over the hock. As she started to go down toward the pastern where the injury was supposed to be, her hand brushed past the hock. She felt a heat she was not expecting.

She brought her hand again from the hip around the side to the hock and noticed a dramatic temperature change. She walked back to the house and got some ice water and towel. She walked again to the sore leg and with an ace bandage wrapped her hock with ice folded in the cold towel.

Paige followed the leg down to where the coronary band wrapped around the top of the hoof. She applied a mild pressure to the back of the hoof, right at the base above the frog. Babe dropped her head and stood relaxed. She held it for about two minutes and then she stroked her leg.

She took off the cold press and dipped it back in the ice water. The towel was warm to the touch. She re-wrapped the leg and then went to throw more hay over the fence. The mare shook her head and yawned and then began to eat.

Charlie pulled up in the driveway. He got out with his bag and stood on the outside of the fence. "Morning, Paige," he said as he looked at what she had done.

"You noticed that hock hot, too?"

"Yeah, I thought that it was odd. It looks like everyone is focused on the pastern and the stress there. I think they forgot to look at the hip and the hock. I couldn't help but notice the heat there. Thought I might put out some of the fire."

"I brought you some of the DMSO. It is nasty stuff to smell, and if you get it on your skin, you will definitely know it." Charlie grinned.

He put on a pair of plastic gloves and drizzled some on an old rag. He walked to Babe's sore hip and put the rag just in front of the hip joint. Babe lifted her head and cocked back her ears.

Paige didn't know if she was going to kick or if she was enjoying the stuff. Shoot it was just medicine on a rag. It couldn't be that bad.

Charlie stroked her hip all the way down to the hock three times with the potion on his rag, and then he walked away. Babe did not move. She stood there like she was thinking. Her expression was of dislike, yet she was not moving or showing any discomfort.

Charlie looked over at Paige. "Well, I think that might help out a little. If you want to, you can put some on her hind foot, too. It will help with the circulation and healing, a little goes a long way."

Paige nodded her head. Charlie started to hand her

the glove he had on, and she looked at him kind of funny.

"You don't have to use it, but it is probably best if you do."

Paige took the glove and went to take the used rag from him. As she reached for it, the rag fell out of his hand and started falling to the ground. Without a second thought, Paige reached with her ungloved hand and caught it. On almost instant contact, Paige tasted something odd in her mouth. She made a funny face, confused.

Charlie started to laugh. "Get the rag out of your hand."

Paige looked at him and then back at the rag. It did not register.

Charlie told her again, "Paige, grab the rag with your gloved hand."

Paige again looked at him as the taste was getting stronger. Then she did what he had requested and took her gloved hand to grab the used rag. Her face looked awful as Charlie started to laugh.

"What is that stuff?" she asked as she clucked her tongue up and down moving her jaw. "That is just nasty."

"Like I said, a little goes a long way!" He smiled again. "Here," he said as he turned on the hose for her to wash out her mouth and rinse her hand.

Paige grabbed the hose and took a swig of water to rinse out her mouth. By now it was all the way through her mouth. "Man, that tastes like oysters or something." Showing her dislike for shellfish. "No wonder why Babe looked like she did."

"Cures what ails you," Charlie said. "Are you better?"

"No, but I am a lot smarter."

Charlie grinned as he held open a plastic Ziploc bag, and Paige dropped it in.

"Chicken," Paige chided.

"Nope! I'd say smart!" Charlie remarked.

They laughed a little as they stood propped against the fence watching Babe eat.. Then without thought, Charlie sighed. "Jim said that Craig woke up yesterday."

Paige's heart went to her throat.

"Is he okay?"

"I don't know. Jim says Craig doesn't have any memory. That he forgot who he is and where he lives. He forgot everything."

Paige couldn't imagine that. "No way!" She had heard of that happening before but not to anyone she knew.

"Jim wanted to go over there, but he just can't with his leg. He said it was good that Alison and Lori are over there taking care of him. But I think in his heart he wants to go over and see if he could help."

"I wish there was something I could do…" Paige felt guilty for leaving like she did.

"Jim sounded a little stressed when Alison told him that she was going to move Craig in with her until he could remember who he was."

Paige felt a surge of panic. "That would be the last thing Craig would want to do."

"Well, either that, or Lori said she could move into his apartment and stay with him for a while to see if she could help his memory."

"Who is Lori?" Paige asked.

"I don't know. I think Jim said she was the sister to Craig's late wife." Charlie paused. "I think I am talking too much." His face flushed with embarrassment, yet he kept talking to finish his thought. "I just think Jim would go over and help support Craig if he had someone who could travel with him."

Paige was quiet. Could she do it again? Could she go over with Jim and help out a little?

Babe stomped her front foot. It was the first time this morning the mare had moved. Paige heard the phone ring at the house. "I gotta answer that," she said as she began to jog toward the house.

Out of breath, Paige reached for the receiver, "Hello?"

"Hello, Paige, this is Janis."

"Hi, Janis! How are you?"

"I am doing pretty good this morning. Still a little shocked but I can't even begin to tell you how much yesterday meant to us as a family and as therapy for Lilly. What an amazing day."

"How is Lilly? She sure did sleep yesterday after seeing Babe."

"She did! She slept so hard she didn't get up until this morning." Janis paused for a moment. "Actually, that is why I am calling. She is asking for Babe this morning and the book is not working anymore."

Paige had already expected that, with what she had learned and studied from the ranch. "Janis, although Lilly does not quite interact with you like you expect, she does understand and can comprehend more than you may realize. To help slow down her anxiety, let her know that when she gets her toys picked up, she will be able to come out and see Babe. See how that works for you."

Janis was quiet for a moment. "Alright..." she said tentatively.

"Be confident in your decision and let her work it out."

"Well, okay. I will."

"Why don't you come out this morning, and we will see how things go? I am curious as to how Babe is going to interact with Lilly today."

They set up a time and a schedule for Lilly to do her "chores". They would come out after that.

She walked back out to where Babe and Charlie were. Babe was still not eating. "Janis and Lilly will be out later today. I think this is going to change a few lives just having that little girl around here."

"I think it already has." Charlie replied. "I know it has changed mine. I am looking forward to the chance to work together again with the two of them. What you're doing here, Paige, is a beautiful thing. I gotta get back and take care of the chores at Jim's and see what he has scheduled for today." Charlie walked back to his truck and started the engine. "Tell Janis hi for me."

Paige nodded. "Will do." She headed back in the house, grabbed a cup of coffee, and sat on the porch to watch Babe and Libby. Her mind drifted to the conversation of Jim's desires to go to New York with a travel companion. She thought of Alison and of the woman holding Craig's hand, Lori. Could she do it for Jim, for Craig and for the betterment, no matter what the outcome might be?

The breeze teased her hair, and she watched the tree limb shadows dance on the ground. She thought of Tom's mother's words. *Do what I can, as honestly as I can, and be smart enough to let the Lord take care of the rest.* She picked up her phone and called Jim.

19

The phone rang twice before Jim was awake enough to answer it. His leg had been giving him fits all night. He had finally fallen asleep in his chair. He glanced at the clock. He had slept four hours, and his voice was still a little groggy. "Hello?"

"Hey, Jim, it's Paige. Charlie and I were talking this morning, and he had mentioned that Craig had woken up yesterday. Something about him not having any memory?"

Jim cleared his throat. "Yeah, I wasn't going to say anything for a few days in hopes I heard some good news and things had changed."

"Sorry, Jim." Paige paused. "I don't mean to pry. That was not my intention." She stumbled over her words. "I just thought I would offer to go with you if you wanted to go visit him." Paige shook her head in frustration with herself. *Boy, way to be smooth, Paige. Just blurt it out like an idiot!*

There was silence on the other end of the phone.

Paige couldn't take the silence. "I am so sorry, Jim. How rude of me to call like this. Can we act like this phone call never took place?"

Still nothing on the other end of the line.

In an almost panic, Paige tried again. "I'm so sorry, Jim. Please forgive me. Goodbye." Paige started to hang up the phone and was preparing to chastise herself for her rude behavior.

"Paige! Paige! Paige, wait!"

Paige heard her name just before she clicked down the receiver and brought the phone back up to her ear. "Yeah?"

Jim was all choked up. "Paige, I can't even begin to tell you what that means to me." He hesitated again. "I have been thinking nonstop of how I could get over there to see Craig, and I just couldn't figure out a way by myself. Are you serious about going?"

"Serious as a heart attack!" Paige said. "I thought I was overstepping my boundaries by calling."

"No, not at all!" Jim said as he sipped some cold, four-hour-old coffee and about gagged. He cleared his throat again. "I would be honored if you would go with me."

"Looks like we have some planning to do," she said as she looked out over the horses. "Lots of planning. So, when do we want to leave?"

"Well," Jim stirred a little, "when can we leave?" He paused for a moment. "I will buy your plane ticket."

"I can get ahold of a friend of mine and see when we can get a flight." Paige said with confidence since she had just done this very thing less than a month ago. "It will be pretty expensive if you want to go at the drop of a hat, but we can get there in the next few days. Fly out of Boise."

"Well, Paige, the sooner I leave the better I will feel. Charlie can take care of the things here."

"I wonder if he wouldn't mind taking care of my place, too," Paige continued. "If not, I could get Mom or Dad to do it." Paige's mind was racing with thoughts of what could be done. "Let me call the travel agency and see what we can do."

"Sounds perfect," Jim said with a confident demeanor. "Talk soon."

They hung up the phone, and Paige instantly called and started making arrangements. They had two days before they could fly out. The flight left a little after seven in the morning.

As Paige got off the phone, she heard a car pull up. Looking out the window, she saw the mustard-yellow Subaru.

Janis got out of the car and instantly opened the back door and started unbuckling Lilly.

"Babe! Babe! Babe!" Lilly could hardly contain herself.

This time Janis was smart enough to have a tether on her so she could contain Lilly without the girl getting away.

Paige noticed the black mare lift her head and look in their direction. Then she did something completely unexpected. Babe nickered at the little girl.

Janis was trying to contain Lilly, totally oblivious of the mare's reaction.

"Wait," Paige said.

Janis stopped. "What?"

Paige watched as the mare took a couple of tentative steps toward the excited Lilly.

Janis did not recognize the effort the mare had made, but with Lilly leading the way, they followed like a marching band. They stopped on the outside of the corral. Lilly was attempting to crawl through the fence.

The mare dropped her head over the fence. Lilly reached out and hugged it as tightly as her little arms could hold. As if by magic Lilly became extremely quiet.

Paige crawled through and took Lilly by the hand.

Lilly began to scream at the thought of losing the touch of the black mare. Panic surging through her body as if someone was cutting off her arm.

Paige was firm. "You're alright, Lilly," she said as she lifted the little girl over the fence and brought her to the mare's side like Charlie had done.

"Babe," Paige said quietly.

Lilly laid her head against the mare's neck, closed her eyes and held on, as she repeated, "Babe".

Babe began to nibble the hay Paige had thrown in earlier that morning.

Paige squatted down in front of the mare's massive front leg so if she decided to move it, she would not step on Lilly.

Janis stood watching. Nothing could prepare her for the quietness and peacefulness of her daughter. Her heart was filled with emotion and confusion. How could her daughter love something that she herself was so afraid of? It made no sense, but here it was right in front of her, as black and white as words on a page.

Lilly opened her eyes, still holding the neck of the mare. She looked through the fence and saw Libby grazing in the makeshift paddock.

She mumbled a little bit, trying to figure out how to say the word she had said at the library, "Powameeno." Her voice was quiet and steady, "Momma, powameeno." She took her hand and worked the fingers so she could point at Libby.

"Yes, Lilly that is a palomino," Janis said with as steady a voice as she could muster.

The little girl buried her face in the mare's neck, holding on while Babe continued to eat.

Janis reached through the fence and out to the horse. Babe's head was almost as big as Janis was tall. She touched the mare's neck with her hand. Then she lifted the long, black mane and put it all on one side of the neck, as if attempting to fix a child's hair.

The mare turned her head in her direction, and Janis moved back for a moment uncertain of the large horse's intention. With the fence between them, she cautiously reached in front of the horse's face to straighten the shaggy, long forelock of hair. The fence seemed to have given her courage enough to touch the animal, but there was no way she was getting in there with it.

What in the world? Paige looked at the mare and noticed that one of her eyes was sewn shut. How could she have lost an eye? "Oh my God!" She couldn't hold back the emotion or the shock of her oversite.

"You okay, Paige?" Janis asked.

It shot Paige back to reality. "Janis, can you go and get me the phone off the desk in the house? I really need to make a call."

"Sure." She looked at the mare one more time, totally unaware of what Paige was seeing. "What kind of magic do you hold?" she asked the mare.

The mare swished her tail in complete satisfaction.

"I will be back in a minute." She headed to the house.

Paige looked at her eye. There was no weeping or swelling. There was no look of trauma to it. But for certain the eye was gone. How could she have missed that? In all honesty, the horse was not concerned with its eye, but it made sense why she kept turning her head the way she did. With all the long mane and her forelock that came almost to her nose, it was completely hidden. Paige wanted to check with Tom and see what he had to say about it. She couldn't remember if Mike had said anything or not. She only heard half the words he had said in the first place.

Babe shook her head, and the forelock fell back over her bad eye. Lilly had her eyes closed, subconsciously rubbing her hand back and forth on the black neck.

Janis came back with the phone, speaking out loud, deep in thought. "I have taken this girl to doctors, therapists, counseling and Lord knows what else to fix her and make her whole." She handed Paige the phone. "And all it took was the one thing I was most afraid of in this world."

"Why are you afraid of horses, Janis?"

"When I was a kid, one of my best friends got killed riding a horse. I swore on my mother's grave I would never have my children around horses." Janis paused. "Sarah begged and pleaded with me, but I would not waver. Now look at me, petting a horse twice the size of a standard one. What magic do they weave within their manes? What mystery do they have behind their eyes?"

"Janis, I think that there is more to this than Babe helping Lilly."

The mare raised and turned her head, looking at Janis. Janis began to back away.

"Hold steady, Janis. Let her see you."

Janis froze in her tracks, her eyes wild as Babe touched her with her nose and then breathed in. With the size of her lungs, the air sounded like she was going to inhale Janis, who was frozen to the spot, holding her breath. The mare smelled Lilly the same way. Then, unconcerned, she turned back to continue eating.

"Oh my Lord! It is one thing to stand next to them, but it is a whole other event having them look at you. Thank God for the fence," she said. "I have never in my entire life felt so scared yet noticed such kindness and gentleness."

Paige looked at the mare. "Well, we have one mystery that I would like to find an answer to." She dialed the vet clinic.

In a short conversation, she had the answer she was looking for. Babe's eye had been plagued with a cancerous tumor at the age of three. She had not had an eye for seven years.

Janis was shocked as she pulled the forelock back to reveal an eye socket, sewn shut. "Oh my goodness! Who would have done such a thing?" She was almost panic stricken with the thought of having one eye.

"Janis, I want you to understand one thing, alright?"

Janis didn't look at Paige. She couldn't take her eyes off the horse.

Paige reached out and touched her shoulder, "Janis?"

Janis looked at her, her breath a little short from what she had just seen.

"This horse is no different than who she was a few minutes ago. It was a choice that had to be made over seven years ago to save her life. She is standing here before you with your daughter hugging her. What better job could she have or what more love does she need?"

Paige paused to let it sink in a little. "It is important to know, Janis, Babe is still a horse. She is not human. She senses you, she recognizes you and she can at times support you, but I do not want you to think that she is human. She is a horse. She feels, she hurts, she gets happy and sad, but all of that is from a horse's perspective, not from ours. Does that make sense?"

Janis nodded her head, but she said, "No."

"At this point," Paige pointed out, "just know she has an instinct of fight or flight within her core being, and she will use it to the best of her ability in an instant because that is all she knows how to do. Basically, it is do or die. It is like the wire cuts on her chest, she could not rationalize the effects of engaging in a horse fight or choosing flight right through a fence."

"Why do horses fight?" Janis asked, trying to get her bearings about her and her mind back into the conversation.

"The same reason why anything fights—to claim a higher standard, to create respect or if they sense weakness. And from the sounds of it, the horse that she got in a fight with knew Babe was hurt and wanted to push her out of the pasture. The weak do not survive in some horse herds. They get pushed out. That is why a lot of times we cannot see a horse in pain until it is so severe they can't hide it any longer. They know by instinct that if they show pain or weakness they will get pushed out of the herd or left behind."

"Yet in others, they thrive," Janis said as she looked down at Lilly. She was playing with Babe's hay, mumbling to herself.

"I think this mare needs your daughter as much as you two need her," Paige stated matter-of-factly. "I think your daughter and the mare are very much alike. Both are misunderstood in the world they live in, yet I think they understand each other on unspoken terms. I think after Babe went through the fence and got hurt, she thought she had nothing to live for and was willing to die. But for some reason, Lilly's interaction yesterday shifted that." Paige looked down at Lilly playing at the feet of the mare. "And Lilly, well, I think she understands that."

Lilly listened to Paige's words. She was hearing that Babe needed her and that Babe had been hurt. While that was going through her mind, she also realized she had been heard and understood.

Janis sighed. "So, what does that mean? Do we come here every day?"

"Well, I don't know that for sure," Paige responded. Which brought up the thought of having to leave for about a week. "I have to go back to New York for about a week, Janis. I am going to have Charlie come over and take care of Babe and the rest of the horses here. Do you think you would be able to trust Charlie working with you, Lilly and Babe?"

"Oh, yes. Of course. I so appreciated him yesterday."

Lilly was playing with the mare as she was eating. Lilly would pick up a couple blades of hay and hand them to Babe, and Babe would gently take them from her hands. Her big lips slapped together to take the strands from the girl.

Lilly would be quietly babbling to herself, practicing. "Charie, Babe," she'd say. "Black Babe. Pawomeeno."

"Momma, Charie. Momma, Charie..." she was quiet and direct in her practicing. "Sarah, pawomeeno." Every time she would pick up sprigs of hay to give to Babe, Babe would lip them away, grinding slowly. Lilly would say another group of words, mumbling incoherently.

"If Charlie doesn't mind, I think we need to come

here every day," Janis said as she smiled down at Lilly.

"I will find out more tonight. See what Charlie is up to and if he has time."

They had stood out by Babe for about half an hour with Lilly caressing and rubbing the mare, babbling in her own little way.

Paige looked at her watch and noticed that time was getting away. She had errands to run.

"Lilly," Paige said directly and firmly, just as Susan had taught her. "You are going to see Babe tomorrow, okay?"

Lilly repeated, "Babe."

"Yes, you come see Babe tomorrow."

Lilly got up and hugged the big horse again around the neck, burying her face and listening with her eyes closed. Then without a thought she repeated Paige's word, "Tomorrow." Lilly began walking back to the car.

Janis followed absolutely speechless.

Babe raised her head and watched the little girl go. She nickered. Lilly stopped in her tracks, turned, and pointed a finger at the horse. "No! Tomorrow!" Then she turned and continued to the car.

The mare watched her for a moment, shook her head, took two steps to reach her water and began to drink.

Paige's gaze tracked the little girl who was determined to follow the rules. So, she and Janis followed her to the car.

"What just happened?" Janis asked as they walked down the path.

"I think Lilly just told Babe not to worry she will be back tomorrow."

Lilly opened the car door and crawled into her seat, pressing her thumb and middle finger together habitually while she rocked back and forth.

"That is what I thought," Janis said as she looked over at Paige a moment and then back at the horse. "You know, I think that dang horse understood."

Paige grinned. "I think so, too."

They continued to the car, and Janis reached in the back door to buckle her in. Lilly still rocked back and forth, touching her thumb to her middle finger. "Tomorrow," Lilly said.

"Yes, Lilly. Tomorrow when your chores are done." Janis winked at Paige.

Paige grinned back.

"Chores." Lilly repeated and then began to hum to herself.

Janis got in her car and started up the little lawn mower engine. With a smile on her face she waved goodbye to Paige.

Paige could hardly believe the difference in not only the little girl but also in Janis. "What magic do you make?" she asked as she looked at the mare quietly eating her bale of hay. Paige walked back down to see how much water she'd drunk. Half the trough was empty. With all that mare was eating, Paige noticed the hollowness of her body was beginning to soften. Her bones didn't look so prominent.

As she turned on the water, a question came to mind. What was it that Lilly felt when she hugged the neck of that horse? After she turned off the water she crawled in next to the mare as she continued to eat. Paige knelt down, wrapped her arms around Babe's neck, closed her eyes and listened. There was a deep, repetitive whoosh-goosh, whoosh-goosh, whoosh-goosh. A strong and steady heartbeat and the subtle grind of her chewing. She listened deeper and found Babe's breath going in and out. The draw of air, so powerful to extend her massive rib cage, and the flurry of wind that was released on the exhale. For a few moments Paige was lost in a symphony, a rhythm of power, beauty, of vitality and life, beyond words or understanding.

She actually didn't know how long she had stayed there, but when she opened her eyes, it brought her back to reality. She stood up and stroked Babe's neck. "Thank you," Paige said. "If that means anything to you, thank you." She patted the mare's neck and headed to the house to get her keys.

20

Lilly had been bursting at the seams with enthusiasm. Although her repetitious swaying was excitement needing to be in motion, she was now beginning to understand how she was able to communicate. She really liked Charlie, it seemed like he understood her and was not scared of her uncontrollable outbursts when she was stimulated with too much movement or noise. Lilly had begun to realize she had to go into her own world and zone out, find a fuzz or a piece of grass, something to take the busyness away. She might not be able to control her body all the time but around horses she felt at peace. There was a quietness that was understood between the two of them. Neither one needed words. A stillness, something she had never felt before. Lilly craved it, for the first time in her life she felt heard, beyond the stimulation of life. People seemed to fast, always talking, too much action, always doing, and doing way too fast.

As Lilly spent more time with Babe and Charlie she began to feel heard, maybe understood, she started trying to say more words, repeating them over and over again, under her breath. Subconsciously developing focus and determination.

Charlie recognized Lilly trying to communicate. He remembered working with young colts and how he had softened himself to see the *try* horses gave him when he started them in halter, or taught them to lead or saddle. He could see Lilly try, see her frustration and responded to her attempts, they were similar. It was not that he compared her to a horse, but when he saw her try to say something he supported her and would repeat it to her with an acknowledgement and understanding. He recognized that she started to focus more and more on how her mouth worked and how to control some of her outbursting emotions. He didn't talk to her like she was stupid or retarded.

Lilly was communicating the same as others do. She realized if she focused hard enough and blocked out the outside stimulus she could talk.

21

Paige called her Mom when she got into the house. Patricia answered the phone.

"Hey, Mom, do you have a few minutes to talk?"

"Sure, honey, what do you have going on?"

Paige hesitated. "Well it looks like I will be taking Jim to New York." She stopped and waited for whatever her mother would say.

Patricia didn't miss a beat. "When are you leaving?"

"Friday morning out of Boise."

Do I need to take care of any animals?" she asked.

"If you wouldn't mind, I need you to take care of two."

"Two? Which two are they?"

One four-legged and one two-legged. My Blue dog and Abigail Marie.

They both laughed.

"Are you going to be alright? Can I help you with anything?"

"No, Mom. I am good. Jim really needs to get over there and see what is going on, and I am the person to do it."

"Who is going to do your chores? We can run over and do them for you."

"Charlie said he would take care of things, Paige smiled. "And I bribed him with a little bit of the strawberry rhubarb jam. He loved that stuff last night."

Paige filled Patricia in on what had happened with Lilly and Babe. "It was amazing, Mom. I can't believe the difference already."

Patricia chuckled over the phone. "It sounds wonderful, Paige. I am so happy that you have that horse, and what a connection with Lilly."

"Yes, I know I can't believe it. Say Mom, I have got to go start packing, Love you."

"Love you too, sis, I will come by and pick up Abby."

"Perfect Mom see you in a bit."

When Paige got off the phone, she packed. She would take the bare necessities tucked neatly in a duffle bag. That way she would be able to help Jim with all of his things too..

When Abby came home, Paige explained that she was heading out one more time to the East Coast to help Jim get around New York and see Craig.

"Is Craig going to be alright?" Abby asked, concerned.

"I think so."

"Well, would you tell him hi for me when you see him?"

"Sure I will. Better yet, why don't you write him a note and I will give it to him," Paige stated.

"Can I give him a picture?"

"Sure, that would be a great idea."

"We can give him a little care package so he has a

little bit of home with him," Abby said as if the idea was already done.

Paige went out, did the chores, and loaded up her travel supplies for her journey. She came into the house and wrote Charlie a note explaining her chores and that Blue would be staying out with her mom and dad. But he would already know that since that was where he was living. She grinned at her note. "Well, I guess there is something to be said for being an overachiever."

Abby came back in with a couple of small stems of sage brush and alfalfa hay. She put each into a baggy and sealed them shut. Then she grabbed a couple of cookies out of the freezer. That should do it, she thought as she put them in a little satchel and pulled the drawstring closed. "Scent from home… Good to go," she said as she dropped it in Paige's overnight bag.

22

Under the circumstances, with the permission of Alison to stay at Craig's place. Lori spent a good four hours cleaning it up. Lori had gone shopping. She had bought a few candles and a couple of modern art pictures to cover the bare walls. She'd bought matching floral sofa and chair covers, some flowers and a couple plants. She couldn't believe that he had let the place go so badly. Finally, she stripped his bed, replaced them with new sheets and a comforter, and washed the blankets. Now she thought she could stay there without her skin crawling with bachelor bugs all over everything. "I can't believe men," Lori moaned under her breath. "They live like slobs."

She knew he would like it. It had a touch of class, simple and elegant. Not at all like the bachelor pad she had walked into.

She tossed all the boxes Craig had meticulously packed back into the baby's room. She glanced at the crib folded against the wall and hesitated a moment.

When Lori found an envelope with Paige written on it, she flipped it over a couple of times debating. She put it with a couple of magazines on the top shelf of the closet with Craig's dirty cowboy hat. Yet, as she began to close the door, she stopped, reached back up and grabbed the envelope. She turned it over a couple more times, walking back into the front room. *What would it hurt to read it?*

She poured herself a glass of wine, still holding the envelope. She sat down in the chair, draping her legs over the armrest, and opened the envelope.

The note was written on standard notebook paper. She carelessly flipped it back and forth, looking for something more. *He couldn't even write a note on stationary paper*, she thought. *Men.* She started to read.

Dear Paige,

I am writing this from the heart.

She continued to read, and the words melted into her heart. She wished she had someone to love her like that.

When she finished, there was a slight pain in her heart, silently folding it and slipping it back in the envelope. Maybe he wasn't a slob, maybe he just needed a woman. She leaned back in her chair and thought Craig Curry was like a sexy character in a real-life romance novel. No wonder her sister loved him so much. He would be perfect if he would learn to clean the house.

"Just a little tweaking," she sighed. Maybe it wasn't too late. She could possibly get him to see her differently. He had a history with her and her sister. She could certainly put on her best charm. And another bonus was that Alison liked her. She downed the last of her wine at the thought.

There was a closed picture frame on the end table. Lori went over, picked it up and opened it. It was her sister Lisa. She looked at it for a few moments and then closed it. She carried it to the baby room and put it on the top shelf of the closet with Paige's note. Lori turned out the light and shut the door.

She had sat down for only a few minutes when the phone rang. "Lori, this is Alison. Did you find everything in the apartment?"

"Oh yes. Everything is fine here. I rearranged a few things and added a few décor items. I think it is pretty comfortable."

"I am sure he would want you to make yourself at home," Alison said. "If you need anything, honey, you just let me know. Sometimes that boy of mine forgets what it is like to have a little class. I have tried my best to make a gentleman out of him, but he is a little hardheaded."

"Well, I kind of like them a little hardheaded. What fun would that be if they were a 'yes ma'am' kind of guy?"

Alison laughed. "Well, if he's anything like his father, it might be a little more than what you bargained for."

"Oh, I don't know, Alison. I can hold my own, I think. He has a good heart, this one does. With a little tweaking I might get him to like the things I do." Lori paused for a moment. "I kind of fixed that up a little already. I am sure he will like what I have done to the place."

"Well, I sure hope so. It would be so nice for him to have a life again. After losing your sister, he has never been quite the same", Alison paused, "so, when are you going back to the hospital?"

"I thought I would take the night off, so probably tomorrow morning sometime." Lori poured another glass of wine.

"That would be great. I have meetings all morning, so I won't get down there until sometime in the afternoon."

"I think I could fall in love with your son." Lori took a drink of wine. It went down smoothly.

"Oh, Lori, my son would be lucky to have you, honey. You have been a Godsend since my ex-husband can't even get down here to help out at all," Alison began to vent. She sighed. "You know he always copped out on everything. He just didn't want to leave his little hole in the wall—that place he calls home. I am sure of it."

"Don't you worry, Alison. I have everything under control. I can't imagine you doing this all by yourself."

"Thank you, honey. Call if you need anything."

"I will, thank you. Goodnight, Alison."

"Goodnight, dear."

Lori took another sip of wine as she hung up the phone, *that "dear" thing has got to go,* she thought, leaning back in the chair with a sigh..

23

The next two days went a little smoother. Craig was getting stronger and more alert although he had no memory. The doctor wanted to start seeing him out of bed for small amounts of time. The swelling was down in his brain and his vitals were stable. He could even hold a conversation. He looked forward to having Lori come in and visit for couple hours a day. His mother had given permission for her to stay in his apartment. It seemed to be alright. She brought his photo album of his past life and shared old stories with him.

"I am a cop?" The label was kind of exciting to him, yet he felt like he didn't fit the description in his mind. Something seemed to be missing.

"Yes, going on six years," Lori told him. She showed him a couple of pictures of Lisa and him at a Christmas party three years ago. Tears streamed down Lori's cheeks.

Craig reached up and wiped them away. Then he gave her a tissue off the bedside table.

"Thanks." Lori sniffed.

Craig patted her hand, "It is alright."

"I know, I know. I don't know what came over me." Lori shifted in her chair. "Look, I have a couple of appointments I have to attend, so I will be back tomorrow, alright?"

"Sure, that is fine." Craig was getting tired anyway and wanted some quiet time.

"Here, I will leave this for you. See you tomorrow." Lori left his photo album with him. "Keep trying. You will get your memory back, and we can laugh about old times."

She got up and grabbed her jacket. As she started to leave, she walked over, bent down and kissed him on the lips. "See you later," she whispered.

Craig was surprised. He watched her go. He touched his lips and then reached up and scratched his head, confusion swirling inside his skull. Was this the woman he loved? She was pretty and seemed nice. Inside he felt part of his life was missing, like an unexplainable hole.

He picked up the album and thumbed through it, noticing there were a lot of pictures missing at the beginning of the book. Some of the pictures were shifted and loose on the page.

His eyes were heavy. He would ask about them later. He laid down and before he could even think, he fell asleep.

***

Three days of being out of the coma and still no memory of who he was. Craig sighed as he started to get out of bed… feeling weak he grabbed for his walker.

A man in a NYPD uniform came strolling in with balloons, a get-well card and photograph signed by the entire force. "Hey, Craig. Remember me? Got a present from the force. Some other guys will drop by in a day or so."

"Umm, thanks, and you are?" Craig looked confused at the cop who was holding holding a photo.

Surprised, "Um… I'm John, uh… your partner…"

Craig looked at the photo. There he stood with the force, alongside John. "You had me scared there for a minute. Thought I did something wrong."

John laughed, "nope, just coming to check on you. They said you were awake."

Craig looked at the photo again. "Huh, there I am in Blues and everything." searching his memory for some recognition.

Ignoring the comment, John continued…"yep, you've got a lot of guys rooting for you." John strolled around the room as he tried to think of something to say.

Craig realized that John's Jersey accent was more prominent. Why would he know that? Craig didn't say anything. He was getting used to the appearance of strangers coming in his room and expecting some miraculous "Aha moment!" Or, "I remember you." But there was nothing but strangers saying they knew him with the pictures to prove it.

"Boy, Craig," John stumbled. "When you got back from Or-ee-gon, I thought you had it all in the bag. You were full of life and spunk. I am sure sorry you are in here. It doesn't seem fair."

"Oregon? Why did I go to Oregon?" Craig asked. His words still drawled a little. He noticed he said Oregon differently than John. Maybe it was because his throat was still scratchy.

"You went to see your dad!" John sounded surprised. "Boy, you really don't remember anything!" He shook his head and rubbed his chin.

Here John could handle murders, robberies and muggings, but when it came to friends in hospitals, he seemed like a fish out of water. He swaggered around the room like a kid off the streets. "You were pretty messed up from some things that happened around here. But we won't go into that."

John cleared his throat. "When I came, after the anniversary of your wife's death..." John realized he probably shouldn't talk about that either and paused a moment. *God what should we talk about?* Then he continued, "...Uh... to take you out for a beer, you said you drank Crown Royal because that is what your dad drank." He paused again.

"You and Lisa had planned to go to Or-ee-gon after the baby was born and we got to talkin', I asked you if your tickets were still good, because you had bought them a year in advance. You came back in the front room and said you were going home." John stopped there for a moment. "When you said that, Craig, I thought you weren't comin' back, and I would be lookin' for a new partner. But two weeks later, you come back with a tan, a cowboy hat and stories of how a horse tried to buck you off... what did you call him? Sugar? Lugar? Booger? Yeah that was it. Booger. Never would have thought that a name for a horse.

Craig was intrigued, soaking up the story. "Maybe he was a booger to ride." He laughed. "I rode horses, huh? Are you sure it was me?"

"As sure as I am standin' here," John said with a grin. "You talked of a little girl Abby, and a wild mountain lion and a baby horse you called Cougar." John stopped again, searching though his memory. "You had some crazy stories."

Craig was racking his brain trying to remember but nothing came to mind. It sounded like he was two people in one body—lost between the world of yesterday and today.

The stories that Lori and his mother told him were of art, the police academy, and Christmas parties. They never mentioned him playing out in the wild, wild West.

John recognized Craig's photo book. "You had them in your album." John picked it up, thumbing through the pages. "You showed me your bronc riding pictures from high school, your dad, and where you used to live in Or-ee-gon."

The way John said Or-ee-gon was like dragging fingernails down a chalkboard. Craig could hardly stand it, and for some unknown reason wanted to correct him.

John thumbed through the book again. "That's funny. They were in here the last time I saw this book." He thumbed through the book again. Spots were empty where pictures used to be. He put down the book. "They were here. I know it." John fanned the book looking for loose pictures. He saw the confusion on Craig's face, "well maybe you have another book at home." He put the book down, then changed the subject. "So, when are you getting out of here? They can't hold you forever."

"They are thinking I can probably be released tomorrow or the next day. Say, John," Craig paused for a moment, unsure how to finish his question, "did I have a girlfriend?"

"You? No, not that I know of." He was starting to feel more at home and casual with Craig than when he first arrived. His casual swagger and raw humor was coming out as the partner and friend he was used to conversing with. "But, hey, who am I to know of these things? You could have one in Manhattan or hell even in Or-ee-gon. I wouldn't know. I am just your partner, not your lover. Ya know what I'm sayin'?"

Craig grinned. He liked this guy. "When I get out of here, we are going to have to go out and get a beer. I think I am going to like being your partner."

"Hey! Hold up there, cowboy!" John gave him a smirk. "You can't be my partner until you figure out which way to point a gun." He glanced at his watch. "Hey, I better get outta here. I gotta get to work." John looked back from the doorway. "Why did you ask about a girlfriend?"

"Well," Craig started, "there is a girl staying in my apartment that has been coming over every day. I kind of enjoy her company. My mother really likes her and said it was okay for her to stay there while I was in here."

"You getting' along with your mom alright?"

"I seem to be, sure. Why?"

John kind of shrugged loosely and bobbed his head. "Good, that's good." Then he disappeared out the door.

Craig felt good. John was like a breath of fresh air. What was this Oregon thing? That is a long way from New York. Horses and cows and cougars, what an adventure that would be to remember.

It was after dark, and Lori wouldn't be back until tomorrow. He took his walker and made his way to the window. His right leg still didn't want to work right, *Got to give it some time.* The lights of the city were bright, but the light that caught his attention was the fingernail moon hanging silently like a beacon. A shooting star raced across the sky and disappeared next to the constellation Orion. Why would he know that constellation?

He turned his back to the window and crawled back into his hospital bed. Maybe things will be clearer tomorrow, he thought. His eyes grew heavy as he lay his head on the pillow.

24

It was three in the morning when Paige pulled into Jim's driveway. The kitchen light was on, so she walked up and knocked. Jim crutched to the door. Paige looked at him, he kind of reminded her of John Wayne. Well, John Wayne on crutches. He had his new Stetson hat, a denim jacket and jeans.

He was not only tall, he walked with an air about him that made him seem bigger than most men. With a boot on one foot and a cast on the other. His duffel bag lay next to the door, and he reached down to pick it up.

"Are you ready?" she asked.

"As ready as I'm gonna get," Jim said as he started to crutch his way to the truck. "Called Alison last night. She will meet us at the airport and take us to the hospital."

"Sounds great, Jim. I would hate to have to find my way around. It is a whole other world over there," Paige said, relieved that they didn't have to find transportation there. It was a busy world, and she felt like she could get swallowed up if she had to try to navigate around there.

They drove in the dark of morning, watching as the dawn made its way from dark purple, to bright pink, then pastel, to a golden pink, until it finally made its way over the mountain into a bright white orb of light, making the shadows of night whimper and fade.

In about two and a half hours, Paige pulled into the Boise airport, dropped Jim off at the front and went to part the truck in long term parking. They dropped off their luggage and had time to get a quick bite to eat before they found their gate.

As they boarded the plane, Paige took her seat next to the window. Jim took a deep breath and tried to get comfortable. He was in the aisle seat where he had a little leg room, but his leg seemed to be swollen in the cast. He fidgeted a little bit and tried to figure out how he was going to be comfortable on this flight.

"Nervous?" Paige grinned at him.

"Well, I don't know if it is nerves or what. I just wish this thing had some reins so I could steer it a little. I don't think it's going to work off of leg cues."

"Well, just pretend." Paige looked around for a moment, took the strap off her purse and clipped it on to the webbed mesh holding the magazines on the back of the seat in front of them. "Sit deep and roll with the motion. Hold on to this." She handed him the purse strap rein. "When you feel like he is taking his head, just hold him steady and pull his nose around." She smiled at him as he looked at her little contraption.

He took the rein and played with it a little to get the feel before they began to move. "I got this," he said as he saw her smile. "I ain't scared."

Paige leaned back in her seat smiling as she looked

out the window at the wing below her. *Not much of a view*, she thought as she propped her head against it. Craig entered her mind with the memory of what she had seen the last time at the hospital. *Can't go there*, she told herself and turned back to Jim mastering the moves of his high-headed seat.

"Have you ever flown before, Jim?"

"Nope, the highest I ever flew was off of a bareback horse they called Hangover. Yep, near as I could tell, he threw me ten feet in the air. He had me bucked off before I could get my spurs rolled over his shoulder." Jim shook his head with a high respect of the horse. "I felt like I had a hangover for a week after that ride. Boy, could he buck."

"Just think of this as a good ride as we take off. Go with it and think of the arm rest as your saddle horn. You can grab it at any time."

"I don't need no saddle horn."

"Just trying to help you stay in the middle." Paige smiled as she winked at him.

The plane began to move as the stewardess came over the speaker. Jim listened and read the manual as she said her speech. *His seat was a floating device...what?* maybe he didn't know his geography like he thought,. He looked at the emergency exits and then saw her put on her seat belt as she too got seated before takeoff.

The engines began to roar. "Never thought I would ever fly," Jim said. As the plane started down the runway, he felt himself being pressed into the back of the seat and felt the thump, thump of wheels. Then as if by magic, there was a smooth glide and the ground began to fall away as the plane lifted off. He noticed he had let go of Paige's makeshift rein and grabbed for the arm rest.

Paige grinned at him.

"Just getting a feel for it. That's all," he whispered.

Paige's wing dropped and Jim again grabbed for the "horns" on both sides of his seat.

Paige leaned back. "Look..."

Jim glanced out the window as they made their turn toward the east. He was silent. For the first time in his life he had a bird's-eye view of the world.

"Is this what you saw when you got thrown from Hangover?"

"Don't know. Kind of had my eyes closed," Jim responded. "When I opened them, it was all dirt, hide and hooves." He watched the figures of people and cars fade away to buildings and streets, then roads, and then a quilt pattern of farms and ranches etched on the skin of the land, and boundaries. The Creator's art of land, water and the insignificance of ownership...

"This is incredible," Jim mumbled and for a moment his life fell away into nothing but land contours of rolling hills, sage brush, creeks and rivers, then it disappeared as they climbed through the clouds.

"Well, we have a couple hours before we land so you can appreciate it all you want."

Without much warning, the plane began to bounce a little in the turbulence.

The captain came on the intercom and announced that there was going to be a bit of a headwind, and they should be out of it in a few moments as they gained altitude.

A mother was trying to get her little girl to quiet down. The child was beginning to get cranky from the bumpy ride.

Looking down at the purse strap, Jim reached out and grabbed it. He pulled it snug and said, "Easy, big guy. Easy."

The girl looked at him for a moment.

"His trot is a little bumpy, but he's a pretty sure-footed guy," Jim stated as he looked over at her. "Do you want to steer him for a while? You've got to have good hands."

The mother looked over at the big cowboy. The little girl turned away from him but quieted down.

Jim gave the mother a wink and went back to riding his imaginary horse. "Easy, Flipper," he said quietly. "You don't want to scare your rider."

The plane settled into a smoother gliding flight.

The little girl looked over at him again. "Flipper is a dolphin," she said boldly.

"Kaitlin!" The mother looked at Jim. "You have to be polite."

Jim winked at the mother again. "Well, what should we name him then if Flipper is already taken?"

The little girl thought for a moment and then said, "Bucky."

"Are you sure that is a good name?"

Kaitlin nodded.

"Well, then, Bucky it is," Jim announced. "Do you want to take the reins?"

She nodded her head.

Jim unclipped the purse strap that Paige had attached and handed the rein to the little girl.

The mother mouthed, "Thank you," silently.

Jim grinned.

"Are you a real cowboy?" the little girl inquired.

"I don't know for sure what you mean, but I have some cows, I ride horses, and I am real."

"What are your horses' names?"

"Well my favorite is Mouse. Right now he is a young one, kind of like Bucky here, who wants to get his way. But we have to hold him steady and show them how to be good and safe. Then I have Booger and Cougar..."

"Grosse... Booger..." The little girl wrinkled her nose.

"You bet, cause he is pretty slick and hard to stay on when you ride him.

Kaitlin laughed at Jim, "your funny." as she tried to attached the reins.

"Thought my name was Jim , but you can call me Funny if you want to" Jim winked at her.

She giggled at him as her mother took the rein and attached it like Paige had to the seat in front of her daughter.

"Now hold it steady. That's it. Not too hard because you will hurt Bucky's mouth."

Kaitlin looked at him and grinned at the thought of playing horses with a grownup cowboy.

The plane started to buck in the turbulence again. In a surge of panic she started to pull real hard on the reins.

"Hold him steady, thats it, easy, Kaitlin, easy. You don't want to scare him. Just hold him steady till he gets the feel of you. Talk to him let him know that you got this."

The plane balanced out again as Kaitlin began to talk. "Easy, Bucky, be good. Good boy."

The mother grabbed the seat, then looked over at him with a worried smiled.

Jim tipped his hat, "Jim," he said for an introduction.

"Claire. Thank you. I knew this was going to be an interesting ride. Neither one of us has ever flown before."

"Well I guess that makes three of us," Jim said as he straightened his leg out into the aisle for a moment.

"How did you hurt your leg?"

"Well, would like to say I got bucked off or something of that sort. Well I guess I did get bucked off, bucked off a step." He grinned.

Claire laughed a little. "Sounds pretty dangerous."

"You have no idea."

Paige smiled at this kind man who knew no stranger. She leaned her head back and closed her eyes.

***

As the plane landed, Claire gave back Paige's purse strap and thanked Jim again for his kindness.

"Well, it kind of helped me out a little to watch Kaitlin handle Ole Bucky there."

Kaitlin smiled at him as they left their seat. "Thank you."

25

Instead of Alison picking them up from the airport as she had promised, there was a small-framed Asian man holding a sign as they walked out of the terminal that read *Curry*. Jim walked up to him. "We are Curry."

"Please come this way," he said in a strong Asian accent. "Ms. Alison has me take you to her."

They headed for baggage claim twenty minutes later, and Paige grabbed a little cart for both of their duffel bags and her overnight bag. The driver took it from her and they followed like two lost pups.

The driver informed them as they walked, "Ms. Alison thought it best if you stay in hotel instead of her house, so Mr. Jim could get the rest he needed. She didn't want to overbear Mr. Craig in his healing process, as she put it. I am to call her when you get settled, so Ms. Alison will meet with you before you see Mr Craig. She wanted to prepare you. She is worried that it might throw him into shock…"

The driver looked like a little kid standing next to Jim, he kept his eye averted to where they were going.

The words didn't sit so well with Jim. He didn't fly clear across the United States, so Ms. Alison could put him on hold until she said it was time.

As they got into the town car, Jim asked, "So what's your name?"

The driver looked curiously at him, "David."

"Hi, David. This is Paige and I am Jim. Are you Ms. Alison's private driver?"

"Yes", the driver answered. Looking nervous, yet he was excited to be standing next to a man in a cowboy hat. "Are you a real cowboy?"

Jim looked at him for a moment. What was this real cowboy stuff? "Well I own cows if that is what you are asking."

"How many cows do you own?" he asked, excited to actually meet a cowboy.

"That is like asking how much money you have in the bank," Jim stated flatly, "There are certain things…"

"Three hundred twenty-two dollars," David answered.

Jim looked over at Paige, who was grinning ."How long have you driven for Ms. Alison?"

"About four years." He said in his Asian accent, looking back in the rearview.

"So, David, do you know Craig?"

"Yes, I do."

"Do you know where he's at now?"

"Of course, he is at Bellevue Hospital on First. I dropped Ms. Alison off there before I get you."

"Before we get settled where Alison wants us to go," Jim stated, "would you take us to him?"

"Well I can, Mr. Jim, but it might get me into trouble, Ms. Alison said you to go to hotel." he reaffirmed.

"Ah, just tell her I held you at gunpoint."

David's face went white.

"David that is a joke, I don't have a gun... I just mean we will take responsibility for you taking us to the hospital.

David nodded his head, gave a stressed smile, straightened himself and looked in the rearview mirror one more time.

Paige glanced at Jim and gave a half smile.

David drove in silence, glancing every once in a while to check his safety status. When he pulled up at the hospital, he seemed relieved when he asked, "I should wait here for you? Call me when you are ready, yes?" David's hands were shaking as he handed Jim a business card, anxious to be away from this cowboy.

Jim got out of the car and grabbed his crutches. His leg ached with the swelling that filled his cast. He looked down at Davids' small frame and said. "Sure. We will do that. By the way, David, let's make it four hundred twenty-two dollars in the bank, alright?" Jim shook his hand and gave him a hundred-dollar bill. "Thank you."

"Thank you, Mr. Jim!" David said. His voice gave way to the appreciation.

Jim turned with one more bit of advice for the young man. "Just don't go around asking everyone how many cows they have."

"Okay, no cows," David answered shaking his head. "No cows. I will wait for you, yes?"

"Yes, we sure would appreciate it if you would wait." Jim replied.

Paige was on familiar territory now. She knew what to do to find out where Craig was. As they crossed through the atrium, Paige adjusted her speed for Jim and his crutches. She knew he must be hurting by the way he got out of the town car. They made it to the information desk and asked for Craig Curry's room. The attendant gave them the room number and the directions going up to his floor.

As they headed toward the elevator, Paige noticed a wheelchair sitting in a cubby. She grabbed it and patted it for Jim to have a seat. He obliged willingly. She elevated his foot and wheeled him down the corridor to the elevator.

"You should have been a nurse. You are kind of good at this," Jim remarked with a little relief.

"Thought of being a vet once, but didn't have enough practice," Paige said with a smile.

When they arrived at the nurse's station Paige again inquired about Craig.

The nurse looked at Jim and then at Paige. "Family?"

"Yes," Jim said proudly.

The nurse looked over the top of her glasses with tired eyes, pointed down the hallway toward the loud commotion and gave the room number. "Follow the noise," she said exasperated, going back to her paperwork.

Paige began to push Jim down toward the voices. One of them sounded like Alison. Paige was surprised to remember her voice.

"I don't care what you think you need. You are not moving back into your apartment unless you have someone there. I have already made arrangements for you to move in with me until you are better. Or like I said," Alison's voice was high and shrill, "Lori said she would stay with you."

"No! I don't want anyone staying with me. Hell, to be honest, I don't even know you!" Craig had woken up agitated and confused.

He questioned the empty picture spaces in his book. Getting a response from his mother, that she was not wanting to confuse him with a history that doesn't exist anymore.

When he had pressed her, she began to get huffy, which had now escalated from a simple inquisition into a full-blown argument similar to that of a mother telling her little boy what to do.

"You are my son, and you will do as I say!" Alison retorted with authority. "You are not well enough to live alone in this city."

"I don't need a babysitter!" Craig was frustrated, confused and borderline mad. "You are forcing me to live with this girl who talks of a past that I have no idea about. For the last three days she and you have been telling me stories of who I once was, yet hiding photos of my past like you are ashamed of who I was." Craig hobbled across the room and looked out the window. "I feel like I am two people." He said honestly, "I feel like I can't live up to your expectations. I can't think when I am with you guys, like I should be ashamed of..."

"You will live with me or Lori, and that is final!"

Paige had stopped, she couldn't breathe. They both were listening to the conversation. Jim moved the wheel of his chair with his free hand and Paige, reading his silent cues, obliged by pushing him closer to the room. She wheeled him to the edge of the door, but Jim raised his hand to stop her. Paige looked down and realized Jim was going to get up. He got his crutches positioned, rocked forward, stood erect, and took a breath.

Paige thought for a moment the man had grown another foot taller.

Jim stepped into the doorway. "Enough," he commanded in an authoritative tone. He had heard enough of the badgering and bickering back and forth.

Alison and Craig both jumped at the bold voice, seeing the big frame in the doorway.

Paige's heart was racing as she stood in silence.

Alison turned to Jim. Anger, frustration, and determination filled her. "I told the driver to take you to the hotel." She looked at Jim. "I have this under control without you."

Jim looked at his ex-wife. "Alison, sit down and shut up." Then looking at his son, "And you, sir," he paused. "This is a hospital for the healing, not a boxing ring that you can go rounds in. If you want your apartment, go and get it. It is not up for discussion."

"I was trying…" Alison started.

"I know what you were doing. You were trying to run everyone's lives." He looked at her for a moment. "And it stops now."

Craig looked at this big man. He knew him, but who was he?

"Craig, get your things, it is time for you to go home."

Craig stood at attention, but then a question entered his mind and he tentatively asked. "Which home am I going to?" He hoped this big man would know the right answer for him.

"That is not for me to decide. Make up your mind and go. Go with your mother or go back to your apartment. I don't care." He paused for a moment then said, "If neither of those suit you, you can come home with me back to Oregon."

Craig looked dumbfounded. Could it really be that easy?

"In Oregon, you got a horse that needs ridden and hay that needs baled."

"Don't you dare take my son from me!" Alison said as she began to stand up.

"Woman, you stay out of this. It is not your choice any longer. Craig is a grown man. He can make this choice on his own." Jim paused and looked at the young man before him, whoever he might be today, and then continued. "He has seen more pain in his lifetime than anyone in this room. You don't have the right to force your lifestyle any longer. You don't own him." Jim looked back at Craig. "Make up your mind, son. There are sick people who need this room."

Lori came walking in the room. She pressed past Jim and Paige. "Alison, who are all these people?" She stood next to Craig and put her arm around his arm, almost claiming ownership. "I could hear you guys all the way down the hall."

Craig spoke up. "That is my father." He looked toward his dad and saw a blonde woman with the bluest eyes standing behind him. The same woman he had been dreaming about. "And Paige," he said quietly. "You have a palomino horse."

Paige didn't say a word. She just nodded.

Lori instantly thought of the letter she had found in Craig's apartment. *This is the girl he thinks he loves?* Her jeans, cowboy boots and button-down shirt screamed that she was a redneck from the sticks and didn't belong in the city.

He stepped away from Lori and looked at his dad again. "You are my dad, Jim, and you live in Oregon." He started to laugh a little at the thought that he might remember something.

Lori walked up to him and quietly said, "Well, aren't you going to introduce me?" As she grabbed his arm again, she glanced at Paige. *Just a plain girl who doesn't have a touch of fashion sense. What in the world could he ever see in her?* She snubbed her head past Paige and walked up to Craig's dad.

"Oh sure," he said as he looked back over to Paige. His eyes locked on to hers for a moment of recognition. "Um, Dad, this is Lori. Lori this is Dad." He stepped away from Lori again.

"A pleasure, I'm sure." Lori held her hand out like she had a broken wrist, her hand palm side down.

Jim looked at her fragile manicured hand, but didn't offer to take it. What did that mean, *"Pleasure, I'm sure?"* This was a lifestyle that didn't belong to him. It felt manufactured and fake. But he wasn't going to be fake. He had things he needed to do and places he needed to get to. He wasn't going to waste his time trying to figure out a lifestyle or play the game. "Good to meet you, Lori. Thanks for taking care of our son."

Craig looked over at his mother. "Mom, I think I am going to take my chances in Oregon."

Alison looked over at Jim and then at Craig. "I despise you, Jim Curry!" she spat. "And for you, Craig, you are an ungrateful, arrogant son. After all that I have done for you and all that we did here at the hospital. I even had Lori go and redecorate your apartment! And you drop us for a man you barely know. He shows up here just in time for you to get out of this despicable place."

Craig looked at his mom for a moment. "I appreciate all that you have done for me, and I love you for it. But I am going home." He again looked at Paige, and their eyes locked again. She had tears forming and she tried to blink them back.

"I have something for you," Paige said as she stepped forward. "This is from Abby. She took the satchel out of her purse and handed it to him. It was a picture of Abby and Cougar standing together and a simple note. *Hope you get better. We miss you. Love, Abby.*

"She thought you might like the smell of sagebrush and alfalfa…" Paige told him as she shifted her weight.

Craig looked at Paige and then down at the brunette girl in the picture. He was confused yet the feeling of happiness filled him.

"Thanks." Was all he could think of to say. He opened the satchel and scent of sagebrush filled his nose, he smiled at the feeling. His mind filled with a thousand images and words that were mingling and trying to get out.

"Okay, now that our mind is made up, let's start taking action," Jim said as he crutched over to the wheelchair. "Grab your gear, son. We have some packing to do."

26

Janis felt herself being lifted on a horse. *I can't do this!* She looked over and saw Sarah and Lilly waiting for her. They were giggling. *Yes, I can!* she thought courageously as she nudged the horse forward and it lifted up into a lope, flowing free and effortlessly. She was free, riding with her girls! She looked back and saw a man watching them ride off. He was smiling at them. She looked on the other side of her and now the man was riding with them. He reached out his hand to her. *Should I take it?* She hesitated but then ever so slowly reached out, brushing fingertips.

The alarm clock went off and startled her awake. She hit snooze.

Janis rolled over in bed tucking her pillow under her head. "I don't want to wake up. Please just let me stay in that dream." Her eyes found the clock. "Please just five more minutes. I don't want to get up."

She closed her eyes as she pulled the covers over her head, wishing she was a child again and her mom would let her sleep in for another hour. The next thing she knew the rhythmic *beep, beep, beep* from her alarm clock woke her for the second time. Janis leaned over and shut it off, inhaled a tired breath, swung her feet over the bed and touched the cool floor.

She had a half hour before she needed to get Sarah up for school. That is when the house would come alive with deadlines and breakfast. She needed coffee, so she padded to the kitchen to make a pot.

She sat down at the table and began to write in her journal. It was silly for her to write. Who would want to read the life and times of a divorced mother and her two children. She thought for a moment. *Maybe she wouldn't even write this morning* . But as the thought crossed her mind, her fingers picked up her pen and began. *The Adventures of Autism and Me.*

Who had the answers she needed? Or did she need answers? What were all these questions...? These were questions plaguing, not plaguing, but making her question herself and have to get out of her head. Here she was putting them on paper to see if they fit her anymore. Was she finding hope or was it all a trick so she would start to dream again that there might be answers out there? And what about a horse? How could a horse help her Lilly? A giant horse.

She kept her pen moving, half numb of what she was writing.

When she put her pen down, she looked at the clock, padded back down the hall to wake up her daughter. As she opened up the already cracked door, she found Sarah writing in her own notebook.

"Well, good morning! What are you writing?"

Sarah looked up at her mom for a moment. "Oh, nothing important, I was just jotting notes down about Lilly and our lives before horses."

"Really?" Janis stated, surprised.

"Yeah, more like feelings and emotions and the things that you have tried before we met Babe." Sarah paused for a moment. "I don't know... just kind of writing."

"Well, I do that too." Janis looked at her daughter with new eyes and maybe some sort of connection.

"I know." Sarah said as she closed her notebook and slipped the pen in the binder. "You write every morning."

Janis was surprised that Sarah would notice. "How did you know that? I usually write when you are sleeping."

"Mom, you do it every day. How can I not notice?" Sarah replied with a sigh.

"I didn't know you knew. But I guess if that is the worst habit you pick up from me, I should be happy."

Sarah rolled her eyes and smiled.

"Well, get up so we can get you breakfast."

Sarah threw her blankets to the side and got out of bed. "Can I have coffee with you this morning?"

Janis was surprised. Who was this girl crawling out of her daughter's bed? "How about hot chocolate?"

"Aw, Mom. Can't I just have one cup with you?"

"I think hot chocolate is what you can have."

They sat at the kitchen table, and Sarah stirred a dollop of whipped cream in her hot chocolate. "Mom, I have an idea for a school project." she paused. "What if we... Can we... with Lilly doing so good..."

"What is it, Sarah?"

"Well… it's just an idea… Let me show you." Sarah got up from her chair to get her notebook she had been writing in. "Well, Mom," she started again, as she returned and sat down. "I was talking with Abby and we thought it might be a good idea to monitor and record Lilly and Babe." Sarah thumbed through her notebook, looking for the layout the girls had started.

"I don't think we want to put Lilly on display, Sarah." Janis didn't want anything to do with her daughter being treated like a circus act.

"Mom, no one will know, we will just take photos of her and write down what she is doing and how the horse and the Lilly respond to each other. Kind of keep a diary. We will take the pictures and write what happens."

Janis looked at Sarah. She had not seen her daughter so excited about doing a project. "What made you think of doing this?"

Sarah thought for a moment, afraid it might just be a silly idea to admit where the inspiration came from. "Well, from Anne Frank's Diary." She paused. "When I picked up that book, Mom, I thought, what could a girl say to change the world or that would be put in a book? She was just a simple girl, living a young girl's life free to dream then locked into captivity so to speak. A prisoner in her own house, screaming to get out."

Sarah paused a moment. "And as I think of Lilly, she is kind of the same way. You help her the best you can but there is something hidden, and we don't know how to help." Sarah rambled on. She had to get this out. "This might be Lilly's only voice to bring awareness through horses, or animals. Just thinking that Lilly was in there somewhere and not just a shell of a person with no feeling." Sarah paused for a moment, surprised that Anne Frank would really bring out so much in her and now she is blurting it all out to her mom. "Now I look at it and think of all the things you have to do every day and thought if it could help another mom to not feel so alone and maybe help give them some answers." Sarah was quiet. "I don't know. I just thought it might help. If not, it was nothing but a couple of pieces of paper and some pictures."

Janis was speechless. She had no idea Sarah was that emotional over Lilly. She thought Lilly just got in Sarah's way. Janis had put sugar in her coffee as she listened to the idea. "I don't know, Sarah. Let me think about it for a while. I just don't want to have Lilly treated like a clown." She thought for a moment, in argument. "Look at how that woman acted at the library."

"Mom, that is exactly why I want to do this project. Because if we don't, and everybody hides their kids with autism, no one will know the difference."

Janis was quiet. Who was the adult here? She glanced at the clock. "Shoot, Sarah, the bus will be here in ten minutes! Go get ready for school. We will talk about this later."

Sarah got up and headed to her bedroom while Janis

slapped a couple of pieces of bread in the toaster. She walked over, took a sip of coffee, making an awful face, realizing she had forgotten to stir.

Before Janis could think, the bus tooted its horn. Sarah grabbed her toast, jacket and backpack before sailing out the door.

"Ride the bus to Paige's place tonight. I will be there with Charlie," she called as she heard the screen door slam.

"I will," came the reply.

She watched her daughter get on the bus and then turned and sat at the table with her half-cold coffee. *What if they documented Lilly and Babe? Her daughter was growing up. Where had the time gone?*

Lilly wandered out of her bedroom, "Babe," she stated.

Janis had to smile. It had to be the first word out of Lilly's mouth this morning. "Yes, Babe," Janis' day had begun. She got up, grabbed a diaper and washcloth, and walked toward her daughter. "How is Lilly this morning? Let's get you cleaned up."

27

Charlie woke up to the creek babbling behind the barn. He heard one of the horses stomp. He had a cozy, little place in the tack room of Abe's barn. His bedroll sat on a couple of grass hay bales, he had little coffee pot and single burner that he plugged in on the leatherworking bar. In his cooler he had bacon, eggs, peanut butter, jam and butter.

Fall air was getting a brisk feel to it, as if ole man winter was giving him a heads up to the coming months of cold and snow. He pulled his wool blanket up. Flick noticing the movements jumped up on the makeshift bed and lay next to him. Charlie stroked Flick's head for a few moments.

Charlie knew winter was another month away or so, but when October hits, all weather is fair game in God's book. He patted the dog's head one more time and crawled out of the warm blanket to put his feet on an old Navajo rug, he had taken with him from his old place. When he was dressed he made himself a pot of coffee from the water out of a jug that he had gotten from the little creek out back.

He went out and fed the horses then came in to make breakfast. He grabbed his cast iron skillet and turned his little single burner on, threw in some butter to melt and walked out and filled his jug again with water. He came back in and tossed a piece of bread into the frying pan to fry as he got his bacon to cook after the bread. Then he fried up his egg. Breakfast was served in less than five minutes.

He knew he didn't have time to mess around this morning because not only was he helping Abe around the place, he had Jim's place to look after, then over to Paige's while they both were gone to New York. He didn't have any idea how long they would be gone, but he didn't mind the extra work. He was saving enough money to rent a place for the winter, and he loved who he was working for.

***

The morning hours sped by, and before Charlie knew it, it was time to go back to Paige's place and meet up with Janis and Lilly. He didn't know what to expect in this session that Paige had lined out, but he thought he would just be there to catch Babe and see what Lilly imagined and wanted to have happen. He had never been around a child with autism, so he would just be there for her and see what kind of adventures he could help make happen.

The afternoon air was a little chilly, so he pulled on his wool sweater and Levi jacket as he got out of the truck. He walked into the barn to get a rope for Babe since Paige had not had time to get a larger halter for the horse. He grabbed a brush as he walked out the barn door to the paddock where Babe stood. The mare glanced at him as he entered the corral, eating the last of the hay he had put out for the morning feeding.

"Hey, Babe," he said as he brought the rope around her neck. He brought out the brush and began to brush down her neck. He looked at the stitches and scars on her. She was healing nicely. He ran long strokes down her neck and front legs, then over her back and hips, and then down her hind legs.

As he finished, he heard the little lawn mower of a car coming up the drive. As Janis pulled in, stopped and turned off the key, Charlie could hear Lilly clearly repeating Babe's name.

Janis worked to get Lilly out, but Janis was too slow, Lilly started struggling in her seat as she tried to get out of the seat belt. Janis tried to quiet the child. All of a sudden Janis paused, and for the first time ever, she knew Lilly had to figure this one out for herself.

Lilly started to scream and rock back and forth in an effort to get out of the car to see Babe. Janis regained her composure and said with a firm voice, "Lilly, wait until I unbuckle the seat belt. I can't do that with you squirming."

Lilly didn't want to wait. She wanted Babe now. She started to scream again. There was a tingling throughout Lilly's body that almost felt like she was crawling out of her skin if she couldn't get out.

Janis stopped and looked over at Charlie, knowing if

something wasn't done immediately, Lilly would blow into a full-out tantrum.

"Wait, Lilly," Janis said again, hoping that would slow her down.

Lilly's tantrum escalated, "Babe! Babe!"

Janis had enough, "Not until you sit still, young lady!"

Lilly fought against her restraints, not patient enough to wait for her mother. She fought harder writhing in her seat then banging her head on the back of it.

It was almost like Lilly could feel Janis's anxiety. She needed to stay calm and direct, she took a breath and blew it out slowly. Something inside her said that *this is where Lilly was mentally.* Janis just had to wait for a moment and put new rules in place for her daughter. "Wait, Lilly. No Babe until you sit still." Janis didn't know if it would work, but she had realized in the last few days that Lilly understood more than what Janis thought she did, and her anxiety fueled the tantrums.

Charlie watched in silence.

Janis gave one more attempt. Be firm and honest, she reminded herself. "Lilly, if you don't sit still, we will go home, and you won't see Babe." Janis said this with so much confidence and authority, she surprised herself. Lilly stopped.

With those words, Lilly's body became quiet. The tingling stopped, and she focused for a few moments on being quiet. Her body seemed to respond. "Babe," she said quietly.

"Yes, Babe and Charlie. Lilly is a good girl," Janis said as she quietly undid the seat belt and lifted Lilly out of the car with her little cord around her middle so Janis could control her if she started to run.

"Babe!" Lilly said again as she started to run toward the horse. The energy she felt toward the horse was almost more than she could control.

"Yes, Babe and Charlie," Janis said as she made the little girl walk up to the horse on the outside of the fence.

Charlie smiled at Janis. "She is a busy one isn't she?"

"Sometimes I think busy is an understatement, especially when it comes to this horse."

Lilly reached through the fence as Babe gave a low nicker of acknowledgment. Charlie grinned.

"Lilly," Charlie said in a low tone. "Do you want to see Babe?"

"Babe," Lilly said looking at the ground. She was trying to make sense of the words she wanted to say. She took her thumb and middle finger and tapped them together to keep focused. With little hesitation, she reached out to Charlie.

Charlie took her in his arms and propped her on his hip. That was not good enough for Lilly. She leaned as far over as she could so she could put her head on Babe's neck.

Charlie put Lilly down and watched the interaction.

Lilly wrapped her little arms around the horse's neck, leaned her head at the throat line, and closed her eyes. Babe wrapped her head around the little girl and stood there quietly, once in a while grinding her teeth or letting a breath out. She did not move a foot or shift her weight at all while the little girl held on for dear life.

Lilly's little hand moved back and forth on the bony neck of the mare, not saying a word. For five minutes she stood there in total silence with her ear next to Babe and her eyes closed.

Then Charlie whispered to her, "Lilly, do you want to sit on Babe?"

Janis looked at Charlie wide eyed.

"Babe," Lilly said calmly.

"I don't know if I want you to do that," Janis said. Her voice was a little shaky with uncertainty.

Charlie looked over at her and winked. "What little girl doesn't want to sit on a horse, especially this big, black, beautiful Babe? Besides," he said, "this ole mare loves this Lilly girl."

He glanced around a moment and then took off his jacket followed by his wool sweater and laid them on Babe's back. "Here, Lilly, jump on up here." Charlie brought her up and lifted her onto Babe's back. "Just like a real cowgirl."

For the first time in her life, she was something besides damaged, something more than, *No Lilly*. She was a cowgirl! Lilly shrieked with excitement, and her hands began to flail in the air with unmistakable bliss. Her smile beamed across her face, radiating pure joy.

Janis' heart was in her throat. She couldn't breathe,

she gasped as Charlie lifted her daughter up onto the back of the huge horse. How could he be so confident with that big animal and her fragile baby. She would have never considered putting her up on a horse.

Lilly sat up there in complete heaven. She threw her head back, looked at the sky, and waved around like a wild bronc rider.

Charlie needed to calm her, or he would have to get her off of the mare. He didn't want to take advantage of Babe's kindness. "Easy there, Lilly girl," he said with caution. "We don't want to scare your horse. Let's try to use our inside voice and slow ourselves down a little bit. I don't want to have to take you down yet."

Lilly understood in an instant. She closed her eyes and dropped her hands. Then she lay forward on the mare, putting her head down on the neck.

"Babe," Lilly whispered. Babe stood there with her eyes half closed. She hardly even flickered an ear at the girl on her back. Charlie had his hands on Lilly so if Babe did decide to move, he would just pull her to safety.

Janis watched her daughter's expressions. She had never seen her daughter so happy, had never heard her squeal for joy, and so content. This man that was holding on to her. Who was he to take this much time with a child and thoroughly enjoy little Lilly's company?

Janis finally found her voice. "I can't believe this."

Abby and Sarah came walking up the drive and saw Lilly on the big mare. Abby grabbed her camera out of her backpack and took a couple of pictures.

Sarah couldn't believe her eyes. "Mom!"

Janis looked over at her. "Can you believe this, Sarah?!"

Charlie looked over at the girls walking up. "Hey, girls. How was school?"

"Good," Sarah said as she looked at Lilly. "Lilly, what are you doing up there?"

"Babe," Lilly said as she opened her eyes. "Cowgirl!" she gurgled, trying to shape a new word.

Charlie grinned, understanding the attempt. "Yep, a natural cowgirl." Charlie felt a lump in his throat. "In a few minutes, this one is going to have to get down so we can go feed and get our chores done."

"Chores," Lilly repeated, and a sense of duty filled her heart. Lilly had a job to do.

"Yep, fun is over. Time to get the chores done," Charlie repeated. He lifted her off Babe, and Lilly stood next to Babe's head that was hung down to her height. "Nice, Babe," he said as he put his sweater and jacket back on.

"Nice," Lilly repeated. To keep her focus longer she kept her eyes on the foot of the horse, tapping her fingers and thumb together.

Abby took some more pictures as Lilly responded to Charlie and Babe. Abby noted her posture, her gestures and actions.

"Nice, Babe." Lilly attempted again

"Yes, Lilly... nice, Babe," Mimicking Charlie, Janis repeated Lilly's words.

Babe shook her head and yawned. Janis jumped back, thinking the mare might want to eat her.

"You girls want to help with chores real quick? Then I have to get to Jim's and get his chores done." Charlie looked over at Janis. "Is there anything else I can do for you this evening?"

"No, I think you did far more than what I was expecting." She paused for a moment. "You do know how to take a girl out of her comfort zone."

"I hope in a good way, Janis," he replied as he buttoned his denim jacket. He turned to the girls. "Sarah, why don't you fill the water trough here for Babe while Abby grabs her blanket. Miss Lilly and I will bring her some hay. Come on, Miss Lilly, let's go do chores." He extended out his hand, and Lilly took it as he started walking to the barn.

Lilly felt like she was important. She beamed as she rocked back and forth, working hard to control the energy in her body. Charlie did not make her feel small or worthless. Boldly she giggled, "Chores."

"What do you want me to do?" Janis asked almost feeling left out.

"You just supervise tonight. Tomorrow you get to get the hay, so you better come with us to learn where it is."

Janis followed them to the barn like a little girl, trotting to catch up.

28

It had been a week since Craig had returned to Oregon with his dad, and still very few things seemed to be coming back into his memory. His motor skills were still off. He was frustrated with the effort of doing the simplest things around the house.

The doctor had told them it could be up to six months to a year for him to get everything back. He was not to lift or strain himself in any way for three months. Working with physical therapy, he struggled with certain motor skills. His right hand felt weak and his right foot felt heavy and lazy as he walked. He tried to maintain a positive attitude and do what was asked of him, but inside he felt angry and slow.

He should know these things and was frustrated that the challenges of handling the simplest chores seemed agonizingly tedious. His headaches would leave him dizzy and weak. His vision fading in and out. Craig would sit at the table during the day and try to put a puzzle together, putting pieces of his life together through cardboard pictures, forcing his fingers to work and grip.

Craig had become withdrawn and isolated. He didn't want pity or special treatment, but that was all he felt he was getting. Someone had to drive him to his doctors. He would send someone in to get groceries... He had lost his independence and his confidence.

Today Craig felt pent up, antsy and frustrated, sitting at the kitchen table looking at the collection of confusing puzzle pieces scattered across it. He tried to put a couple pieces together, but couldn't make them fit, he couldn't seem to focus. Rubbing his eyes, with a burst of frustration Craig swiped the pieces across the table. Half of the puzzle fell to the floor. "This is stupid! Completely stupid!" As he got up and paced around the kitchen.

Craig slipped on his shoes and walked out the door into the brisk, dew-filled air of fall, and headed toward the barnyard. The horses came to see him. They nickered as if he might feed them early or turn them out. He looked at the large animals, almost afraid to pet them, but he forced himself to interact. *I used to ride you...* he thought. He took a breath and then crawled through the fence and stood next to the big bay, Booger. Instead of walking away from Craig, the ole horse stood still and waited. Mouse faded away to watch.

Craig touched the horse's cheek. He looked at the bone structure of the horse's face. It seemed odd to him how it was all bone and blood vessels. He ran his hand over the eye and down the middle of the face. Booger stood quietly, letting this man explore and rediscover a life he used to know.

Craig brought his hand down to the end of the bony

structure and onto the soft palate of the nose. Booger sighed and closed his eyes. Craig brushed up against Booger's whiskers and felt the velvet softness of his nostril as warm air blew out.

Then the man looked back at the horse's body. He ran his hand down Booger's neck, feeling the shagginess of winter coming on. He felt the bone of the withers and continued down along his lean back to his hip. Feeling, breathing, seeing as if for the first time the structure of this large animal.

He knew this animal that had carried man for centuries. One who carried kings through battle and pulled brides to be wed. This species that allowed children to play at their feet, yet could strike a cougar dead. Who could run for miles across open range, yet walk at man's side. Who helped stampede buffalo with the natives and carried ammunition of war. This animal as gentle as a lamb or as fierce as a lion. A feeling of sentimental respect filled Craig's heart was standing before him. Craig knew all of this, but he could not remember this horse who stood before him. This horse who was waiting for Craig's memory to return. No judgment or anxiety, just companionship and patience behind his bold brown eyes.

What an amazing animal, a mysterious and amazing animal, he thought as he patted Booger's neck. Craig walked back up to the horse's head and stroked his face one more time. Booger's liquid brown eyes were quiet and calm, as he sighed again. Then he casually lifted his head draped it over the top of Craig's shoulder as Craig reached up to stroke his neck again. He pressed Craig closer to his shoulder, and the man reached around and wrapped his arms around the horse's neck.

Craig felt tears run down his face as the horse stood there holding him in this odd kind of press. As he felt the emotions release, as he realized the horse was giving him a hug, the best he knew how. He stroked the horse's neck, pressed his head against his mane, and closed his eyes.

"What a mysterious animal you are, a beautiful, mysterious animal." He collected his thoughts, took a breath, and then released the horse. He patted the brown neck one more time. For some reason, he didn't feel like he had to have all the answers. He could just be without talking or explaining. He just was.

He sat with the horses as they picked meager morsels of hay left on the ground. He watched their lips lift each stem of hay up with talent he could only imagine. He listened to the rhythmic chewing. He got up from the feeder, brushed his hands along his four legged friend with the feeling of gratitude, then walked to the barn.

As he crawled through the fence, he noticed some bailing twine that was braided and rolled up hanging on a beam in the barn. He took them down and looked at them for a few minutes. The braid looked familiar. They were a set of reins. He played with them a little bit, feeling the weight and texture. It felt good to him as he twirled them around a little and tossed the ends up and down. He looked again noticed how tight and straight the braid was. It felt oddly familiar in his hand, then hung them back up on their peg and headed back to the house. His legs felt weak and he felt lightheaded. He needed to sit down for a little while.

As he walked onto the porch, he saw a gunny sack sitting in the corner of the mud room. As he looked inside, he found narrow strips of rawhide coiled up and a can of beeswax. Curiosity and ambition got the better of him.

He poured himself a cup of coffee, took the gunny sack outside on the porch and sat down. Craig took out each strand and began to wax the dry strips. His warm hands felt the rawhide and wax mold and melt together. He really didn't know what he was doing, but it felt good and natural.

He played with them for a little bit and before he knew it he was braiding the strands together, a familiar rhythm found his unconscious hands. He hooked it on a peg on the porch and continued. With his mind busy, Craigs anxiety fell away. It didn't matter what he thought or remembered or that he had a bit of a limp. He just did what he was doing, and it felt good.

A UPS driver pulled up in the driveway and pulled out a box, it was one of his boxes he had shipped in from his old address. It had been pretty beaten up. He signed for it and brought it onto the porch. He took out his pocket knife and cut open the tape. There laying on top was his photo album and an envelope that said Paige on it. Without thought, he lifted it out of the box and sat down to read it.

Dear Paige...

The words didn't really make any sense to him. Was he in love with that girl?

He scratched his head as he re-read the words on the paper. Then he put it back in its envelope and slipped it in his hip pocket. He dug through the box and found a tube with the sketched art work of a buckskin horse with hazel brown eyes. There was a war bridle on him and the words on the bottom, *From the Heart... P Cason.* Boy, that girl can draw, he laid it out flat, and stared at the detail for a few moments. He dug further into a life he didn't remember, a life that intrigued him, yet frustrated him at the same time. Why couldn't he remember? He found Abby's satchel, he grinned at the picture of her and Cougar who now stood out in the pasture with his bachelor buddy, Mouse. He grinned as he pulled out the dehydrated sagebrush.

Charlie came pulling up in the pickup, Craig casually waved at him as he unloaded some hay for the calves.

"Hey, Craig." Charlie stated as he pulled up to the house.

"Hey". Craig answered back.

"You up for a drive today, I got a couple of things to do if you want to tag along."

"Oh, I don't know." Craig had been kind of antsy all day, he put things back in the box. "I s'pose I could go for a little drive with you."

"Well, come on then, we're burning daylight." Charlie

grinned as he stated the famous line, heading to the barn to turn out the horses.

"Alright, give me a second." Craig grabbed the box and took it into the house, he would go through the rest later. He grabbed his jacket, jogged to the pickup and got in with Charlie.

29

Paige had come back to a whole new scene as Abby filled her in on the details of her and Sarah's project documenting Lilly and Babe. The pictures Abby had were incredible—deep and touching.

"Abbs, you have an incredible eye for taking photos. These are beautiful," Paige remarked as they sat down one evening.

Abby beamed. "I didn't know I would have so much fun with a camera. Sarah and I are having a good time doing this project. And now I am having fun taking pictures of other things that I see."

She pulled out some pictures that Patricia had developed of Charlie and Babe, the barn with hay in it, Libby peeking around the corner of the barn with half a face.

"Yes, Abbs, I think you have quite a little talent." Paige thumbed through the photos. "You capture our life pretty good."

Abby beamed.

After Abby went to bed, Paige stayed up for a while going through her paperwork from Susan. The layout over at the therapeutic ranch was a lot different. No space like what was here. Paige had room to plan and develop and used her imagination to sketch out a dream. If Susan had kept up a horse school and working farm for challenged kids, why couldn't she do something here? Her imagination began to kick in. Paige started sketching plans.

As she had listened to Abby and Sarah and the changes with Lilly, she questioned how it could be something as simple as a horse could make Lilly feel like she was heard. What would a dog do? With all the differences in the spectrum of autism, some might work with equine therapy while others would not, and this would not only affect autism but a vast amount of people with different challenges in life. Just like Buttercup the pony with Tia or Crystal, learning to move and strengthen her hands or Rocket and his ability to give speed to Danny... and what about Oscar? The charm, hard work and volunteers. What could she offer?

But if she just offered assistance for what it was and let the people come to her, maybe she would be able to help some other families out there that were having the same feeling of lonesomeness and helplessness. She started brainstorming, writing down all the thoughts in her mind of things that she might be able to do.

Her eyes got heavy from the lack of sleep over the last few days along with the time change from the East Coast. She put down her pen and started to get up. Blue was sleeping at her feet, not wanting to be left behind again. Paige reached down and stroked her dog's head.

"Blue, you are such a good girl." Blue looked at her as if she were looking into her soul then licked Paige's hand. They headed down the hall to bed. At the head of the bed on the floor, Blue turned several times trying to get comfortable. Then Paige heard the thump of the Border Collie-Australian Shepherd crossbreed lay her body down with a sigh. Paige closed her eyes. It had been a day.

***

In the morning, after she had poured herself a cup of coffee, Paige looked at her scribbles from the night before and sat down at the table. As she read through her list, the one that had popped out at her was a benefit horse show. She thought of the possible logistics involved and whether she could actually pull it off. But how much fun would that be to create a little horse show for autism? What would she have to do?

She started drawing up a list of things needed and support she would have to have to make it happen.

Abby came into the kitchen. "Don't you ever sleep?" She yawned and stretched, sitting down across from Paige.

"Apparently not," Paige said as she thumbed through the papers and jotted down notes. "I just can't believe the changes in Lilly. I am so hopeful that this will change her life and offer Janis some much-needed answers. But what if this went bigger, Abby? What if we could get the community involved?"

Abby was hopeful that her project would be of help. "Sarah and I are recording Lilly's progress and documenting it for a school project. I am gonna take pictures and Sarah is going to do the writing of it. I'm not much into writing, you know."

"Yeah, I noticed," Paige chided. "I saw your grade on your English paper. A 'C' isn't what I call a scholar paper."

"I know. I think the teacher has it in for me."

"Oh no you don't," Paige stated matter-of-factly. "You can't blame the teacher for your writing. You waited until the last minute to finish that paper, and that is not the teacher's fault."

"Well, she could have given us more time."

"You had a week. You just didn't want to do it."

"Well, nouns, pronouns, verbs, adverbs, adjectives… Blah, blah, blah!"

"You will think blah, blah, blah if you don't pay attention. There is a reason for how English is written and the grade that follows. Just because you don't want to do something doesn't mean you can only do it halfway, Abbs. We do things all the time that we don't want to do, but we get it done, just by focusing on it and doing the work." Paige looked at her for a moment, knowing she sounded like a broken record. She had said these things before when school had started. How could she get Abby to understand?

"I just don't get it!" Abby whined. "Why do they make us do things we don't like? Why can't we just focus on what we do like?"

Paige thought about it for a moment. "Okay, so you don't like writing. What do you like?"

"Horses."

"Let's say you wanted to write to the American Quarter Horse Association about Piper. Say... you would like to put him in for horse of the year because of all he has taught you and things you have done with him." Paige searched for some kind of connection the girl could grasp. "Or, say you could win a thousand-dollar scholarship for writing a story about him. Would you want to do that?"

"I can get a scholarship for writing?"

"That is how you get scholarships, Abbs, but you have to understand the language and try to figure out the rules of language."

"Would you want to write to American Quarter Horse and tell them about Piper?"

"That would be cool."

"Well, that could be a project for you to do to help you learn your writing. Do something that you are passionate about and work within the rules."

"What if the rules don't make any sense?"

"Then question them, find out. That is what the teachers are there for. We can sit down tonight and go over a few of those and see if we can get things lined out."

"Would you do that?"

"Sure, why wouldn't I?"

"Well," Abby paused, "I didn't think you knew any of that stuff."

"Why wouldn't I? Just because I work horses and am not in an office?"

"Well I just thought since you don't write or anything like that, why would you need to know that kind of stuff?"

"Abby, when I write proposals and ideas and business letters, I use it all the time. I might be a little rusty, but I did the work assigned to the best of my knowledge. I also think Sarah might be able to work with you, too. Maybe you could ask her. Have a study night or something."

"That would be fun."

Paige tapped the table, "Well, better get out there and feed the horses before the bus comes. I will get you some breakfast."

Abby slipped on her boots, grabbed her jacket, and headed out the door, she took a deep breath and inhaled the sweet smell of Fall. She was so looking forward to Saturday morning. It would be a relief from school.

Abby thought about Paige's talk inside. She always thought school sucked. It always seemed to be in the way of what she wanted to do. But maybe if she tried a little harder. She thought of Abe when she first started riding Piper, how he asked her how long it took for her to learn to walk. He explained, asking if she just gave up and scooted around on her butt all day.

She smiled at the memory. "I get good at what I work at." She walked off the porch, and Blue followed her. Abby reached down and stroked her pillow-soft head. Blue's ice blue, Aussie eyes looked up at Abby as she wiggled her docked tail butt back and forth. Abby grinned at her as a burst of energy flooded her emotions. "Scoot on my butt... I can run!" she laughed with a sense of pride.

"Race you!" Abby challenged Blue and took off running across the yard. Blue chased at her heels. Abby got to the barn door laughing and roughed up the happy dog's coat. Blue jumped up and down on a race well done. "I beat you. I beat you!" Abby sang.

Blue bounced around and barked at her competitor.

Paige watched from the kitchen window, smiling with satisfaction and thinking of when Abby had first come into her life. The crutches were a thing of the past now. With a very mild limp and therapy, she was a strong girl who had overcome so much. How fulfilling it was to have her be so ingrained in Paige's life now.

Paige sliced two pieces of homemade bread and dropped them into the toaster while the skillet heated up for the eggs. A scrambled egg sandwich for breakfast sounded good, she thought as she sliced a couple pieces of bread for herself. Stirring the eggs and sprinkling in some seasoning, Paige started thinking of what could be done for a horse show and who to call.

Abby came in the house, grabbed her sandwich, and was out the door to the bus stop.

Paige finished her breakfast and made a few phone calls about her idea of a horse show. Before she knew it she had a list of names, a couple of sponsors, and some donated items. She picked up the phone and called Janis.

"Hey, Janis. I have an idea that I want to run by you. Tell me what you think."

"Alright," Janis said, feeling comfortable and bold enough not to get too nervous at Paige's voice.

"I had a thought last night of doing a horse show in tribute to autism. Maybe begin some kind of funding program and help bring awareness to autism or handicapped kids."

Janis was quiet for a moment. "Um, I don't think I can help you out with a horse show. I don't know anything about horses and I am just now starting to be brave enough to pet Babe." She paused again with her honesty.

Paige didn't hesitate to give her pitch. "Well, I don't think you need to know anything about horses at first. I need someone to make phone calls, write invitations and get ahold of the newspaper, radio and that kind of stuff. Do you have a computer?"

"Yes, I can do some of that stuff."

"Good," Paige piped in before Janis could think about it. "Alright then. Let's get talking to some of the horse people and get a date set. When you get here today, we can talk and make out a plan. I have a couple of people I need to get ahold of this morning. See you this afternoon."

"Alright, see you later."

***

Janis hung up the phone and collected her thoughts. Oh boy… What just happened? If she was a smart woman she would have just said no. But look at the difference in Lilly and even Sarah. Janis drummed her fingers on the table and then slapped her hand like a gavel. "I can do this." If I were to set up a horse show, who would I call? She thumbed through the phone book, picked up the phone and dialed a number.

"Baker County Fairgrounds. This is Angie."

"Yes, Angie, my name is Janis, and I am helping put on a horse show for a benefit to bring awareness to autism. Can you help me out?"

As if Janis had dialed the magic number, Angie said, "Well, I would be delighted! What date are you looking at?"

"Well, that is where we might begin. What dates do you have… and by the way what do we need?" Janis asked. "I have never done this before, so can you walk me through the prelims?"

Angie was enthusiastic, and her energy was contagious. "You bet." She began to fill Janis in on the information she needed and a few people she could contact. "If you drop by the office, I have some contacts and some papers that will help you get the information you need."

Angie suggested a few extra classes so that Lilly could actually participate in the show—Lead Line class and In Hand Trail class.

Janis had to stop and think about that. "Yeah…

Ummm… I don't think Lilly would be able to do that."

"Well, she doesn't have to," Angie stated, "but she is no different than any other kid. She just wants to fit in. Besides it would help bring awareness and let the other parents understand that they can do the same thing. If she gets scared or something, you can always take her out of the class."

Angie was so matter-of-fact that Janis had a hard time arguing. "How do you know that?"

"Because my best friend works with autistic kids in a daycare in Idaho. She challenges them every day with different projects. You ought to see them light up when they do something special. And it sounds like Lilly has found her special thing."

They finished their conversation, and Janis had a little time to digest what was said and the notes she had taken. She had some time to think about it anyway. Lilly riding in a class. Boy, how things changed so fast. Less than a month ago she was isolated in her home with two children, depressed and scared. Now here she was helping to put on a show of the thing she was most afraid of. She had to laugh. Janis looked at her watch. She had two hours before she met up with Paige.

By afternoon, with the help of Angie, Janis had the layout for the show with the typical classes, Showmanship, English and Western Pleasure, Equitation, Trail and cow classes. She also had all the paperwork and instructions on certain classes. *Looks like we are putting on a horse show!* she thought as she got Lilly in the car.

30

Paige had spent the morning getting sponsors and spreading the word of what she was going to do to the ranches in the outlying areas. Now that the word was out, flyers needed to be made and a date set.

Paige heard the school bus stop and realized she had spent the entire day working on the horse show project. Time had seemed to stand still. She gathered up all of her papers and put them in a folder. She would sit with Janis a little later to get the latest scoop.

She heard the lawn mower engine of a car coming up the drive and looked out to see Janis drive past the two girls walking up the drive. They both waved at her, giggling and talking.

Paige walked out onto the porch and saw Babe lift her head to nicker in recognition of the car.

Not far behind Janis came another pickup. Charlie was pulling in. On the passenger side of the pickup was another man with a cowboy hat and sunglasses, Craig. Paige had to still herself. She hadn't seen Craig since he had gotten home. She had heard that he had locked himself in the house and didn't want any company or to go anywhere.

She had asked about him once, and Charlie had said

he was fine. He mentioned Craig was frustrated that he couldn't remember anything. He also mentioned that Craig didn't get around very well because he would get lightheaded and had frequent headaches.

She had asked if there was anything she could do. Both Jim and Charlie said the same thing the doctor had. "Time. Just give him time." What did that mean? She had chosen not to get involved and do what they asked. She would have to wait and see what happened.

Now here he was in the pickup with Charlie. Her heart began to pound as memories flooded her imagination, yet she knew he really didn't remember her at all. The little bit of history they had was buried deep and may not ever surface again. So if that was the case, she had to wait. If the opportunity arose, they would have to start again or maybe never again.

Paige looked down at Janis and Lilly. "Hey, Janis," Paige said. "I will be down in a minute."

"Okay." Janis had gotten Lilly out of the car and began walking toward the corral, Lilly tugging on the lead her mother had so craftily created.

"Babe! Babe!" Lilly wailed.

Abby and Sarah strolled up talking and stopped at Charlie's pickup. "Hey, Charlie."

"Hi, girls. How was school?"

"Oh you know, same-ole, same-ole," Abby stated.

"Yeah, I know. Just keep it up, okay?" Charlie encouraged.

Craig looked at Abby and recognized her from the picture Paige had given him at the hospital.

"Hey, Craig!" Abby greeted through the downed driver's side window.

"Hey…" Craig couldn't think of anything else to say.

He had thought that somehow being around familiar things he would be able to remember much easier, but that was not working well for him. Now here two girls were standing in front of Charlie. Craig felt tongue-tied, not knowing how to talk.

He looked on the porch and saw Paige standing and looking in the pickup at him. What was he going to say to her? He wished he had stayed home. Visions flashed before his eyes. He took off his sunglasses and blinked, taking two fingers and pressing on the sides of the bridge of his nose. *Damn headaches*, he thought as he pressed harder. It wasn't a bad one, but he could blame it for staying in the truck.

"You gonna get out?" Charlie asked as the girls had surrounded him.

"No. I think I'm gonna stay here for right now. I've got a headache," Craig responded halfheartedly.

"Is it a bad one?" Charlie asked Craig.

"No, it will pass. Just do what you got to do, Charlie. I will wait here."

Charlie had seen Craig with headaches, and this time something was different—no pressure under the eyes, no blotchiness or paleness to the skin.

"These girls don't bite if you want to get out and stretch your legs." He turned to walk to the corral with the girls.

"Is Craig alright?" Abby asked concerned.

"Yep, just has a little stage fright. He'll get through it in time," Charlie answered as he neared the corral where Sarah was standing next to Babe outside the fence. The mare had her head down toward Lilly, who was petting it through the fence.

He smiled as he walked up to Sarah. "You're getting pretty good at this, huh?" He was happy to see her.

"Well, Lilly is not taking no for an answer, and I see her changing every day."

"For the good, I hope."

"Yes, of course." Janis blushed.

Abby had the camera, clicking away at different angles of Lilly. She turned the camera and snapped a few of Charlie and Janis talking.

Craig sat in the silence watching Charlie interact with the girls, a woman, and a colorful child next to the fence of a big, black Percheron mare. *This was a stupid idea to come*, he thought.

Paige walked past the driver's side door on the way to the corral and stopped. "So you came here to play a little, huh?"

"No, not really," Craig answered. "Charlie was taking me for a drive and this is where we ended up."

"Oh… Sorry you are stuck here."

"I don't think we will be here too long," Craig answered. That did not come out like he wanted it to. He turned away and didn't look at Paige, shame or something similar filling his heart. He didn't know for sure what it was but he felt uneasy with this woman.

Paige tried to ignore his abruptness and tried to lighten the emotion. "Run over any pedestrians lately?"

"No, not lately..." he answered, confused by the question. "Wait! I was the pedestrian." She didn't even ask how he was doing. "I was the one who got hit by the car, remember?"

"Not when I rode with you." Paige paused thinking back to a little over a month ago on their first date and the rock he almost hit with his jeep. "Just checking. I hear those New Yorkers are quite the drivers. Gotta duck and dodge from what I have heard."

"I suppose. At this point I couldn't tell you." He was getting a little angry at the thought of being asked stupid questions. "Because I don't know. But I figure I can hold my own if I need to."

"Well, you must not be able to, if you let two little girls scare you into staying in the truck. Just kinda looks like you scare easily," Paige chided as she walked past, half teasing.

Craig got out of the truck and followed her, half angry at her teasing. "It seems that I have forgotten my whole entire life, and I can't remember things like I should," he blurted. "Seems like you have forgotten that too. Remember? You picked me up at the hospital."

"Did I?" Paige stated matter-of-factly. "Can't remember." She continued walking. "You sure that was me? What was I wearing?"

Craig followed after her as he thought back, a little confused. *It had to be her.* "You were wearing a light blue, button-up blouse, blue jeans and your hair was pulled back in a ponytail like it is now. And your eyes were the purest blue I have ever seen." He stopped, embarrassed from saying that out loud.

Paige stopped and looked at him. "Huh, seems like your memory is good to me. So what other excuse do you have?"

Craig stopped and watched her walk away. He thought people were going to feel sorry for him for not having any memory. He didn't want their pity... but he didn't know if this was what he wanted either. He was very confused. He watched her enter the paddock, put a new halter on the draft mare as the little girl played, and hugged the black horse.

He turned to go back to the truck. What the heck? This was not the reception he had expected, and he knew before he left the ranch that Charlie had something up his sleeve. *Just going for a drive...* hmpf. He made it back to the pickup door and looked over his shoulder at the gathering around the black horse. He kicked the tire, took his hat off and slapped the door. His mind was churning up memories, confusion and anger all at once as he turned and walked to the corral.

He strode right up to Paige, "I will have you know, Ms. Cason, as soon as I get my memory back you will be one of the first to know."

Paige handed Charlie the lead line of the black mare and walked out of the corral toward the barn. Craig followed. Paige grabbed a brush and handed it to him.

"Why are you so worried about yesterday when today is right now?"

"Well, because I can't remember yesterday."

"You are making memories right now, Craig. Why worry about the past?" She paused for a moment. "What did you do this morning?"

"I went out and saw the horses and braided some rawhide, had coffee and visited with my dad."

"You braiding again? Sounds like good memories to me." Paige grabbed another brush and halter and headed back to the paddock. "How did you know how to braid?"

"I don't know, I just did it." Craig followed trying to digest his confusion and frustration, then spoke up. "You know I am not worried about my memory as much as wandering who I was before the accident. I was supposed to be a bronc rider, a rodeo star, a police officer, a husband..." he paused. "I was supposed to be all of that, but I ain't any of that without a memory."

Paige looked at him for a moment. "That doesn't make a whole lot of sense, Craig." She whistled for Libby, and the mare came trotting in. "You are who you are, not what you do."

Craig felt overwhelmed. "Don't talk to me in riddles."

Paige continued, "When you follow your heart instead of your head, that's what makes you who you are. You are fighting with your head as if it has all the answers, but your heart is where you know you should be." Paige paused. "Like the day we walked in the hospital. Everyone was giving you reasons why you should stay, but your heart made it clear to you that you belong in Oregon, and the choice was made. Now you are here and you want to let your head do the thinking instead of your heart. You want to figure it out, argue with yourself about who you used to be and that you're weak for not remembering. Yet you are here right now, making memories. You are not the choices you make. They are only actions of what you believe. It doesn't matter who you were yesterday or a year ago. Your life is what you do today."

Paige had the halter on Libby as they walked to the barn. She put grain in the bucket and started brushing. Craig did the same on the opposite side.

"I got to give Charlie this brush. Be back in a few minutes." Paige left him there.

Craig kept brushing Libby, *was this the girl he was supposed to love? No way, No way would she be the love of his life. She is way too obnoxious, too cocky....* He thought of the letter he had written, *Lori seemed more like the gal he would be attracted to! At least she tried to understand him losing his memory!* he thought to himself. *This gal here was way out of line, she didn't get it at all.* He brushed a little harder on Libby.

Paige had no idea where all that came from. She wanted to be more understanding, but she was more than a little frustrated that the man who was so confident and kind, was hiding behind his loss of memory like he was afraid of who he was. The memory thing she could understand, but the fear he was playing on was an act, and she wasn't buying it.

She came back to the barn and grabbed the saddle to put on Libby. Without a word, Craig grabbed the blanket and positioned it correctly. When Paige threw the saddle on Libby's back, he reached over and grabbed the cinch and finished saddling the mare without hesitation.

"I really like this mare, Paige," trying to find something nice to say, as he finished cinching her up.

"I know. You already told me that." Paige smiled and winked at him. "Do you want to ride her?"

"I don't think I can…" Craig's anger was subsiding, he couldn't stay angry at this girl. He thought for a moment and then countered, "You know I probably could ride her around here a little. See what it feels like."

Paige grinned. "I think she will take good care of you."

Craig led Libby around a little and then checked the cinch, reached out, and let the stirrup leathers out about four notches.

"What? You saying I have short legs?"

He looked at her, grinned, and then let them out another two. "Nope, just thinking it will be easier getting on with the stirrup closer to the ground." Without any thought or hesitation, he stepped up on the mare, grinning.

Libby came to attention, arching her neck ready to go someplace. Craig beamed. Just feeling the horse beneath him brought back familiarity. He turned her around a few times without thought and headed down the driveway.

Paige just smiled as she watched him ride away, silently hoping someday he might remember—if nothing else at least remember her.

She started to walk away when she found an envelope on the ground where Craig had been. She bent down to pick it up, her name was on the outside of it. She turned it over a few times. Then casually opened it, the date on it was the day of his accident… her hands began to shake..

Dear Paige,

I am writing this from the heart. Life is filled with change, and our lives are led by the choices we make after the changes. I have been trying to put the pieces together here, and pack up to move on, but it seems so hard to do. For these last few weeks I feel like I have been two people divided by past and future. When I look at all of the history here that I had in this life, to close the door on things I once had and the things that could have been or should be has brought me anguish and sadness. Yet today, I am looking beyond tomorrow. I am blindly searching for an uncertain future. I dream of you almost every night and I feel your hands hold me. I can't shake that feeling. I woke up talking to you more than once and found myself hugging a pillow.

I put the last of Lisa's and the baby's things in a box last night and am calling Lisa's sister, Lori to come and get them. I guess my life is finished here.

I want to start a new life with you, Paige, if you think you want to give it a go. You are with me wherever I am and whatever I do. I want to share everything with you. You are like water to me, forever flowing and making things grow. When I look up at the stars, I hold the memory of us at the creek staring at the Milky Way. I can't imagine my life without your smile or your blue eyes glittering with mischief and life.

All my love forever and always,
Craig

Paige swallowed hard, her vision blurry. She held it to her heart for a moment, and said a silent prayer. *If it is meant to be, Lord, bring him back to me.* She looked at his handwriting once again, then folded it back up and slipped it back into the worn envelope..

He was not the same man he was before the accident... Paige wiped her eyes. She would give it back to him when he got back. She put the brush back in the tack room, waited a minute for her eyes to dry and walked over to where Charlie and Janis were. Time to get busy again. Charlie had bought a little helmet for Lilly and had buckled it on her head. Abby had her camera out snapping pictures as Charlie lifted the little girl onto Babe's back.

Lilly leaned forward and lay over the mare's withers with her arms hanging down each side of Babe's neck. She closed her eyes as she felt the lub-dub of the mare's heart. "Babe."

Janis looked over at Paige for a moment. "I can't believe I am letting him do this, but it seems so right. To have her here and all the excitement."

"It is a beautiful thing," Paige agreed as she watched Charlie handle the girls.

"I have to tell you, Paige, about the horse show when we are done here."

"Well, we can go to the house and get something for these guys to drink. I think they have this under control."

Janis walked with Paige into the house, got a pitcher of lemonade and a dozen homemade cookies out of the freezer along with glasses for everyone, and brought them out to the porch.

Janis hollered from the porch. "We have some lemonade and cookies when you are done." She smiled and looked over at Paige. "I could get used to this."

Paige poured the lemonade while Janis went to the car and grabbed her folder of the notes she had taken earlier that day. Then she sat down with Paige.

"I talked to Angie at the fairgrounds today and she was extremely helpful," Janis began. "We have the layout of the classes, the rules, and everything we need to pull this together." She pulled out the papers. "All we need is a date, sponsors and volunteers."

"Perfect," Paige responded. "I knew you were the right choice for the job."

Janis was excited and beaming to be doing something constructive in her life. For the first time in a long while, she had value beyond a mother struggling to make things right. She looked back at Charlie with the girls and Lilly and smiled.

"Where did you find that man?" She was afraid to say Charlie's name. It might give away the silent crush she was feeling inside.

"Charlie? I think he found us, actually." Paige looked in the direction of the corral. "He is something alright— helpful, honest and loves what he does."

Charlie had ahold of Lilly's thigh and the back of her jacket. With cautious words Charlie softly spoke, "walk on." The big horse carefully put one foot in front of the other. Lilly felt the motion and screamed with delight. Babe stopped.

"Hold right here," Charlie coaxed, grabbing the mane. "Hold right here."

Lilly reached down with both hands, grabbing Babe's mane.

"That's it! Good girl, now hold on." Charlie nodded to Abby leading, he spoke again to the mare, "walk on." who again responded by cautiously stepping forward.

Janis couldn't watch. "Oh my goodness they are leading her! I can't watch." She turned her head for a moment. Trying to stifle the panic in her heart.

Sarah called out, "Hey, Mom, look! Lilly is riding Babe! She is riding just like I did!"

There was no panic, no fear, no anxiety—only laughter and happiness. Janis turned and glanced at the large mare with her fragile little child riding her. Charlie securely holding on to Lilly who was in complete bliss of the motion.

Janis looked at Paige with a nervous grin. "Guess there is no going back now, is there?"

"Nope, I don't think so," Paige agreed as she watched the little parade.

Sarah had the camera. "Lilly, look over here. Over here, Lilly." Sarah snapped a couple of shots. "Charlie, turn so we can see your face," Sarah coached. "Abby, turn Babe's head around." With direction from Sarah, they all posed for a picture.

Charlie had stopped the big mare, with pride he stated. "You did it, Lilly. You rode Babe!"

Lilly was not done riding, in a firm voice she stated as Charlie had done, "Walk on."

Babe took a step forward, Charlie grabbed Lilly's thigh and walked another round. "You are a smart one Miss Lilly, you are a smart one." He repeated as they came to a stop.

Lilly was giggling and squirming around as Charlie went to set her down on the ground.

Lilly rocked back and forth with energy, focusing her eyes on the ground. She never wanted to be small again. She blurted out the words as best she could, "Again! Again!"

Charlie heard Lilly's words, clear and pure. There was no guessing what she wanted.

Janis looked in surprise at her daughter. Lilly really understood! She tried to hide her excitement the best she could although tears filled her eyes. Janis resigned her position from a mother hen to an onlooker. "Don't look at me," she hollered to Charlie. "You heard the girl!"

Charlie grinned. "Just checking." And he lifted Lilly again on Babe's back. "One more time and then we have to do chores," Charlie stated.

"Walk on," Lilly said with complete authority.

The old mare responded to the little girls command, perfectly content to be a part of something so special. Charlie walked along side, aware that this little girl's life had just changed.

31

Craig rode the yellow horse down the drive, across the highway and into the timber. He didn't care where he was going. His mind full of emotion and frustration. *What is with that Paige?* he thought. *She just doesn't get it. How am I supposed to live with no history? Arguing with my mind... What did that even mean?*

He rode, oblivious of his surroundings and letting Libby choose the way. He just wanted to get away from all of that busyness at Paige's house.

Libby traveled across a quiet little meadow and on up to a spring. There she stopped and looked back. For the first time since he left the road, Craig looked around. He saw the spring and dried rutted tracks around it. Something looked familiar about the spring.

He stepped off Libby, feeling a little lightheaded, he leaned on the saddle as he looked back the way he had come. An image filled his head of a blonde girl running out of the timber on a palomino horse. A flash of wasps, a flash of him carrying someone to the spring. *"Don't you die on me, Paige! Don't you dare die on me!"* echoed in his mind.

Glimpses of his first horse, rodeos, birthdays and hospitals came tumbling in. Then his Marriage, the accident, driving his black Jeep with Paige beside him, dodging the pedestrian rock, of hauling hay and images of Cougar the colt. Like a soft wave, memories came flowing in and filled his mind.

This place was where he'd covered Paige in mud, His eye caught a glimpse of something shiny in the dried dirt. He reached down and chipped at the mud, picking up Paige's crucifix necklace. He held the fine broken chain in his hands. He knew this cross. *Make a wish*, words he had said at one point in his life. The one time he had hoped he would be that wish.

Craig noticed the tire tracks of his Jeep, where he'd come back to get her. Libby bumped him with her nose. He looked at the palomino mare standing next to him. "I know you," he said as he stroked the mare's neck, fixing her mane. "I know you." Craig gave a half laugh, half sob as he lay his head on Libby's neck and closed his eyes. Putting the necklace in his shirt pocket, Craig stepped up in the saddle and headed back the way he came. Memories continued in waves as he stroked the mare's neck. Then with a grin spreading silently across his face, he asked Libby for a lope. She responded, eagerly heading home.

As he reached the highway, he asked Libby to slow down. He took a deep breath of fresh air. He knew this highway. He knew the pothole that needed to be filled on the edge of Paige's driveway. As he rode into the view of the house, he recognized the porch and the woman sitting on it. Flick and Blue came bounding over to greet him. That porch was where he gave Paige a kiss. *I kissed her.* He smiled at the thought.

Paige looked up at the man riding her horse and recognized something had changed. His posture was different. There was a confident air about him. He rode up to the gate.

"How did you like your ride?" Paige asked tentatively.

"The best ride ever," he replied with a twinkle in his eye. "No pedestrians."

Paige smiled at him. "Didn't have to duck and dodge?"

"Nope, no semi-trucks either. Just me, a palomino horse and a little thinking."

Paige grinned at him. "Are you back?"

"I am back," he said as he stepped off Libby. His legs buckled underneath him, and he grabbed the horn to hold on for a moment.

Paige was off the porch and through the gate. "You alright?"

"Little lightheaded, I think. Maybe too big of a day."

"Abby, come and grab Libby for us, will you?"

Janis and Paige each grabbed an arm and helped Craig to the porch.

Abby and Sarah came running up, "Everything okay?"

"Yeah, Craig just had a big day," Paige explained.

Craig turned to Abby. "Don't worry about me, little sister," he said as he was being escorted to the house. "Not every day I get to fall in a beautiful woman's arms." He grinned.

When they got him seated on the porch, Paige went in and wetted a washcloth to put on the back of his neck.

"I could sure use a glass of lemonade," he said.

Janis poured him a glass as Charlie came up on the porch with Lilly. "You alright, bud?"

"Sure, Charlie. I just wanted to see if I could get a little feminine attention here."

"Well, that seemed to work alright. I wished I would have thought of that." Charlie winked at Janis.

Janis blushed.

Charlie grabbed a glass of lemonade and sat for a few minutes while Craig got his bearings. "You gonna be alright?"

"Yeah, the doc said this would happen for a while. I probably shouldn't have gone for a ride, but I am not going to complain."

Charlie noticed a difference in Craig, but he didn't say anything. He looked over at Janis with Lilly sitting on her lap.

"Lilly, did you tell your mom that you rode Babe today?"

Lilly turned her focus on the ground and touched her middle finger with her thumb as she focused on the words she wanted to say. "Ride... Babe... ." She rocked back and forth in excitement.

"Yes, Lilly, I saw you ride Babe. You are a good rider." Janis looked over at Charlie.

Lilly beamed at the thought of being heard and

clapped her hands in excitement. "Did you tell Charlie thank you?"

Lilly again looked at the ground. These prompts from the people around her were making Lilly feel like they wanted to listen to her. She again touched her middle finger tip with her thumb to stay in the moment. Not looking at anyone, she forced out her words with confidence, "Thank... you...."

"You are welcome, Ms. Lilly. You are sure welcome."

The title of Ms. Lilly brought a smile to Lilly's face. She rolled her head back and clapped her hands. In that moment she was just like her sister. She babbled in excitement.

Sarah and Abby came up from the barn after putting Libby away.

Abby stated as she grabbed a glass of lemonade, "Chores are done."

"Thanks for putting up my horse, Abbs," Craig said. "I am feeling a whole lot better."

"Your horse?" Paige piped in.

"Well, she would be if you didn't own her. Besides, I think she likes me better than you," Craig stated matter-of-factly.

"In your dreams," Paige said with a smirk.

Charlie cut in, "Alright, you two. Don't make me put you in timeout."

Paige looked over at Charlie and then pointed to Craig. "He started it."

Craig started to say something when Charlie cut him off, "Ott!"

Craig clammed up and smiled.

Sarah and Abby both giggled.

"Well, I guess we better be getting back, Craig, before your dad starts to worry and somebody goes home with a black eye. I told him we would only be gone about an hour or so and it has been a little over two."

Craig looked over at Paige. "Thanks for lending me your horse today. I am really glad we came out here."

"Craig, I am glad you came out too. I hope you get to feeling better."

"The doc said it was going to take some time, but now that I have a memory, I don't feel like there is a hole anymore."

"You remember?" Charlie chirped. "No balloons, or party? No hangover or headaches, just 'Bam', you're back?"

"Guess so, Charlie. I mean I was fighting a bit of a headache when I got here but I am just tired right now. I feel pretty good."

"I'll be doggone! Well, welcome back!"

Craig smiled. "It's good to be back."

"You remember me?" Abby looked closely at him.

"You bet I do, little sister. First time I met you was in this yard when you brought me out a picture of a baby-faced kid in high school. You tried to convince me that it was me. We loaded up Blue and drove to the hospital. Remember?"

"Like yesterday." Abby grinned. "Well I am glad you are better."

"Me too. Me too." Craig slapped his leg and looked at Charlie. "Guess we better get home and see what Dad is up to. Think he is going to want to know I have my memory back too."

"Yep, gotta get chores done and get back over to the Casons'. I want to get that filly haltered this evening."

Paige got up and grabbed the cookies. "Give these to your dad, will you, Craig? Here Charlie take some too, if not, I will eat them all."

"Sure. Can I have a few or do they all go to Dad?"

"I won't count them, so if you have a few it won't be known by me."

They all laughed as Charlie helped Craig down the stairs and to the truck. "You guys have a good evening."

Craig looked over at Paige. "I will call you."

"Alright," Paige replied.

Janis sat with Lilly who had quietly fallen asleep in her arms. "Riding horses sure wears her out."

They took her in the front room and laid her on the couch. Sarah and Abby were working on their project, lining up pictures and dates with Lilly's achievements.

Paige and Janis sat at the kitchen table going through the paperwork of the horse show and getting things lined out. Within two hours, dates were set. With the help of the girls, a poster was designed and announcements prepared..

32

Charlie came to help as Paige doctored Babe's wound one evening, a few days after Craig's memory had returned. Janis was out there helping put the last touches on the paperwork for the show. She casually walked down to the corrals to watch Charlie brush Babe and put more medication on her hip. She enjoyed watching him around horses. He seemed so natural.

Janis began to talk about the work that she and Paige had completed for the horse show, expressing the excitement of accomplishing something she would have never dreamed she could do. Janis stood on the opposite side of the fence and reached out tentatively to touch the horse.

Charlie had watched Janis with Lilly. The way Janis made sure that everything was taken care of. How she was dedicated to being a mother, how she helped Sarah keep up with her homework and invited Abby over to work on the project of Lilly and Babe. Abby and Sarah had filled notebooks with images and notes of communication, challenges, and triumphs of a little girl and a horse. He admired Janis' stamina and courage through all of her adversity. She kept trying to make a better life for her children.

"Angie mentioned that Lilly should participate in the horse show," Janis stated uncertain of what that really meant. "What can Lilly do in a horse show? She is just a little girl."

"Well, as far as I can tell, she is a smart little girl. She knows what she wants and what she can do. She could ride in it, just like Angie said, Janis. Someone could lead her in the trail class, and she could do the walk trot class."

"How can we do that? She doesn't know how to ride." Janis sounded frustrated.

Charlie shrugged his shoulders. He knew the next words were going to be pretty touchy, but he was going to say them with confidence and determination. "Well," he took a breath, "I am thinking if you led Babe in the class, Abe and I could be spotters."

Janis responded as Charlie had expected. "There is no way that I will lead that horse in a show! Not with my child on her."

Charlie didn't respond. He let her think about the possibilities, but possibilities were not on her mind at all.

Janis was expecting a fight or a challenge about her decision. She thought of her ex-husband and how he made her feel stupid and insignificant. She felt anxiety filling her, expecting Charlie to respond the same way. Since Charlie didn't argue, she said it for him because she knew it was coming. "I can't."

"What do you mean you can't? Could you mean you

don't want to?" Charlie asked quietly, no defiance or resistance, just truth.

"No! I mean I can't!" Janis felt panic and anxiety all at once. "I can't walk out there in front of all those people and parade around with that huge black horse, acting like I know what I am doing and with my daughter on her back." Janis had worked herself up into an argument without anyone to argue with. She was chastising herself for her own fear and weakness.

"Janis, what if I helped you lead Babe? I could show you. You don't have to do anything you don't want to. But you are not alone. What if you tried to lead her without your daughter? What if you just lead her to water, or to the barn, or something? What if you just walked beside her as we went for a walk?"

"Well," she argued, "what if she falls off?" Janis retorted, her imagination running wild. "What if I trip and fall? What if the horse spooks?" Janis was remembering her friend's death so many years ago. The memory was trying to hold her in her old belief that all horses were dangerous.

"Let's not get too far ahead of ourselves. Let's just see how Babe leads with you. Let's just see if you can walk beside her first. Then we can work up from there."

"I can't, Charlie! I just can't!"

"Okay then don't. It is as easy as that." Charlie heard the desperation in her voice. "You don't have to do anything you don't want to."

Janis looked at him. *He's lying. I know it. He is going*

to guilt me into it or make me feel weak or stupid. That's just what men do. She felt helpless.

"Janis, do what your heart tells you. If you don't want to do this, then don't. It's alright. I understand." Charlie stood quietly.

"No, you don't, Charlie. You don't understand anything!" Her heart was pounding. "I am alone in this! I am the one who has to keep my girls safe! I am the only one they have to count on! I have spent the last six years alone and I think I have done alright." She felt like she couldn't breathe, yet now that she had started, she had more to say. "I can't get hurt or afford for them to get hurt. I am all they have! They are all I have!"

Tears fell as sobs came from her lungs. *Why am I crying?* she wondered. She had no idea, but she was not going to give in to this man. "You don't know shit, Charlie."

Charlie watched her for a few minutes. He felt almost helpless at the thought of the hurt and anger this woman was showing, of baggage she had been harboring behind her eyes.

He reached out to her. She wrenched away from him, raised her fists to resist, and Charlie closed his eyes as she pounded her fists on his chest. "You don't know anything!" Then she fell against his frame, sobbing like a child lost in emotion and hurt.

"I will be there for you if you want me to," he whispered.

Janis sobbed until there was nothing left. She felt

weak. Charlie didn't move. He just held her. Janis finally relaxed against his chest, and she could feel his heart beating—calm, strong and as true as his arm around her. She could feel him breathe and could smell his shirt.

"Better?" he asked as he stepped away to look at her.

Janis blushed. "Yes... sorry about that." She stepped away from him, half ashamed of her actions.

"Don't be sorry. You did nothing wrong."

"I just hollered at you like this was all your fault." Her face reddened. "Then I beat the heck out of your chest and cried like a baby." Janis looked at the ground.

"Oh, I see, and you're the only one in the whole world who has ever done that. So shame on you?" Charlie grinned. "You kind of hold yourself up to a high standard. When is the last time you cried? I mean really cried?"

"I don't have time to cry! I have got to keep my head on straight. I have to be strong and do the right thing." Janis' anger started to rise again. She didn't like this talk. She didn't like feeling vulnerable, especially to a man.

Yet she said what was on her mind. "I can't just drop everything and run off. I can't just call in sick because I have a headache. I can't lose my temper in front of my kids." Tears streamed down her face. "I have to have a standard. I have to have limits and stay strong. There is no one to do that for me. It is me and me alone."

Charlie listened. "Well, if that is how you see it, I guess Paige and I are wasting our time being in your company. Since you are doing it all by yourself, all alone. We are no more than a couple green road apples on the ground right here." Charlie kicked a horse turd in front of his foot. "I thought we were doing something wonderful together, but I guess that isn't what you are thinking."

Charlie turned to walk away and then turned back to Janis to finish his thought. "You know, when you are ready to let go of yesterday and all your hurt and your pity party. When you are ready to enjoy the life you have, the children, the laughter, the family, let me know. Life is struggles and happiness. That is all life is, a roller coaster between the two and the decisions you make between them. That is all I got, Janis. I love to see your kids, exploring things, learning what is offered to them, challenging themselves, but for you, you have locked yourself in a box of history and fear. Let me know how that works for you."

"That is all I have!" Janis spat as tears rolled down her cheeks, holding onto her belief of her world.

"No! That is all you are looking at. All you want, safe in your own little world of not trying or not stepping outside your box. We are right here waiting."

"But what if it doesn't work? What if I can't do it?" The fragments of the wall that Janis had spent six years building was beginning to crumble.

"Then you start again. You pick yourself up and start again." Charlie looked over at Babe eating hay and then at Flick playing with Blue. These words he spoke were just as much for him as they were for Janis. "Look at this right here and now. With all you imagined of leading a horse and the fear that followed, when right now, a perfect day, a perfect time and an opportunity to share your knowledge and experience with other women, other families with kids who need a little extra help." Charlie began to tear up at the emotion of finally letting go of his past. "You were never alone, Janis. It just felt like you were."

Janis turned and looked at Babe eating. She kicked at the ground. "Well hell." She turned away from Charlie and began to walk toward the barn. For the first time Janis was beginning to realize she had been holding on to Lilly's autism as a crutch. A reason to hold back in life, for herself. *That can't be true,* She thought. *I love Lilly and want the best for her.*

Charlie watched her walk away. He wanted to ask where she was going but just watched instead.

"Are you coming?" Janis asked as she stopped at the tack room. "I am not gonna get good at this if I don't have a teacher to teach me how to lead that mare. We have a horse show to prepare for."

"I will help if you want me to." Charlie trotted after her with a grin on his face. "What do you want to get?"

"Well I thought I would start with a brush and work up from there."

"Well… it sounds like a good place to begin." Charlie's voice was wispy as he vaulted the fence and jogged to get another brush. He smiled. "Bristle side down," he said as he handed it to her.

Her hand was shaking as she took it.

It dawned on him just how hard this was for her. "You ever used a brush before?"

She looked at him to see if he was joking. "Yes!"

"On a horse, I mean." He looked sheepish.

"The first and last time I brushed a horse was when my best friend got killed." Janis' voice sounded distant. "I vowed never to touch another horse in my life."

Charlie couldn't say anything. He just walked with her. He opened the corral gate and let Janis go through. She stopped next to the fence, fear gripping her as she heard the latch click on the gate.

Charlie took her hand. "Come on. We got this."

Janis followed his cue and allowed him to lead her across the corral where Babe was eating.

They walked up next to the big mare, and Janis just stood there trying to figure out where to brush first.

Charlie coughed. "Um, come over here on her sighted side so she can see you and what you're doing." He pressed Babe's shoulder a little so he could get Babe in the right place. "Since she's missing an eye, it is best that she sees you and understands your motion so she will know you when you are on her blind side." Charlie brushed Babe's forelock to the side so Janis could see Babe as the mare looked at her.

"Hi, girl, my name is Janis," she began "How will she know it is me instead of you when we are both on her blind side?"

"Well, I guess I don't know for sure but I feel better

letting her learn my habits and brushing techniques along with my voice on her sighted side first so she knows she can trust me on the off side. I just don't do anything different when I communicate with her."

"What do you mean communicate with her? She's broke, isn't she? She does what she does because you told her to, right?"

"Yeah, she does, but it is more out of suggestion and respect than out of being told what to do."

"My girlfriend Debra said you have to make them do what you say, no matter how much they don't want to. I think that is what she was doing when she got killed."

Janis hesitated as her memory filled her mind. "We were going to ride her horses to town and get a soda. We came to the railroad tracks and her horse stopped." Janis started reliving the accident. "He didn't want to cross the tracks. Debra said that he has to do everything she says when she says it without hesitation. Then she took her long rein and started hitting him with it. He jumped around the side of the tracks as he tried to get away. That horse reared up and tried to turn around but got a shoe hung up in the tracks. He just started falling over backward with no way to get his foot loose, and he toppled onto the tracks. It was like in slow motion, and Debra went down with him. She hit her head on the steel rail." Tears formed in Janis' eyes. "I couldn't move. I couldn't stop it. It was so unreal, like watching a movie or something." Janis felt the tears run down her face. "I got off the horse I was riding and just stood there not knowing what to do. My horse took off toward home.

"There I stood helpless while a horse was reeling on the tracks with a dead girl underneath him. Someone came and grabbed the horse to quiet him while they got his foot free. My friend just lay there in the mess of it." Janis' eyes were distant. "After that, it was all a blur, ambulance, people and sirens." She started to sob. "I am so sorry, Debra."

Charlie put his hand on her shoulder and listened. After a few moments he spoke up. "I am so sorry, Janis. I had no idea."

Janis brought herself back from the memory and wiped her eyes. "I didn't do anything. I just stood there."

"Was there anything you could have done? For God's sake, you were a kid, Janis."

"I should have done something. I remember it like yesterday. I should have done something other than stand there."

"Would it have changed the outcome?"

Janis was quiet as she thought. "Well no… but that is not the point. I just stood there, Charlie, while my best friend lay there and died. Shouldn't I have done something?" The wind had shifted and blew strands of hair across her wet face.

"If this was Abby or Sarah that lost her best friend, what would you say to her about it?" Charlie questioned.

Janis searched her heart. "That is different…"

"Is it?" Charlie questioned. "God forbid, if your daughter was with her best friend when she died and she 'just stood there', and she felt the same way you do now, what would you say?"

"Well…" Janis swiped her hair back off of her face as tears fell. "I would tell her that it wasn't her fault. I would tell her that things happen because they happen, I guess." She was quiet.

"What if she said she couldn't, that she felt responsible, because she didn't do anything? Kind of like what you did."

"No! She shouldn't waste her life when she had no control over the situation."

"Can't you do the same thing for yourself instead of holding on to it for the rest of your life?" Charlie questioned.

Janis looked at him, her eyes red from crying. "I have never forgiven myself for that." She sighed in understanding and looked down at her hands. "I had never thought of it like that. I don't think I ever talked about this before." Janis paused in recognition. "I don't even think I told my ex-husband."

The reality was sinking in to Janis as a deep-seated release came from within, and she sighed again. "Wow, I hadn't even realized how much I had been holding on to that."

Charlie took her hand. "Let's take Babe for a walk."

Janis gripped his hand and took the halter rope in the other. She looked at the mare. "Come on, Babe. We have a horse show to get ready for."

Babe softly took a step beside her handler with no hesitation.

33

Abby knew she had to ask Mr. John Greenly if she could enter Piper in the show. Abe told her that Piper didn't belong to him personally, Mr. Greenly had just lent him to Abby while she was staying with them.

"Well, since I am going to be staying with you permanently, can't I keep him?" Abby asked as she stroked the horse's head.

"Nope," Abe stated as he filled his pitchfork with another load of hay and headed off to one of the boarding horses.

"Why not?" Abby spouted off. "I don't understand."

"John Greenly allowed you to use Piper to learn to ride, Abby. He was not a gift. He was lent for a while. Kind of like when you lend someone your coat or jacket, or something like that. It is borrowed and returned, for better or worse." Abe looked over at the girl's distorted face. "Have you ever lent something out and not gotten it back?"

"Well, yeah," Abby answered, "a sweater that my friend had used."

"Did you want it back?

"Yeah, but she said she lost it."

"How did that make you feel?"

"I get it," Abby answered halfheartedly. "I get it." Then her eyes lit up with an answer to her dilemma… "I wonder how much Piper is worth. Do you know how much Mr. Greenly paid for Piper?"

Abe looked at her for a moment, thinking of how to answer her question. Then he thought he had better answer as honestly as he knew. "A little over five thousand ten years ago."

"Oh!" was all Abby could get out. "I guess I had just better ask to ride him in the show then."

"Yeah, there will be a day when you can buy a horse, but for now let's just learn how to ride one."

"There will never be a horse like Piper."

"No, don't think so either, Abby. He is one in a million, so let's just enjoy riding such a gift and then return him back where he came from."

"Okay." Abby began to realize it was not going to be easy to send Piper back, but she was going to enjoy him while she had him. So while Abe continued doing chores, she grabbed the wheelbarrow and pitchfork—Abe called an apple picker—and started to clean Piper's corral.

***

Later that afternoon, Abe told Abby to call Mr. Greenly.

Abby grabbed the phone book, looked up the number, and dialed it on the spot, not knowing for sure what she would say.

"Hello," came a voice on the other line.

"Mr. Greenly?" Abby answered, all of a sudden gathering up her courage.

"Yes"

"This is Abby Sorensen, um… I am staying with Paige Cason, and I have your horse," Abby rambled.

"Yes, Abby, how is Piper doing?"

"Oh, he is doing great. I love riding him! Um… I was wondering…" Abby was trying to stay on task. She felt her heart in her throat. "Um, there is a horse show coming up in a couple weeks, and I was wondering if I could take Piper in a couple of classes?"

There was a pause on the other end of the line. "Do you think that you are ready for a show?" John asked inquisitively.

"Oh yes, we have been practicing almost every day," Abby stated with confidence. "I would really like to have you come and watch, Mr. Greenly. He is doing so well and has taught me so much."

John smiled at the amount of enthusiasm the young girl had. "I think Piper would love to go to the show with you, Abby. I would be honored to attend the show as well. So, yes, take that horse to the horse show and enjoy yourself with him."

"Thank you so much, Mr. Greenly. I am so excited!" Abby couldn't contain herself as she almost jumped up and down for joy. "I will do the best I can. I promise."

John felt a warmth in his heart as he listened through the earpiece of the phone. He could feel her enthusiasm. "I know you will, Abby.

As she settled down, she hesitated for a moment, then spoke with certain confidence on an uncertain topic. "Um, Mr. Greenly, are you wanting to sell Piper?"

John paused. "Well, Abby, I don't know. I was kind of thinking about it. Why do you ask?"

Abby's heart sank at the thought but she pressed on. "Um, I was kinda wondering how much you were going to ask for him?" Abby was quiet as she anticipated the answer. "If he was for sale, anyone could buy him... right?"

"Yes, that's the way it usually works Abby, horses are a big expense, and a huge responsibility. Are you looking to buy a horse? What does Abe think?" John knew what was going through her mind, but he wanted her to have to work out what she was thinking and put it into an action, no matter what the answer was.

Abby looked over the table at Abe. He didn't look up from his paper, so she continued. "I have saved some money and was thinking about it. I wanted to ask Abe and Patricia, but I wanted to know how much first before I asked." Abby felt desperate. "He would have a good home."

"You talk it over with Abe and Patricia and make me an offer," John replied with no emotion.

"Okay," she replied, a little concerned. *What offer do I make?* she thought as she looked over at Abe across the table again. He took a sip of coffee, appearing oblivious to the conversation. "I will talk with them and let you know. Thank you for letting me use your horse, Mr. Greenly. He is a really good boy."

"You bet, Abby, glad you are enjoying him. Let me know what you guys decide, and we will talk with you later."

"Okay, goodbye." Abby hung up the phone and looked over at Patricia wiping the last of the dishes to be put away.

"Well," Patricia stated, "what did he have to say?"

"He said I could take him to the show and that he would come and watch." Abby glanced over at Abe as he put down the paper.

Abe leaned on the table and looked over at Abby. "So you are wanting to buy a horse and are thinking that Piper would be your best bet."

Abby had never been talked to like a grown up before. She paused before she spoke, half anticipating that she was a child that was going to reprimanded for her actions. She leaned back in her chair to maybe create a little distance in the conversation they were about to have.

"Well, I was just thinking, maybe, um…" she hesitated again. "I wanted to know how much money it would take to buy him. I don't want anyone else to get him if he is for sale." Abby blurted it out to release her anxiety, remembering the way her mother would have talked to her.

Abe waited, he gave no response, Abby continued to voice her case. "I have some money saved, Abe. I can get a job and earn more I am sure."

"How much does he want for him," Abe asked to validate the silence.

"He said to make him an offer." Abby was surprised that he was talking to her about the decision she was wanting to make.

"So it looks like you better be thinking what he is worth and how much you have. Take into consideration what it is going to cost you to keep him fed and groomed."

"You guys already have hay and grain right here." Abby started thinking that was already done. She didn't need to get that. So what else did she need?

Abe smiled. "That hay is for my horses. I have enough hay to get the horses I have through the winter. To add another horse will take another three tons of hay."

Abby had no idea what three tons of hay looked like. *Anyway, he was in the pasture right now, so why did she need to feed him hay?* She thought.

"So what does that cost?" she asked disheartened. She hadn't thought of that part. All she wanted was to keep him forever. It felt odd for her to sit at the table with grown-ups and come to some kind of decision without it being made for her. She looked up at Patricia who was coming to sit down at the table with a tablet.

"Let's make out a budget and see what it will cost you to have a horse. Then we'll make a plan from there if that is what you want to do," Patricia said as she opened up the notebook and put it in front of Abby. "If a horse eats fifteen pounds of hay a day and there are thirty days in a month…" Patricia began.

Abby waited for Patricia to write it down. Patricia

just sat there waiting. *Crap, I have to do the math.* Abby picked up the pencil and began jotting down notes and calculations of what it was going to cost to keep a horse.

"Now we have to add a trim every six weeks and getting shoes on him at least three times a year," Patricia continued. "Now we need wormer and vaccinations…"

An hour later, the figures written, Abby looked at what it would take to maintain keeping Piper. She had no idea of the expense of a horse or the amount of hidden money that went into what Patricia and Abe did. Yet here it was in black and white before her.

"I can do it! I know I can."

"You're about five hundred dollars short," Abe stated.

"I can get a job and work around here…"

Abe looked at her, "Let's give it some time and see what happens. Keep up with your grades, your school work, and your chores. Let's see where that gets you."

Abby was a little disheartened, yet she felt confident in her discussion. She realized love was not going to pay for the responsibility of owning a horse. It was an investment, supporting a living being and making sure she would have the money to continue to support, feed and take care of such an animal. She might love Piper, but could she support that love by providing wellbeing, beyond love?

34

Craig had gotten up early, almost giddy with memories. It felt like a weight lifted off his shoulders as he prepared coffee and watched the sun come up. He played with the puzzle on the table and thought of his dad's response the night before.

"I knew you were in there somewhere," Jim had said.

"Yep, I was. I guess I can take that off my bucket list now. I don't want to do that twice." Craig laughed.

He had never had a bucket list, but he had heard some people had written certain goals they wanted to achieve in their lives and marked them off when they had experienced them. He never thought he would have been one of *those people*, but now those people didn't seem so odd.

He thought of what he wanted to do today and what he wanted to do tomorrow, and the day after that, and next week and a year from now, ten years, thirty years, of all the things he wanted to do. One name kept coming into his mind, someone who he would want to share it with.

In the fresh Fall morning, he wanted to go for a run, but he thought better of it and thought maybe a stroll would be better before his dad got up. He put on his boots and walked outside. He walked out to the barn and grabbed a halter for Booger and a can of grain, just like he always had as if no time had passed. He poured the grain in the feed bucket and walked out to the corral and through the gate.

Booger took one look at Craig's posture and the halter, and he turned to walk to the other end of the corral. Craig followed, playing the regular game of walk away with him. As per habit, Booger made it to the corner and then turned to face his pursuer. Craig caught up with him and, with a grin, presented the halter. Booger dropped his nose in it, giving up on the game for the day.

"Don't worry, big guy. I ain't gonna ride you. I just want to brush you out and play a little. That's all." He buckled the halter and then turned to walk away. Booger followed quietly as they strode to the barn grain bucket.

As Craig brushed the big bay, his mind wandered to Paige. It brought a grin to his face as he thought of the memories they had together. And the silly names they had given each other. Sir Saves-A-Lot. He kind of chuckled to himself at her name for him. His imagination turned loose at the thought of a knight in shining armor coming in to save a damsel in distress. And how the knights that he had read about as a kid would ride in and do exhibitions and ride Friesian horses, rearing up in the field of battle. Fighting good over evil. He shook his head as he grinned. How fun would that be? He brushed the thick neck of Booger.

It all started with a nickname for Paige, and her grand entry, She Who Runs with Horses, flitted in his mind. Yes, that pretty much summed up Paige Cason. She was in constant motion, doing, being, creating and achieving. Yet just like the horses around her, there was a grounded nature within her. An awareness beyond words and energy maybe. He thought about it and then, with a grin, gave Booger some long strokes with his brush as he shook his head to get those silly thoughts out of his mind.

As Craig brushed, he bumped Booger's coronary band, just above his hoof with his foot. Booger moved his front foot back and stood that way for a few moments. "Oops, sorry about that, buddy," Craig said as he continued to brush.

Booger didn't move his front foot back into position, and Craig all of a sudden had an idea. What would it take to get him to bow?

He went and got a stock whip out of the tack room and came back over to Booger. He took the handle of the whip and touched the same front leg. Then he tapped on it, and Booger moved his leg back.

Well, that is pretty cool, Craig thought as he moved the horse around a little bit and tried it again. Over and over he would tap the leg, each time asking for a little more with less attempt or effort from himself. He was surprised that he could get that front foot clear back to his hind foot and Booger would hold it. *How is that even possible?* he thought as he played. When he had finished playing, he led Booger back to the corral, happy to feel halfway normal. Although he was weak and a little lightheaded, he was feeling like he was going to be okay for the first time in a long time.

As he made it to the house and got up on the porch, Jim came out with two cups of coffee as he leaned on one crutch.

"Hey, Dad, I could have gotten that for you," Craig said as he reached out and grabbed at the cups.

"Nonsense. I ain't crippled—just wounded," Jim stated. Then he looked hopeful. "But I do have a couple of hot cinnamon rolls on the counter."

"Well, if you are inviting me to have coffee and a cinnamon roll with you, I will take you up on that."

Craig entered the house to get the rolls on the counter. He grabbed a denim jacket for his dad to keep off the chill from the fall morning air.

As they sat on the porch, Craig looked across the pasture. He saw something moving on the far end of the pasture. He looked again.

"What is that, Dad, going along the tree line?"

Jim looked and saw a herd of elk moving restlessly along, mainly cows and calves. A young spike carelessly came out into the opening while the rest stayed within the trees. Jim could hear the soft mew of the cows as they kept in contact with the herd.

"That herd of elk comes through here about two or three times a month this time of year," Jim said as he took a sip of coffee.

"They really come in this close, huh? I would have never guessed," Craig said casually as he watched the herd continue on their way. "Where are they headed?"

"They are headed up to the ridge, I reckon," Jim answered. "I haven't really followed them."

"That is so cool!" Craig responded like a kid.

"Yeah, I suppose. They are amazing animals. They know the lead cow and can sense what she is thinking with just a twitch of an ear or a bob of her head. You can see when they bed down they are each facing different directions and set purposely in lookout positions." Jim took a sip of coffee. "I don't know, being out here just gives a person a chance to see things you normally don't see." His eyes lit up with happiness.

Craig looked at him concerned for a moment, "What?"

"Fall is coming... I just heard a bugle." Jim grinned. "Didn't you hear it?"

"No, I just hear quiet."

"You wait. In a week or so, this whole hillside will be filled with elk song."

"It has been years since I have heard an elk bugle," Craig commented.

Just about the time the words came out of Craig's mouth, a high-pitched scream teased his ears. He came to attention, his eyes wide with excitement. He strained his ears to hopefully hear it again.

Jim's face lit up. "They're baaack." He felt like a kid hearing his favorite song. This was his favorite time of year, and he had his son back. As for the elk this year, they could eat his whole hay lot, and he wouldn't have cared. His son was going to be alright. Despite all the tough times this last couple of weeks, all was going to be good.

Over the hill another high-pitched scream and two grunts—then silence. Both men sat like statues yearning for more, yet there was not another sound or a movement in the trees. They were gone like a ghost in the morning light.

35

It was mid-morning, and clouds had gathered on the west skyline. The hint of rain was heavy in the air. It had been two days since Craig had seen Paige. Picking up the phone, he dialed her number. After three rings Paige picked it up.

"Hello?"

"Hey," he said. "You have time to talk?"

"Sure," Paige replied. She had just taken Abby over to Sarah's so they could work on their project. She had the day to herself and was dreading the thought of finishing up with the show paperwork.

"What are you up to?" he asked as he grabbed his coffee and sat on the porch.

"Well you know same-ole, same-ole," Paige answered. "Getting things ready for the show. It is coming along really well. Your dad said we could use his cows for a couple of cow classes, and he would be the announcer too! I got the judge lined up, got quite a few sponsors, and ordered the ribbons," Paige rambled on giving details, frustrations and challenges. She paused, and the line was quiet. "Craig?"

"Yes."

"Oh, thought I lost you."

"Nope. Just listening."

"Sorry, I kind of get caught up in these things." Paige felt embarrassed that she should talk so much. "So, what are you doing?" She was trying to steer the conversation back to why he called.

"Oh, I just thought I would call and just sit and listen to you talk about the horse show. Sounds like you have everything under control."

"No, not at all. There is so much that needs to be done, but I can take a few minutes and visit if you like, remembering the letter he had written to her and was kind of hoping that he had remembered too."

"Well, I was going to ask you a question if you had time." Craig hesitated for a moment.

"Yes?"

"Well, I was wanting to ask a girl I like out to dinner and a movie."

"What girl did you have in mind? Do I know her?"

"You might. She lives around these parts, has a couple horses and took on a foster girl." Craig hesitated again. "I think she got so ambitious as to put on a horse show too. I can't think of her name but I have kind of had a crush on her since high school. Been too shy to ask her out. Thought you might know her number."

Paige leaned back in her chair. For the first time since she had gotten up this morning, she stopped to breathe. He was really asking her out on a date! "I might…" Her heart was in her throat. "What if I did? Are your intentions true?"

"Actually, she has a pretty nice horse that I like really well, a palomino that I have my eye on. I got to ride her the other day and haven't been the same since. So, I was thinkin' a little Chinese restaurant, a little action film... you know, a typical date. Maybe she would let me ride her again."

Paige chided back at him, "You might want to change that to a romance film, and from what I heard, you tried to take that mare from that gal, claiming her for yourself."

"Well when I see something I really like I can't help myself. Just have to take action and see where that gets me."

"When is this date supposed to take place?"

"I was thinking tonight... if she wasn't busy."

"She has been here all morning. I could ask her if you would like..."

Craig paused for a moment and then grinned. "If you don't mind, you could ask her, or better yet... You could put her on the phone."

"Hold on, let me see if I can get her..." Paige cupped the phone and hollered, "Phone's for you." There was a pause and then her voice came back on the phone.

"Hello..."

"Um, is this the woman with the palomino horse?" Craig asked playfully.

"Yes," Paige answered enjoying the fun. She waited.

"Well, ever since I rode your horse the other day, I have been thinking about you and wondered if you would want to go out for dinner with me tonight?"

"Are you asking me or my horse to dinner?" Paige quizzed. "Just a forewarning, my horse is a vegetarian, but don't tell her I told you." Paige smiled at the thought.

"I was kind of wanting a date with you. But if you want your horse to go, I could bring a trailer and bring my horse too."

Paige laughed. "You are back, aren't you?"

"Never been better… well, I have, but it feels good to be back. I feel like my coordination is coming back too. I should be back together in no time," Craig replied honestly. "Really, Paige, I would love to take you out tonight if you would like to go, just you and me." Craig felt like he was back in high school. "I can pick you up right around six."

"Sounds like a date. I hate to tell my horse that you chose me over her, but hey, she would have a hard time fitting in the front seat."

Craig laughed. "So six will work?"

"I will call Janis and see if Abby can stay at their house. Six will be fine."

"Perfect."

Paige fidgeted the rest of the afternoon, half excited at the prospect of going out with Craig and half nervous at how things might be different. She finally had to regroup herself and focus on the horse show and getting things done. There was plenty to do.

36

Charlie had been working with Janis and Babe, which was come along nicely. Charlie seemed to be in his element, sharing the things he knew about horses. Janis felt like she was in school again, learning new math problems. For some reason she seemed to be laughing a lot lately, maybe even a little glow about her.

Charlie and Paige had set up some obstacles for Abby and Janis to work on with their horses. Lilly had watched as Abby and Sarah rode the horses, watched them serpentine between some poles, side pass and back them up. All of this she absorbed in small increments and listened as Paige and Charlie coached them through the trail class. She saw their happiness when they succeeded, their determination and how they kept trying..

Lilly knew she could do that too if someone would let her. She shuffled around the corral and found small objects to focus on, as she listened, mumbling in her own language. She rolled the words around in her mouth as she formed them, if she practiced enough, she could be heard.

"Abby, you need to face that bridge straight on. Don't come at it from the side," Paige schooled her. "Hold him steady, yeah that's it, straight on."

Lilly listened. "straight on," she repeated quietly as she grabbed at the grass..

"I am trying," Abby wined, "but Piper won't do it. He keeps moving his hips over."

"Take a breath and relax your legs," Paige coached trying to give the girl something to work with. "Your legs are telling him he needs to move his hip."

"No, they're not," Abby argued trying to convince Paige it was the horse's fault.

"Abbs, stop right there," Paige said sternly as Piper dropped his hip to the left again. "Stop…" she repeated with confidence, seeing where she could get the girl to understand her communication with Piper.

"I am trying," Abby responded as she sucked up on the reins. Piper kept moving his feet. His ears were back and his neck tight, swishing his tail back and forth with irritation, wanting to brace against his rider.

"Abbs, close your eyes and take a deep breath," Paige instructed. "Ask him with your mind to stop. Loosen your legs and your grip on him."

Abby was frustrated. *He should be able to do this*. She thought to herself,as she only half listened to Paige's words. Her mind busy with what he wasn't doing. "What is wrong with him? He is being crazy."

Paige asked again with a little more force. "Abby, breathe, think in your mind to stop and relax.

Remember when we rode out in the hills and rode without reins?" Paige had to think of how to get the two in sync in the arena. "Remember how you wanted him to jump or walk over the log. Feel him, Abbs, and feel yourself. You're not holding him quiet and steady. You are asking too many things with too many limitations. Stop your mind and breathe."

Lilly was again rocking back and forth, playing with the blade of grass in her hand. She quietly took a big breath in, and repeated Paige's words, "breathe."

Through the frustration, Abby knew Paige was right, but she didn't want her to be. She wanted it to be Piper's fault, although she was getting to know the horse well enough to know she had something to do with his hesitation and unwillingness to cross the bridge.

Abby closed her eyes, she took a deep breath, letting it out and imagining her time out in the hills, and felt her own legs start to relax. Sitting there for a moment made her finally realize how much pressure she was really putting on Piper. Regrouping she felt herself soften and feel.

In the next moment she asked Piper to go forward on the bridge. She found the left hind leg move forward then left front and Piper walked straight across the bridge.

"That's it, Abbs. You got this," Paige said enthusiastically. "Perfect."

Abby beamed at the accomplishment. "I did it!"

Janis had watched the struggle the girl was having

with her horse and her anxiety began to rise. And now it was her turn to go across it. Janis paused for a moment and looked at Charlie. This was different than when they had led her to the barn, but she didn't think Babe would cross it with her blind eye.

"She can't do this, Charlie."

"Sure, she can. All you have to do is ask her."

"She is going to fall. She can't see it." Janis was getting worried and started fretting about the obstacle in front of her, and looking for something to blame.

"Just give it a try, Janis. Let her have her head and give it a good effort. If she doesn't cross it, we will do something different," Charlie soothed, allowing a little time for Janis to work through her own troubles.

"I can't."

"Then go to something different. There are all kinds of things to practice on." Charlie looked at her and noticed her hands were shaking. "Just walk around it."

Lilly walked up to Janis. "Okay, Momma?"

"Yes, Momma is fine," Janis answered.

Lilly began playing with Babe as Charlie visited with Janis standing next to the bridge. "Breathe," Lilly mumbled to herself.

Janis heard Charlie's words, but fought against them... *Why would a blind horse trust her to cross a bridge?* She thought to herself.

Sarah had the camera out taking pictures and saw a perfect opportunity to get a great shot of Lilly and Babe.

"Hey, Mom, hand Lilly the lead line and step away from Babe. I will get a picture of them together."

Without thought Janis handed Lilly the lead line. "Stay right here, honey," she said as she stepped away from the horse for a moment, watching Sarah handle the camera.

"Lilly, look over here. Move over that way," Sarah instructed, pointing toward the bridge.

Lilly was petting Babe's head, and the pictures that Sarah was taking were amazing shots of the connection between that mare and girl. "Step up on the bridge, Lilly, and look tall and big for me."

Feeling so proud of herself for holding Babe, she boldly said Charlie's words, as she stepped up on the bridge. "Walk on."

Babe followed her command as both child and horse crossed the bridge.

Sarah gasped at what Lilly was doing.

Janis looked over her shoulder. What in the world had she done letting Lilly have that horse? "Lilly, no!"

Lilly began to rock back and forth, hesitant of her accomplishment. But she had done it, just like the big kids... Babe followed her off the other side.

"Lilly you can't do that! No!" Janis said in a panic," Give me that lead line baby."

"No, No!" Lilly said, holding the lead.

"Honey, you can't lead that mare across that bridge. Give me the lead line!" She repeated.

"No, mine!" Lilly boldly replied with confidence as

she stomped her foot, holding tight to her connection to the mare.

"Don't you talk to me like that, young lady! You give me that lead line." Janis was almost panicking.

Lilly was frustrated. How could she tell her mom that she could do this? How could her mom understand that she was more capable than her mom was letting her be? Lilly stomped her foot again and said more forcefully. "Mine" she repeated, "my horse!"

Charlie was standing next to Lilly. "She has got a point, Janis."

Janis looked at Charlie and then at Sarah. Then she looked at her little girl who had determination on her face. In a matter of weeks, this little girl all of a sudden had a voice. A voice of confidence and determination.

"Walk on," Lilly stated, Babe responded to the request with ease.

Janis noticed this little girl was more than an empty shell with no mind. The proof Lilly was a little girl who had goals, and pride, and now a voice! *Oh my God, Lilly has a voice!* Janis realized they just had their first argument.

"Let's see if she can do it again, Janis," Charlie coaxed.

Janis looked at him with hesitation.

"Let's give it a try again." he repeated

Without hesitation, Lilly said, "Walk on," as she turned the big horse around and headed the few steps back to the bridge.

Charlie was surprised that the girl reacted so quickly.

Janis's heart filled with pride and panic all in an instant. "Lilly, you did it! You are such a big girl."

"Horse show." Lilly blurted, she paused a moment to say one more word, "Cowgirl."

Charlie grinned at the thought of Lilly taking this big black mare and walking though trail class, and then riding in trail class with her mom leading her. "Well, looks like we have some practicing to do."

Janis had realized she, as a mother, had not given her daughter a chance to express herself. She had held Lilly helpless. Janis had realized Lilly needed this just as much as she did.

She looked over at Charlie, "Yep, no more chickening out. It is time to make this happen."

Charlie grinned at her, "Yep, I think so."

Sarah held up the camera as Janis took the lead line. "Hey, Mom, look over here." She clicked the camera several times. "Charlie, step up next to Mom. Let's get all three of you in this one."

"Sarah, why don't you get in this picture. I will take the shot," Paige suggested as she watched all that had happened. "I think we just made history today."

Sarah looked over at her for a moment before handing over the camera.

Okay guys work it!" Paige stated as she zoomed the camera in and started clicking film.

As Paige handed back the camera to Sarah, "You going to ride in the horse show?"

"No, think I will just take pictures."

Janis looked at the big mare, "Guess I was holding you helpless too, Babe, not thinking you could see." Janis looked over at her youngest daughter and repeated her words, "Walk on."

Babe stepped forward as Janis walked across the bridge with the big gentle mare beside her.

In the next few minutes, all the years of anxiety Janis had felt melted away. How her being afraid was holding everyone around her helpless. Nothing was what she thought it to be, and it took her six-year-old daughter to show her what fearless meant.

"Yes, Lilly, horse show. We are going into a horse show."

37

Craig pulled into Paige's driveway a little before six in his dad's Dodge pickup. Paige saw him through the window and came out to meet him.

"You ready to go?" he asked as he got out of the truck.

"Yeah, I think I am. Do I need to grab a swimsuit?"

"No, not tonight, at least I don't think so."

"Okay, just checking," Paige said with a grin.

Craig opened the passenger-side door for her.

"Thank you, kind sir."

"My pleasure, ma'am," he said as he shut the door and got into the driver's side. "So a little Chinese food and a movie?"

"That sounds good." Paige paused. "Or…"

"Or what?"

"Well, we could get the Chinese to go and eat out under the stars…"

"Oh! That sounds like a great idea. Any place in particular?"

"Naw, just want to sit and talk and visit with you without any distractions," Paige said matter-of-factly.

"Sounds like a plan. I was having a hard time between romance or science fiction. Neither one sounded good to me, so I was going to let you choose." Craig started the pickup and headed toward town.

"Oh I see, no pressure here, just leave it to me to get the wrong movie."

Craig laughed, "Well yeah, that is the way it's done, isn't it?"

The conversation was easy and pleasant as they pulled in and grabbed Chinese food to go. Craig pulled up at the east side of town and into Ruckels Creek Road going out toward Keating. The sprinkles from earlier that day was just enough to bring out the aroma of sweet sage into the air. He pulled off the dirt road along where his dad had leased land for grazing cattle and turned off the pickup. They sat silently for a few minutes, not knowing for sure what to say. It was almost an awkward silence, and Craig drummed his thumbs on the steering wheel before looking over at Paige.

"Come here often?" he asked with a grin.

"No," Paige raised an eyebrow. "First time I have ever been here."

There was a thousand things Craig wanted to say but all that came out of his mouth was, "Shall we eat? The smell of sweet and sour pork has got my attention."

"Yep, I think that is a great idea." Paige opened up one bag. "You know, I haven't been down this road since we moved."

Craig opened up another bag, "Really? You haven't seen your old place since you moved?"

"No, I sure haven't. I guess it is kind of like selling a horse. You just have to move on."

"Like you would sell one of your horses," Craig chided her.

Paige grinned and looked out the windshield into the open sky. A shooting star sailed across the darkness. "Oh!" she gasped but before she could say a word it was gone.

"I wish we had grabbed a couple of blankets so we could sit out and watch the stars."

"Well, I think we might be able to do that." Craig reached in the backseat and grabbed a bed roll. "Dad is always prepared." He got out of the pickup. "Two wool blankets, a foam pad wrapped in a tarp." He dropped down the tailgate. "Let's eat out here," he said with a tap on the tailgate. "The view will be wonderful."

Paige got out of the truck with the food, and Craig helped her onto the tailgate. They both got settled with blankets and food.

In the silence, Craig finally mentioned the hospital for the first time. "I never thanked you for coming to the hospital with my dad, Paige. That was really kind of you."

"It was a fun time traveling with him. It's about time the tables turned and I got to be the one standing next to the hospital bed. Although, I never thought I would ever see your dad so angry. Boy, when he puts his foot down, everyone listens."

"Yeah, he does kind of know how to get people's attention when he wants to. It doesn't happen often, but when it does…"

"Well, I am glad I went. It was a trip of a lifetime." She paused, "you should of seen him on the airplane, with a little girl and him talking of a bucking horse named Hangover."

"Haha! Yeah Hangover was Dad's last ride, I don't think he got on one after that."

Craig returned back to the memory at the hospital, "I recognized you right off, except I didn't know from where. It was like you could see right through me."

"I was a little concerned with your lady friend there, just sayin'..."

"Why would you be concerned with her? She was my sister in-law and, to be honest, she kind of scares me a little." Craig smiled. "She kind of reminds me of my mom."

"Your mom is a powerful lady."

" Yes she is. She knows how to get things done when it is to her advantage. I admire that about her at times. Other times... not so much. Craig stated. "As of me leaving New York, I might not see her for several years."

"Well I hope it won't be that long," Paige stated concerned.

"Paige, there is a difference between powerful and strong. My Mom is powerful in her own world, but that is all she knows and wants to know. You and Patricia are powerful and strong, in balance you can take a situation and evaluate and with the help of others make it happen with respect between all involved. There is a big difference." he took out the Chinese boxes and handed her one. " I enjoy that kind of living so much more than trying to get ahead by using others. He took his chopsticks out and began playing with his food, "I want to focus on here and now and what a beautiful evening it is."

A breeze came up and blew across his shoulders. He set his sticks down and grabbed a wool blanket, draping it over Paige's shoulders "You warm enough?"

Paige glanced at him with a smile on her face. "I'm golden. Couldn't be more perfect. I have something of yours."

"Oh you do?"

Paige paused then answered "Um yeah, I don't know if I was supposed to have it, but it had my name on it." She pulled out the envelope with his note inside.

"Oh damn, Paige, I had been looking for that." Craig now was nervous, "Um, did you read it?"

"Yes, I did."

"Paige, I wrote that before the accident, I don't want you to judge me by who I am right now. I have a lot of healing left to do. But just so you know, I meant every word of that when I wrote it. And I think I will mean them again. Can you give me a little more time?"

"Craig, I am here for tonight. I had to let you to know that I read it, and they are beautiful words." she handed the envelope back to him.

He grinned at her, "Thank you." He took the envelope and put it in his pocket. "Are you alright, or do you want me to take you home?" Craig was uncertain now of where the evening might head, now that he knew she had read the letter.

"Heck no, I don't want to go home, I am having a wonderful time here with this crazy guy that has a crush on my horse."

"Yeah, well it's too bad she is vegan..." He laughed.

"Was that the deal breaker, her being vegan?" Paige chided

Craig laughed again, "Heck no, she has four legs and can't fit in the front of my truck."

Paige laughed as she slapped his arm, she leaned back, wrapped her blanket closer around herself and looked up at the stars.

He took her hand and gave it a kiss, and laid back with her.

They watched the evening stars, talked of past lives and future dreams.

38

The day of the show seemed to have promised complete chaos for Janis. She was as nervous as a cat on a tin roof. She didn't know what she was going to wear, what not to wear, and the thought of whether Babe would act up brought her near tears of emotion. All of that and Lilly. *Oh my goodness, what have I done, letting this little girl enter horse classes,* she thought as she fought with her anxiety. When she saw Charlie pull into the fairgrounds, all of a sudden a calm fell over her. *I am not doing this alone,* she reminded herself. They were going to show that horse.

Abby and Sarah set up their project, of photos and notes on a cardboard display along with the photo album so people could actually see the results that Lilly had in participating in therapeutic riding. They set up a donation jar for the plans to help other people in therapy riding too.

Abby was in Paige's hip pocket as she unloaded Piper out of the horse trailer. The bay gelding looked around, taking in his surroundings. Abby could not be prouder as she unwrapped his leg wraps and revealed snow white socks. Abe and Patricia came up beside her as she finished with her last wrap.

"Abby?"

Abby looked up and saw John Greenly standing with them. "Yes? Oh! Hi, Mr. Greenly! Doesn't he look great?"

"He looks fabulous, Abby. He looks absolutely fabulous!"

"I am so excited to show him and really happy that you are here. I hope we will do well today…" Abby rambled with all the exciting things happening. "Paige says not to worry about winning but just to go out and play with him just like we do at home."

"That is great advice, Abby, great advice. You go out there and have a great time." John started to leave, but then turned around and faced Abby again. "Oh, Abby, I almost forgot… After you and I talked the other day about selling Piper, I have to tell you, I sold him. After today Piper has a new home."

Abby froze. "But Abe, Patricia and I were talking of trying to buy him. I didn't know for sure what to offer for him…" Abby stumbled through the words as she began to shake, and tears started to form and run down her cheeks.

"Well, sometimes in life you get an offer you just can't refuse."

Abby wanted to run, or scream… Abe's words echoed in her head. He is not a gift. He was lent to you. "Okay." She tried to stifle the sobs coming from her chest.

"You might know the new owner. The last name is Cason…"

Abby looked over at Abe and Patricia, tears streaming down her face. "You bought him?"

"Nope, not us," Abe stated.

John continued, "The name on the transfer is Abigail Marie Cason."

Abby didn't recognize the name at first, but then she looked up at all three of them. "Your adoption went through yesterday. We got the papers today," Patricia said with tears in her eyes. "You are now our daughter!"

Abby jumped up and ran to Patricia, wrapping her arms around her and holding on so tightly at the thought that it could be a dream. She looked over at Abe. "Is it true? Am I really yours?"

"As true as us standing here," Abe stated.

He came in and gave them both a hug and then looked back at the horse standing quietly behind her that John Greenly was holding. "Is he really mine?"

"As soon as you sign the papers and send them in," John told her with tears welling in his eyes too.

Abby reached out and gave him a hug too. "This is better than any Christmas present ever," she gushed as she then reached out and hugged her horse around the neck.

Paige and Samantha, John Greely's daughter, and Craig stood off to the side.

"Paige, I am your sister!" she squealed.

"My little sister," Paige corrected with a smile.

Abby didn't know what to do first, kiss her horse or hug her family. She ran to Paige.

"Hey, little sister, you better get ready for your first class," Paige told her as she heard Jim's voice boom over the speaker.

Some kids were playing with a birthday helium balloon across the way right behind Piper. John was the first to hear it as the balloon burst with a loud bang! John jumped, recognizing the memory of what happened to his daughter. But Piper only flickered an ear at the bang and stood casually where he was.

John glanced at Abe, who stood silent. John tipped his hat to the horseman he called friend.

***

In a day of everything coming together, Patricia had a surprise for her elder daughter, "Paige, there is something that I want to share with you today"

Paige looked at her mother, curious of the change in her voice."Sure Mom, what do you got?"

She motioned to some people in the crowd. Paige searched the faces of friends and family when her eyes came to rest on Sue, and standing next to her was Danny.

Danny couldn't contain his excitement any longer "Ms Paige!" He came running up to her. "I came to see you! Me and Ms. Sue, got to ride a plane and everything!"

Paige could not believe her eyes as she reached out to give Danny a hug. "Yes you did, look at you!"

"Ms. Sue said, since I was such a good worker I could come and see you. And Mr. Abe said I could ride one of his horses in the show, just like a real cowboy. We are staying out at their house for three whole days."

Abe tried to keep himself composed, "Cricket needs a little bit of exercise," he shrugged.

Paige looked over at her father and mother, then she looked over at her mentor and gave her a hug. "Oh my goodness, I can't believe you are here!".

"I couldn't let you go and do this show alone, I thought I would bring a little help with me." Sue explained as she tried to hide her emotions.

"We had to leave Oscar at home," Danny piped in. "He couldn't ride on the plane with me."

"Yeah, it is probably pretty good that he stayed home. He might of eaten everybody's snacks on the plane." Paige grinned at him.

Danny laughed at the thought, "You are funny Ms. Paige."

They all laughed.

The day was a blur of classes, horses, and challenges. Sue helped in the arena, while Danny gave out ribbons. When Danny's class came up Abe was the one who led him in to do walk trot class. When they walked out and Danny stepped off Cricket, Paige saw her father do something he had never done before. Abe reached up, took his hat off and put it on Danny's head.

Paige thought that boy grew three foot taller in an

instant. *Yep a real cowboy,* she thought to herself with a feeling of pride beyond words for her family.

Abby was never prouder to ride in the arena, receiving ribbons and awards on a horse that was her very own.

When trail class finally came up, Charlie led Babe to the arena with Lilly along side of him, Jim began to explain. "This is the reason why we are here today, to bring awareness to young folks who have been challenged by difficult obstacles in their life. They have the courage to face each day, challenge themselves to grow and become part of the activities that we do. If you folks will welcome Lilly and Babe into the arena, they will do their lead through trail class."

Janis and Charlie both walked into the arena beside Lilly as she led the large mare, quiet and accepting. The crowd came alive with applause and whistles, Babe ignored the crowd. Lilly had to focus on her job, pressing her thumb and forefinger together, she kept her eyes to the ground as she walked.

Charlie handed her the lead line, "Okay Ms Lilly here you go."

Lilly took the lead like and said boldly, "Walk on." Charlie and Janis both walked beside her as she walked Babe around the barrel. She then led Babe over the poles, picked up a flag and carried it to a bucket, just like she had practiced at home. She stopped at the bridge and looked over at her mom. "Momma," she said. Janis looked at her daughter, took her daughter's hand. The crowd stood and applauded as mother and daughter crossed the bridge together. Charlie was waiting on the other side. He reached out to the little girl, and she walked into his arms.

He lifted her up. "What a cowgirl you are."

Lilly threw back her head, "cowgirl."

Janis knew now that her life had changed forever. She no longer held her daughter helpless. She was a strong, independent young lady with determination and goals that she was determined to fulfill and capabilities beyond Janis's imagination.

39

The horse show had been a success with the help of Angie and Sue, plus Danny sporting his new hat, and all of the volunteers and sponsors. The cow class finished the day. Paige rode in the arena with Libby to put up the last of the heifers and close the gate.

Jim turned on the microphone one more time. His throat was sore and tired from names and number calling all day long. But he knew the best part was yet to come.

"Well, folks, we have a few more scores to tally for the high-point horse and cow classes.

"And in the arena, we have the lady who has put on a heck of a show here in our little county. The one person who gave uncounted hours of planning and determination to bring awareness and a community together and make this show a success. Can we give a hand to Paige Cason?"

Paige was surprised to hear her name. It took the whole crew to put on this kind of a show. But she waved a hand in recognition. Libby broke into a trot, lifting her head as people from all around the arena and grandstands clapped and hollered for her. She felt her face flush with embarrassment.

Jim spoke up again. "I think we have some unfinished business here, Paige, if you could wait there for a few minutes."

Craig trotted into the arena riding Booger. There was a large blue blanket draped over the sadde and fastened together at the chest with a large silver concho, with Craig bracing a yellow flag. The flag had a picture of large black horse rearing up with a knight in full armor. Booger circled around the arena at a high lope as the flag snapped in the wind.

Paige sat in the middle of the arena on Libby confused. *This is not part of the program. What in the world is Craig doing?*

She looked at Jim for answers or understanding, but Jim refused to look in her direction.

Abe and John Greenly had climbed up the arena fence on cue, about thirty feet apart from each other. Each held out a bar about four feet long inside the arena, attached on the end were medium rings tied on by a fine string. Craig circled the arena again, lined himself up, nudged Booger into a run, right straight toward the rings. Dropping his flag down, he pointed the ten-foot pole at the rings with marksmanship. He scooped up the first ring and, with pinpoint accuracy, scooped up the second ring, as a knight in shining armor would have done to impress the ladies.

People cheered at the exhibition of warlords and mounted knights. The rings fell all the way down the flagpole toward Craig's hand. Craig slowed Booger down as he circled again. Then Jim handed Craig the microphone. "Paige Cason, I have known you most of my life."

Paige felt her face redden.

"You have flickered in and out of my life beyond memory, beyond laughter and sadness. You bring life and happiness beyond measure. You challenge me, encourage me beyond the capabilities I put on myself." Craig paused to keep his composure. "Then you support all of those who come into your life."

He circled his horse around Paige at a walk then stopped, standing directly in front of her. He dropped the flag down next to her hand. Paige glanced at the flag and read, "Sir Saves-A-Lot." She grinned through her uncertain emotion. Next to the point of the pole attached to the flag was a small lace satchel filled with something. She glanced at Craig for a moment, who gave her a nod of approval for the gift.

Paige pulled a string and the small satchel fell into her hand. She held it for a moment, her heart racing with anticipation and curiosity.

As she pulled the laced bag open, Craig continued. "Paige, with all that you know of me, my flaws, my ambitions, my heartaches and my love. I promise to stand beside you, support you, challenge you and never doubt your strength or courage."

She looked down at the bag in her hand, reached in, and pulled out a small piece of paper. Her eyes blurred with tears. She blinked several times before she could see her knight in shining armor, in a cowboy hat and jeans. She looked at the small piece of paper again, which read, *She Who Runs with Horses.* She put her hand up to her mouth, as if to hold in her emotions. Written under those words was, *Make a wish,* as she pulled out a fine silver chain. It was her crucifix cross necklace. She gasped in a sob.

Craig couldn't hold back tears as he watched her reaction. His heart in his throat, he needed to keep it together to finish what he had started. With a slight cue from Craig, Booger bent down on one knee. Craig stepped off his gallant steed and walked up to Libby and Paige.

Paige began to shake as Craig extended his hand as he asked her to get down.

The crowd around them had gone completely silent.

Paige stepped out of the saddle and stood before him. He towered over her frame as he reached out, took her necklace, and draped it around her neck, fastening the clasp.

"You are my wish, Paige Cason." With the microphone still on, he continued, although at that moment it was just her and him as he spoke. He wanted the world to know he was in love with this woman, but as he looked into her eyes, the world fell away. He pulled out a velvet box from his pocket. "With all my heart," he continued, "I am asking you to give me the biggest gift a man could ask for."

He dropped to one knee, his hands shaking, he

opened the velvet box. Within the deep blue velvet, shimmering within the evening light, was a diamond ring. "Would you share the rest of your life and marry me, Paige? It would be an honor to have you as my wife."

Paige couldn't speak. She couldn't see. This man who stood before her, this wish, and all that life had to offer, the frustration, the attraction, the emotion, fear but most of all the love. She could not imagine her life without him.

"You bring beauty in everything around you, Paige, and I want to be a part of that beauty for the rest of our lives. Please say yes."

Paige dropped Libby's rein and draped her arms around Craig's neck. "Yes, I will marry you. Yes, yes, yes, I will marry you!"

Paige felt his arms encircle her and lift her off the ground as he stood. In an instant she was being twirled into a sea of excitement and bliss. Ultimate bliss.

The crowd outside the arena went wild with enthusiasm. Abby and Sarah were the first two to run into the arena and give them a hug. Charlie wiped his eyes and then looked over at Janis and Lilly, who were sitting on Babe, oblivious to the emotion in the arena. He winked at Janis, kind of shrugged as if to say, why not? Janis smiled and nodded. Charlie took her hand and with the other grabbed hold of Babe. "Hang on, Ms. Lilly. We are going for a ride."

Lilly beamed with excitement. "Ride."

Charlie opened the gate to join the girls. Other folks

came filtering in to congratulate the newly engaged couple.

Abe felt moisture on his cheek, as Patricia reached up to brush his tears away. Abe looked down at his wife and kissed her. "Well, it is about time!"

They walked over to the little gate to join the crowd.

As the sunset reflected the golden fall colors at the base of the Blue Mountains, there was peace in the moment. An ancient Indian brave, who lay silently within its snowcapped folds, seemed to smile in his wisdom. For thousands of years, he had his place in the mountains where he silently watched over the people of the valley. All was right, all was good and new adventures were about to begin.

"The development of softness truly is a journey — one with a beginning and a middle, but not necessarily an end."

-Mark Rashid, A Journey to Softness